FINAL STAND

NORTHWEST COUNTER-TERRORISM TASKFORCE - BOOK 5

LISA PHILLIPS

TWO DOGS PUBLISHING, LLC.

eBook ISBN: 979-8-88552-095-9

Print ISBN: 979-8-88552-096-6

Cover design Ryan Schwarz

Edited by Jen Weiber

Published by Two Dogs Publishing, LLC.

1

St. Petersburg, FL. Tuesday 11.12p.m.

The air outside was thick with a coming storm. A heavy and oppressive heat that made sweat slide down the small of her back.

Black leggings. Black, sweat-wicking, long-sleeved running shirt. Beat-up, black Converse shoes. If anyone saw her, she could easily argue being out for a run. At night. In Florida.

Ponytail. Black headband. She'd even stuck a device that looked a whole lot like a phone in the side pocket of her leggings and she had Bluetooth earbuds in.

No music playing.

A woman alone, jogging at night *and* listening to music? Not unless asking for trouble was the mission objective.

Victoria ran down the sidewalk through the retirement community like any other jogger. Two streets ahead of where she wanted to be, Victoria ducked off the sidewalk between two trees.

Second building on the left. Fifth apartment. Sliding door from the tiny, fenced-in patio. It was open a couple of millimeters. Far enough that cool air from inside wafted out through the gap.

"Probably a trap."

She wasn't naïve. Maybe she never had been, given everything that'd happened to her since the day she was born. Then again, after what happened the past few months, she should probably be a little more relaxed than normal right now. She was basically on vacation—though it didn't look like anyone's ordinary idea of taking a break. No one would find her at some beachfront tiki bar celebrating the massive victory of bringing down a whole cabal of dirty FBI agents laced throughout the agency on the West Coast.

Bribery. Corruption. It made her sick, the things people with power did to those who couldn't defend themselves. She had a particular hate for people who were supposed to work for truth and justice—for good—and yet used that position to hurt others. But she'd exposed them. After five years of work, Victoria and her team had brought darkness out into the light of day.

A couple of their suspects had gone to ground, running and hiding like rats headed back to the dark, but the majority had been caught. Victoria had no doubts the others would be rooted out as well. Soon enough.

But this mission had nothing to do with that. Her job with the Northwest Counter-Terrorism Taskforce was done.

Mission accomplished.

Victoria slid the patio door open and listened. Sure, she could use the front door. But what kind of former spy would she be if she walked in the front door, her face on camera for all to see?

She shoved the door closed so all the air conditioning didn't leak out into the night. She might be an old spy, but she wasn't reckless.

Then she made her way between the armchair and coffee table, over to her grandfather's bedroom.

Something's wrong.

Those latent instincts hadn't ever failed her. Not once. Victoria reached for the device in the pocket of her leggings. Before she could get her fingers between the stretchy material and the hard plastic of the stun gun, someone slammed into the back of her.

Victoria hit the linoleum of the hallway floor. Her knee and hip—and almost her nose—cracked the floor. She hissed out a breath between pursed lips as a much heavier body landed on hers.

She wriggled, trying to get him off.

His hands roamed places they shouldn't. "Been waiting for you."

Old fear fingered at the edges of her consciousness, frozen talons waiting to scratch her until she couldn't move from the onslaught.

Victoria bent one leg, planted her foot and pushed off the floor. She rolled to the side and the man slid off. She scrabbled out of reach, pulling out her stun gun as she moved and got up.

Light.

She reached to flip the switch, but he was up. And he was on her again. The press of his body against hers, pinning her to the wall. He grabbed her ponytail, tugging her head back. She winced but didn't let up, fumbling for the switch.

There.

Light flooded the hallway. He moved enough in his surprise that Victoria could twist her arm around. She jabbed him in the side and twisted, following it up with an uppercut that glanced off his chin.

The hallway was wide to accommodate her grandfather's occasional need for a wheelchair. She lifted her foot and utilized the extra space to kick the man in the stomach.

He dropped to the floor.

Victoria tugged off the man's ski mask while he moaned. He tried to kick out at her with his boot. She shifted out of the way, then rolled him and sat on the back of his thighs. From that spot, she could rifle through his jeans pockets. No phone. No wallet. No visible tattoos that might clue her in as to who he was and where he'd come from.

"So who are you?"

This was no random breaking and entering. He was here because she was here.

When he didn't answer, she tried a different question. "How did you know I would be here?"

And where was her grandfather? He should be in his bed sleeping. This guy better have left him there, or he would find out quick, the consequences of hurting someone she cared about.

Victoria reached around the front of his thigh and pressed her fingers into the man's sciatic nerve, halfway between his knee and groin.

He shifted immediately. A hiss of pain. An attempt at escape, to make the sensation stop. If she did let him up, he'd have to try and stumble away with a numb foot.

"Who do you work for?"

Before he could answer, she heard a noise. The hallway. Someone was coming.

Ditching the pressure point, Victoria used the stun gun to zap the man with her into unconsciousness. She pulled the closet door open and dragged him in there. She just had time to pull his feet inside before the voices turned the corner into the hall.

"The light is on. He's probably hiding." It was a woman, though she evidently had a smoking issue. "Crazy old coot says his granddaughter is a spy. Like the CIA, you know? He says she visits him after every mission."

Victoria stared through the crack between the door and the frame, praying they wouldn't see her. No. She already had plenty of evidence to know prayer didn't really work. No matter that everyone on her team now believed. They were all about praying and sharing what God was doing in their lives. She'd already decided it wasn't for her, and she didn't want to be around when they learned it was all a farce.

If she was found here, stuffed in a closet with an unconscious man, then she would deal with it. On her own.

Like she dealt with everything else in her life.

She ducked back deeper into the closet as they walked past the door. Down the hall to her grandfather's room.

"Jacob?"

Victoria waited.

"Jacob, are you here?"

She heard the shower door open, then the click as it was closed again.

"Alert security. We need to know if he's still in the building." The footsteps back down the hall to the front door were much more clipped. The sound of someone moving quickly and taking charge of the situation.

The man on the floor behind her moaned.

They were going to look in here. Of course they would, because they'd have to search everywhere for her grandfather. Which meant she needed to come up with an explanation fast.

She heard the front door squeak, and peeked out. The hall was clear.

Victoria tied the guy's hands behind his back with a winter scarf her grandfather did not need for those humid Florida seasons. She'd been meaning to borrow it from him this year, but at least it would come in handy now.

As soon as he started to wake enough to move, she hauled him to his feet and dragged him down the hall to the bedroom so she could look around.

He hadn't packed up to leave. His suitcase was still here, as was his medication.

"Where is he?"

She shoved the man against the wall beside the window so his nose squished against the paint. Very satisfying. He put his hands on her because he thought he could do whatever he wanted to. She wasn't going to let that go without a little recompense. That was the way the world worked.

She put pressure on him until he winced. "What did you do with him?"

He hissed out a breath between clenched teeth. There wasn't time to get the answers she needed. Not here, at least.

Victoria relieved some of the pressure off the man in order to unlock the window and push it up. It would throw off the cops, or whoever investigated his disappearance, but there was nothing else that could be done.

She shoved the man out the window, then jumped out herself. She yanked him by the arm and walked him across the lawn to a utility shed, picked the lock and then pushed him inside. He stumbled over a lawnmower and ended up sitting on the wheel.

"Talk."

"Not gonna happen." His voice held a slight slur, probably from being unconscious.

"Where is my grandfather?"

There were no other leads to follow unless he talked. This man had been sent here, and she had to know what he knew.

"Are you FBI? Someone with a beef who thinks I wronged them?" Plenty of those in the world. Didn't matter that she'd been working for the US government. She had enough enemies to fill a recital hall.

Sometimes that fact hit her. Like a wave broke over her, and she wondered if she should just give up. Go home...or to a quiet place.

But trouble would follow her there, too.

It always did.

"Who sent you here?" Victoria balled her fist and punched the guy. "Took my grandfather, waited around for me to show up. You have to know who I am. So who sent you?"

Why here.

Why now.

She couldn't get bogged down with the questions.

"Thought you'd strike a blow to his operation." He spoke around bloody teeth. "High and mighty, but not invulnerable."

"So this is revenge?"

"He wants you put down. Fast and hard, he said. Recompense for what you did in California."

Victoria didn't move. She didn't react either, at least not outwardly. She had negotiated with a very bad guy to turn state's evidence against a group of corrupt FBI agents who he had bribed into working for him.

And in return, he'd targeted her *grandfather*?

No. That was just…no.

It had been a last ditch effort to make the best of a bad decision. Yes, she'd let someone that one of her team members cared about swing in the breeze. That had backfired in a serious way. If Sal hadn't gotten to her fast enough, Allyson would have been carved up. Literally and figuratively.

Allyson was safe now.

Victoria had fulfilled her mission objective. She'd uncovered those FBI agents who had been associated with Allumbaugh's bad business. Most had been arrested. Some were still on the run. It wasn't her job to wipe the floor after, even if it was her mess. She wasn't the kind of person they wanted to stay around and help, only to reinforce the fact her presence had been necessary in the first place. No FBI agent wanted to be reminded there had been a disease in their ranks. Official word was that the agency planned to do their own cleanup.

Which left her…where?

Here.

Police sirens rang outside. The cops had been called, possibly even responding to a resident going missing. Or maybe the break-in and possible abduction.

"Where is my grandfather?"

"You think finding him is going to be the end of it?" He grinned, flashing blood and enamel. "He's after blood, and he's only just getting started."

Victoria secured him to a barrel of sand and left a note for the cops to read when they discovered him here.

Two minutes later she was back on her jog, pounding the sidewalk to where she'd left her rental car.

2

He pulled out the chair and sat. "I'm Assistant Director Mark Welvern, Seattle FBI office." He motioned to the man sitting beside him wearing a considerably nicer suit. "This is Dennis Pacer. Assistant US Attorney."

All the while his stomach twinged, reminding Mark he'd had his insides shredded by a high caliber rifle round only a couple of months ago now. *Too bad.* No time to wallow, there was way too much work to do.

The man across from them didn't look up from the table. The two week growth of beard shifted though, a face made for only himself. He knew this was Seattle. He'd been flown here just yesterday. One of six FBI agents they'd recently arrested.

So far, they'd attempted to climb the pecking order of this criminal group. At least, as best they'd been able to figure out who was who and where they fit.

This one was at the top.

"And you're Steven Bordeaux. Born and raised in Tennessee, but you dropped the accent pretty quickly at that Yankee college, didn't you? Criminal justice major." Mark glanced up from the paper. "Guess you didn't learn much." He studied the file again, though he knew it all by heart. He'd been knee-deep in this guy's personal and professional life for hours now. "Joined the FBI. Played at being the good guy, doing all the right things. Under the table, you're taking bribes. Payoffs. Banking cash in a Cayman Island's account."

The man shifted in his seat, handcuffs clinking. Orange jumpsuit. He'd be an old man before he saw the light of day as a free man. What would it take to get him to give up what he knew in exchange for a deal?

"You've lost a lot. I'll give you that." Mark leaned back in the chair, refusing to allow either of the men in the room—or anyone watching through the window, for that matter—know his wound hurt still. Sure, they knew he wasn't yet fully recovered. He was on desk duty only. He was also the boss of the whole office, answering only to the director of the FBI.

Mark continued, "All those cards, fallen down now. Nothing to do but pick up the pieces and try to salvage what remains of your life."

"You're gonna do that for me?" His face was carefully blank.

"You should know by now, you don't get something for nothing." This man knew better than most. He'd been an agent for nearly two decades. Almost as long as Mark who'd spent his forty-fourth birthday unconscious in the hospital a few weeks ago.

"So I roll over on…who? And I get a deal, or something?" A tone leaked into Bordeaux's words. He shifted one shoulder, like a half shrug. As though he had nothing better to do, and there was nothing major happening in his life right now. Like an indictment.

Mark glanced at the A-USA, as though he hadn't already discussed this option with Pacer.

The man sat stone faced as he stared down the corrupt FBI agent. "That all depends on what you have to offer."

"You aren't the one in charge, Bordeaux. You're not the head of the snake, but I think you know who is." Mark folded his arms as though, like the agent in cuffs, he had all day to wait instead of it being after nine at night now, and after a seriously long day.

Actually, it had been a long month.

The dirty FBI agents they'd uncovered had been entirely too coordinated in their efforts to not be in communication with each other—or at the least, receiving orders somehow. From someone. Had they found any indication at all that there'd been messages, coded or otherwise? Nope. Nada. It was starting to irritate Mark, cleaning up this mess. Seemed like with every-thing they uncovered, it was worse than they'd previously imagined.

Men and women who had used the badge—the same one he wore—to hurt people. To try and get rich. Mark said, "We need to know who is in charge and where to find him."

"So I just roll over? Then he finds me in prison, and I bleed out on the floor."

Pacer said, "Protection can be part of the deal. If necessary."

Mark didn't figure that would be effective, given who they were up against—FBI agents with contacts on both sides. A foot in polite society and the other in the underbelly, where people took cash to end someone's life.

Bordeaux shook his head. "If I'm in prison, I'm still breathing. I talk. That's done."

Someone with reach. Someone with the reputation of disposing problems.

Pacer flipped the page in the file and tugged over a slip of paper no bigger than a cocktail napkin. Bordeaux read it as well, though from upside down. The letters were small but block capi-tals. Mark watched him absorb what was there without even asking the question. He saw the flex in the man's jaw muscle as he bit down on his molars.

The paper read *Oscar Langdon*. A name currently number seven on the FBI's Ten Most Wanted list. A man responsible for bombings across Europe and one in Denver last year that'd killed hundreds. A man who traded in black market antiquities, art and artifacts, as well as anything he could get paid to pass along in a deal.

A man whose face nobody knew.

What it had to do with corrupt FBI agents, Mark didn't know. But there had to be a connection. One that seemed above his pay grade, given how it had been done.

Pacer said, "Well?"

Bordeaux sniffed. "You want Oscar Langdon? You think you're fishing in a lake, you don't even realize that lake feeds the whole ocean. You're rounding up all the bass, you don't even realize a shark is going to bite you."

"So help us get Langdon." Mark leaned forward. "Before he *bites.*"

"Langdon." Bordeaux sniffed. "Got no clue, do you? You want Langdon, why don't you talk to Victoria Bramlyn? The woman's been on a fishing expedition of her own, exposing all this 'corruption' like we're the only ones with something to hide."

"Victoria?" Mark shook his head. "That's who you're going to flip this back on?"

She'd done her job, and then she'd left town. He'd left her countless messages, but she hadn't returned a single one. Now he was done calling. He had enough to do, between healing from a gunshot wound to the chest and taking out the trash in his office.

Mark had been forced to prove to the Office of Professional Responsibility that he was still an honorable agent who upheld his oath. Every man and woman who worked here were, these days, glancing sideways at each other almost constantly. Wondering who would be swept up next. Cuffs on. Marched out.

Now it was all about figuring out what the fallout would be. Working on repairing the reputation of the FBI which had taken a serious hit in the media and on social lately.

"Victoria Bramlyn is only interested in one thing. Victoria Bramlyn." Bordeaux leaned across the table. "All she wants to do is prove her ridiculous theory correct. Salvage what's left of her career and her reputation."

Like the FBI? Mark dismissed that idea so he didn't get distracted by more thoughts of Victoria. He knew she'd had an operation go wrong years ago. She'd thought agents from the FBI might have been involved, but since when was that common knowledge? He'd cautioned her to play it close to her, considering she hadn't exactly had proof.

Mostly, he cared about her and she'd gotten hurt. Mark had been forced to deal with the fact her job was seriously dangerous, and she might not actually outlive it. Things weren't much better now. He'd only just learned how to temper his reaction to hearing about her escapades. Along with how she continually pushed him away, "for his own good" as she called it, didn't make for a very happy Mark. It just made for a life where he had plenty of time for overtime, and working long cases into the weekend.

Which he had to admit had benefited his career.

Bordeaux said, "Blaming the FBI for what happened to her? It was Oscar Langdon."

"She believed in a link between Langdon and the FBI," Pacer commented. "What do you think about that?"

"It was probably she who breached security and sold all that information. The FBI was just someone convenient to blame, and now she's at it again." Bordeaux lifted his hands and made air quotes. "'Cleaning out the corruption' like it's not obvious she just wants someone to blame for her mistakes, a way to pass off responsibility. How do you know she isn't in on it?"

"She isn't." Mark realized what he'd said, and what it sounded like, after the words were out.

Bordeaux leaned back in his chair. "Is that how it is? I heard you two were close."

"She's an old family friend." Mark said, "And that bit about responsibility was rich, coming from you."

"Sure she is." Bordeaux said, "And you've got enough work cleaning up the FBI on the West Coast to worry about Langdon and Victoria Bramlyn. Not enough time for all of it, so I guess you'll just have to let that go. Your priority is the FBI, right?"

Mark nodded. "That's right."

And yet, he'd managed to help Victoria before, plenty of times.

Did she return his calls, though? No. No, she didn't.

"Anyway, how do you know Victoria isn't the one who *is* Langdon?"

Pacer said, "What? Seriously, you're telling us Victoria is Langdon?"

"With a guy who could pose as him, a front man. She could pull off being the person behind the screen." Bordeaux shrugged. "You know she could."

Mark did, but that was hardly the point. The woman's skills weren't in question here. "Tell us where you got your instructions from. You coordinated bad men. My count, you had three guys picking up payoffs and leaving them where you were told to, right? So how did you log the money, and how did you know where to do the drops?"

There had to be cell phones they hadn't found. Or an app built in that left no traces of the conversations. Mark was getting more and more irritated the longer it took for them to get an answer. He was even starting to wonder if someone down in forensics was hindering their search for it.

"Victoria Bramlyn isn't the terrorist Oscar Langdon." Mark shook his head. "And that's not why we're here. You swore an oath, and then you betrayed that oath. You know the rules and you know how this will go now."

Victoria had been in Mark's life for as long as he could remember. If there was anyone he was certain was *not* a black market arms dealer, it was her.

Pacer took up right where he left off. "Unless you have something to give us, we can't offer you anything."

Bordeaux stared right at Mark. "Watch your backs."

"Is that a threat?" Pacer asked him.

Bordeaux gave a tiny shake of his head. Not to Pacer. But it was a threat to Mark and probably Victoria as well. *Watch your backs.* She knew that, didn't she? Otherwise there was no way for him to tell her. The woman wasn't dumb. She knew there was the possibility of retaliation. Enough to be taking precautions. Wherever she was, whatever she was doing.

"Tell us where to find the agent, or whoever is in charge of your little corrupt gang."

Bordeaux only chuckled. "Too late to find them now."

Mark's phone rang in his pocket. He stood. "You'll have to excuse me for a moment." He pulled it out as he stepped into the hallway and swiped to answer. "Welvern."

"Yes, Mr. Welvern. This is Bridget over at Gracious Living. I'm calling about Jacob Bramlyn. I'm afraid there's been an incident."

3

Victoria stared at the phone in her hand, thumb hovering over the play button. She just needed a second to collect herself before she finished watching the feed of Mark interviewing that agent. Just a moment, that was all. Just a moment to think before she got back on task.

Her grandfather was missing—she could think of little else. The police were investigating, and she'd sent an email to the committee to find out which detectives were on the case. She wanted to know they were the very best—and if they weren't, well, she had no problem waltzing in and making their lives miserable. Victoria reserved the right to throw her credentials around in any given situation.

Mark had interviewed the FBI agents he had in custody today, so she needed to keep tabs on that.

Then there was her team, reassigned to work—still as a group for the most part—under Homeland Security, at their Seattle office. Niall, the NCIS agent, had a desk at the NCIS office on the Navy base close by.

Her task force. The one that wasn't hers anymore, not officially. She'd formed the group by handpicking agents from all different federal branches. They had successfully combatted domestic terrorism for nearly five years now, working in their own way to fight that fight. They'd arrested some serious players and brought down Kennowich's entire operation, just to name one.

Sure, she'd planned on using Kennowich as a witness in her case against these dirty FBI agents, but that had been a means to an end. He wouldn't have walked free. She made sure that didn't happen to men who hurt people the way Kennowich had done.

Something she would have liked to have explained to Sal, her US Marshal team member. If he actually answered the phone.

She wanted to call him now and ask if he'd help with the search for her grandfather, but she doubted he'd pick up. Even weeks later it seemed he hadn't forgiven her.

Sal and Allyson had both quit their jobs and "retired" to Wyoming. Formerly an ATF agent, Allyson was now apparently working in a coffee shop that was also a bookstore. Victoria had found Sal's name on the ballot for the upcoming sheriff's election. How they'd managed all that in just a few weeks was baffling, but apparently they'd figured out what they wanted. Each other. And they no longer wanted to wait to get it.

A truck door slammed and a family got out of the vehicle that had just parked. The man walked around to the back door and pulled it open. He lifted a child out and carried him to the door of their room while the woman gathered up handfuls of bulging bags. Souvenirs. A day at the park.

Victoria smiled to herself.

How many times had she nearly just bought a ticket to that park just so she could go, even though it would be by herself? She didn't want to think about the photo she'd seen, years ago now, of a family all at Disneyland. Standing in front of that castle, wearing the mouse ears. Smiling. Tired, but so happy.

She looked down at her phone. That life wasn't hers, and she was old enough to know it never would be. Old enough she might even have outlived her ability to have children, considering she was pushing forty-six. Not that she'd want to give her DNA to an innocent human. Talk about a life sentence.

It was why she'd worked to keep a relationship with her grandfather. Because he was her stepfather's dad and also, out of her entire family—what there was left of it—she'd actually liked him, despite how he treated her sometimes. Now he occasionally had no idea who she was, but she still made sure to visit when she could.

He was missing.

Because of her.

She bit her lips together. Sal would help, or at least he had the ability to find people in a way she'd never seen before.

Victoria pressed play on the phone screen, the cord running to her earbuds. The interviewee, Steven Bordeaux, knew he was going down. She wanted to make sure he never walked free after what he'd done.

His sardonic tone filled her ears. "You want Oscar Langdon? You think you're fishing in a lake, you don't even realize that lake feeds the whole ocean. You're rounding up all the bass, you don't even realize a shark is going to bite you."

"So help us get Langdon." Mark's voice. "Before he *bites.*"

She shut her eyes. Just hearing him was like being there, beside him. Even just having his voice echo in her head, talking to someone else. A long time ago, she'd vowed to have him in her life any way she could get him. Lately, that had involved sitting beside his bed while he recovered from a gunshot wound.

"Langdon." Bordeaux went quiet for a second. "Got no clue, do you? You want Langdon, why don't you talk to Victoria Bramlyn? The woman's been on a fishing expedition of her own, exposing all this 'corruption' like we're the only ones with something to hide."

"Victoria?" That was Mark. "That's who you're going to flip this back on?"

Victoria paused the recording again. Pacer had to have given Mark the name Oscar Langdon. She'd made sure that Mark didn't know Langdon was the one behind her last mission for the CIA. The one where she'd been betrayed by someone and left for dead.

That was a different life, and yet it seemed intent on bleeding back into now.

Dirty FBI agents. That was what she'd suspected years ago when everything had collapsed around her. And so she'd had a committee formed in Washington so she could go after FBI corruption under their authority. Now that she'd done it, she could move on. Right? And yet Pacer was throwing around Langdon's name.

What did that have to do with these FBI agents? Unless he thought they worked for Langdon, or that they had at one point. Or Pacer thought the man on the FBI's Most Wanted list *was* an FBI agent.

She shook her head. No.

And yet...

Bordeaux was throwing her name around, trying to get suspicion placed on her. Victoria turned her wrist so she could see the skin on the inside of her forearm. She had every reason to be afraid if they started investigating her and a connection to Langdon. Because when she'd been betrayed, they'd left a breadcrumb in her life that lead straight back to them.

One she'd be hard pushed to argue with.

She needed to call Mark. To warn him that this might get worse. That he might hear her name a whole lot more. She trusted him and had confided in him probably more than was wise. Definitely more than her gag order allowed her to say. But it was Mark. Given all they'd been through, she was sure that trust went both ways.

She pulled the earbuds from her ear and tucked them in her purse. Probably a better conversation to have in person, considering she was going to have to plead her case a little. It occurred to her, and not for the first time, that talking to him was a little like going to confession. Always had been and maybe that would never change. It didn't take her long to get packed up and book a flight for first thing tomorrow.

While back in Seattle, she could check on her team as well. By the time she did both things there would probably be movement on the hunt for her grandfather, and she'd hopefully be able to come back. Have a regular visit where she walked through the front door, and they sat down for some tea.

She slept a couple of hours, then more on the plane. With a connecting flight in Salt Lake City, Victoria had time for an extra-large, black coffee. But not before she used the facilities. They were always packed, normally. She walked farther and found an out-of-the-way bathroom just so she could avoid the press of humanity for a little while. She could get the drink on the way back to her next gate.

The door clicked behind her.

A toilet flushed and an older woman dragged her suitcase out without washing her hands. Victoria made a face no one saw and headed to a stall. She pushed the door open, purse swinging against her side.

Before she stepped inside, someone shoved her.

She flung out a hand, but there was nothing there. After stumbling onto the toilet seat, she turned herself around and kicked up at her assailant, jabbing her heel into the person's thigh.

A woman this time. She cried out.

Dressed like any other traveler. Leggings and a T-shirt. Running shoes.

Victoria dropped the purse and lifted her hands, curling her fingers into fists.

The woman grinned. Never mind that she looked like a muscly soccer mom. "This is gonna be fun."

She launched herself at Victoria in the small space. Victoria swiped away both of the woman's attempts to hit her. She grabbed the woman's shoulders and pulled one knee up into her stomach. "Guess they didn't fully brief you on who I am."

The woman chuckled, though out of breath.

The next blow came out of nowhere. Before she realized what'd happened, Victoria fell against the side of the stall. Head butt. She grunted. Why did those always hurt so much? Usually on both sides. But this woman seemed unaffected.

Her fist darted toward Victoria's left side. Something sharp jabbed into her. When she pulled her hand back, Victoria realized it was plastic ware from a restaurant. Not a weapon security would have seen. She'd probably grabbed it on the way. Following Victoria. Stalking her.

She tried to breathe around the pain as she locked her knees. There was no way she was going to end up on the floor.

Victoria grabbed her purse as she straightened and threw it at the woman. She brought her arms up to defend herself. The purse hit the woman's hands and face. Victoria punched her in the stomach. It hurt a lot, but she did it. Then she kicked the woman again, and when she was down, slammed her head onto the tile floor.

Someone entered the bathroom. The young woman tugged on her companion's arm, probably her daughter, and the two of them left.

Victoria went through the woman's pockets. All she found was a picture of herself. Nothing else, not even ID. Victoria shoved the photo into a pocket in her purse. Then she pulled out a penlight. She lifted the woman's arm and shone the black light on the skin on the inside of her forearm.

Bingo. She lifted her own arm and shone it there as well. Like it would have disappeared since the last time? She shook her head and stowed her flashlight before clambering to her feet with a hiss.

She grabbed a bundle of paper towels and shoved them over the wound, between her blouse and her skin. Who knew what that woman had hit? She held her elbow over the suit jacket she wore and checked her hair in the mirror before leaving the bathroom.

Now she *really* needed that coffee.

Victoria strode out of the bathroom just as security raced there from the opposite direction. She followed the signs for baggage claim and took that way out of the airport, hailing a cab at the curb.

She needed clothes and a new way home if Langdon knew she was here—plus security would be looking for her. Probably she also needed stitches. Then a rental car, which she'd drive to Boise. She could fly to Seattle from there. It would take all day, but what else was there to do? She had to get home.

In the cab, Victoria pulled out her phone and stared at it for a while.

Then she called Talia.

4

Seattle, WA. Thursday 6.47p.m.

M ark showed his badge and got checked in through security at the office of Homeland Security in downtown Seattle. It wasn't far from the FBI office, but he'd had to finish up his work day before he could get over here. Thankfully Talia was still in the office.

The guard handed him a badge. "Know where you're going?"

He nodded. "They're expecting me." Mark didn't need any help. If he ran into the assistant director here, he'd have to do all that posturing. The part where he had to try and prove he was still a good FBI agent, while the man gave him kudos for sticking with it. Then they'd commiserate with each other on how on earth it could have happened, and how long it would take to clean up. It would be even longer before the FBI got its good standing back.

Kind of like how the DEA had to keep their nose clean and their agency out of the news, after stories broke of what agents had been getting up to in South America.

The FBI had a serious PR problem to work through. Agents turning up to crime scenes would have to fight through the

distrust. Judges would think twice before trusting their investigations. Cops would hesitate before calling them in.

Mark sighed as he stepped off the elevator.

"Wow, that's a long face if ever I've seen one." Talia shot him
a smile as she wandered over on her heels.

He smiled and opened his arms. She walked into his hug long
enough for a quick squeeze and then stepped back. "Mason know
you're working late?"

"He has a big assignment right now, so he had to cancel
dinner." She shrugged. "So we ordered take out and I decided to
wait for you. I'm assuming you need..." She waved at her
computer. The skills she had were legendary, even outside of the
federal world. She'd been an NSA analyst and now...

"You guys really work for Homeland now?" There was no one
else in here. The office looked dark and dreary, the only windows
showed the office building next door. No view. Not like the last
office they'd had, which gave them a sweet panorama of
downtown.

This was a step down if ever he'd seen one.

"We have our own cases." She motioned him to a chair and
then sat in her own. "They know where our skills lie and Dakota is
Homeland, so we had an in." Talia shrugged one shoulder. "We're
good."

He studied her for a second, to make sure that was true, and
then said, "Any idea where Victoria is?"

"Florida, last I heard." She glanced at the papers on her desk,
and closed a file. Then she turned a quizzical expression his way.
"Why do you ask?"

He opened his mouth, halfway sure of what he wanted to say.
Before he could get out a word, the elevator doors opened. Josh
and Dakota strode out, laughing and carrying take-out bags.

"You're here." Josh set his bags down and stuck his hand out.
"How are things?"

"Busy."

"And the..." he motioned to Mark's abdomen.

"Recovering. Good time to be doing desk work and weeks of interviews."

Josh nodded. Beyond him, Dakota was mouthing something to Talia. The NSA analyst said, "Mark was about to explain why he's so interested in where Victoria is." She actually folded her arms. "Has she called you back yet?"

She really wanted to get in the middle of that? Also there was the question of why she'd have a problem with it. Though, the fact she seemed intent on protecting her friend was something he could definitely get behind.

"Let's eat. Then Mark can talk." Josh opened all the cartons.

Dakota uncovered paper plates and plastic forks, and Talia grudgingly handed him bottled water.

"Thank you."

He knew she didn't necessarily like where the team was at now. He didn't blame her, since it was pretty much like the band had broken up. Niall worked at the naval base. Haley wasn't their office manager anymore and had gone to work at a bank. Josh and Dakota couldn't even bring their dog into work now.

They all sat, and Josh prayed. After Mark said, "Amen," he asked, "When's the wedding?"

"Two weeks." Josh grinned. Dakota shot him a smile.

"Yeah, yeah." Talia shoved a piece of chicken in her mouth. After she'd swallowed, she said, "Mark still needs to tell us why he's so interested in Victoria."

He ate a couple of bites, realizing he was hungrier than he'd thought. When it had abated a little, he said, "You aren't worried about her?"

"I didn't say that. But the fact is, she can take care of herself."

"Maybe."

Dakota said, "What's that supposed to mean?"

He didn't like the idea that he was going to have to justify himself to them, but since that seemed to be the theme of this month, he swallowed it. "Victoria and I have, in some way or another, always been in each other's lives. We probably always will be."

"I thought you were dancing around a relationship." Talia eyed him. "You're just friends?"

"It's…more complicated than that. But I care about her, and I do what I can to help her be safe. But she's Victoria. I don't always get the whole story." Something they had experienced themselves.

Josh said, "She has her own agenda."

Mark shrugged. "She's always done what she thought was right."

"Like lying to us that the task force was about terrorism when we were actually investigating the FBI the whole time?"

Mark studied Dakota. He guessed Victoria had been uninvited from the wedding at this point. "It wasn't about terrorism? You didn't stop any attacks or arrest anyone that wasn't FBI?"

"Ask Sal." She shrugged. "Victoria left Ally out to dry."

Mark shook his head. This was a serious change of tune if Dakota had switched sides from Team Victoria to Team Allyson. He blew out a breath. "I'm not going to defend her. She wouldn't want me to."

Talia said, "You've known each other for years?"

Dakota waved her fork at him. "I thought you were just someone she knew from the FBI. You guys were working this corruption case from the beginning?"

"Not as such. My getting shot threw a wrench in that, but I'd filled in the director. And her friends in Washington did the rest. The whole thing broke open when I was barely out of the hospital and continued throughout the time I was at home recuperating. I managed to spearhead an investigation from there. Making sure everyone was on the same page and we had what we needed before she took everything to the US Attorney's office."

"And she never thought we'd want to know?" Dakota looked hurt for the first time ever.

Mark said, "She wouldn't have even thought to read you in. It was her investigation, her deal. Your judgment would have been clouded, which would have led to things that could have tarnished your credibility within the federal community."

The truth was, having been a spy meant Victoria was much more inclined to cross lines these agents—or he—would never even consider. She operated under a different set of rules.

Dakota didn't say anything, because he was right. She was all about justice. Victoria had, in effect, saved Dakota from herself by not allowing her to know there was massive corruption in the FBI. She would have gone on a one-woman crusade to root out the problem. And it probably would have destroyed her career. It might have even cost her life. Or her upcoming marriage.

Victoria knew where her team members were; engaged and happy. All of them.

"She would never have allowed you to carry this," he said softly. "She wanted you to be happy."

Talia set her drink down. "What about her? She doesn't get to be happy?"

Mark was never going to tell them about all the reasons why Victoria thought she didn't deserve to have happiness for herself. He gave them an answer that might satisfy them. "She was engaged once." He even shrugged his shoulder, so they'd think it wasn't a big deal. "It didn't work out."

"First I'm hearing of it." Dakota didn't believe him. She looked suspicious.

"Was it you?"

Josh's question surprised him. Mark shook his head. "Another spy."

Mark's feelings about that were his own, belonging to no one but him. Not even Victoria was privy to that. Still, he figured she knew. After all, they'd been in each other's lives through so much, and there was no sign that would abate.

"Sometimes she'll go…under the radar." Mark tried to figure out how to explain it. "But this time, I have reason to believe she might be in danger. The agents I'm interviewing have been pointing fingers, and her name keeps coming up."

Dakota shot him a look. "Is that any wonder? She does what she wants."

"She's your friend."

"Maybe. She *was* my boss. But you know what? Friends trust each other. They share."

He nearly smiled, but didn't think that would be a good idea. "So you shared with her?"

"I told her everything. Because she demanded full disclosure. Did she return that favor? No."

"She has reasons." Victoria didn't trust easily, but Dakota wouldn't accept that. "She does what she can."

"Why do you defend her?"

Mark closed his mouth. Then he turned to Talia. "Have you heard from her?" He wanted to warn her that Victoria was being dragged into the fallout. That was why he'd come, not so he could get grilled about Victoria and give away his feelings for her.

"Why?"

"You said she was in Florida. When was that?"

Talia's eyebrow rose. "Why?"

"Her grandfather went missing. I'd like to know if she was there for that, or if she even knows it happened."

Dakota said, "Bypassing the fact she has family she also never told us about, how do you know her grandfather went missing?"

"I'm the emergency contact at the assisted living home where he lives."

Dakota closed her mouth. Talia opened hers, hesitated and then said, "You are?"

"I told you, we've known each other for years. She needed someone who could be called at any time. Especially while she was on assignment. Sometimes they last weeks, sometimes months. In her late twenties, she went undercover for *two years*."

"She called me at lunchtime."

Mark waited for Talia to say more.

After a full minute, she said, "Fine...she didn't sound all right but called because she needed a flight from Boise to Seattle. She should have touched down an hour ago."

The muscles around his wound tensed, sparking pain. "What do you mean, she didn't sound right?"

Talia shrugged. "She said she was driving. Maybe that's true."

He said, "Anything else?"

Dakota shifted in her chair. "I thought she could take care of herself."

He shot her a look. Josh just seemed uncomfortable, torn between his wife's hurt and the safety of a woman he respected.

"She can." He glanced at the other woman. "Talia?"

She shrugged. "I asked her if she was okay. She muttered something about needing a bear, whatever that means, and then she hung up."

Mark tossed his plate in the closest trash can and strode to the elevator. He jabbed the button and tapped his foot while he waited for the car to come.

"Is she okay?"

He turned back. Dakota was hurt, but she hadn't stopped caring. "There are threats. But then, there always are. She knows that and she's careful. But that won't stop me from looking out for her."

"And making sure she's safe?"

He nodded. "And making sure she's safe."

Talia said, "You know where she is?"

The elevator doors opened. He stepped inside. "Yes."

5

Seattle, WA. Wednesday, 03.22a.m.

I t began the same way every time. Victoria walked down the hallway, the long skirt of that evening gown swishing around her legs.

At the end of the hall was a brown door. Ornate, heavy wood. She pushed it open and stepped into the office, then quietly closed the door behind her. The diamonds on her bracelet glinted in the light.

A safe, behind the painting above the fireplace. The whole hearth was huge with jagged stones worn down over centuries. A castle, in Vienna. She'd had to go on tiptoes to crack the safe, but she'd gotten in. She'd scooped out everything inside. Money, papers, and envelopes. A flash drive. That was what she'd been after.

Then he came.

It must have been a noise, because she turned. He stood right there. Victoria couldn't make out his face, though. Either she'd forgotten it, or her mind didn't allow her to remember. The image was blocked for some reason.

The scene changed, as it had each time before.

Victoria came awake, head pounding, remembering what came next in her reoccurring dream and how she wished it had only been a fabrication of her mind. She'd been knocked out and dumped in a South African prison. It had taken six months for Mark to find her, just a few days before she'd planned to escape. His way had been less painful. The only clue she had as to what had happened—or why—was the red mark that she discovered on her arm after she'd first come to. The only sign she'd been given a tattoo was the angry skin. UV light revealed what it was.

Langdon's mark.

Victoria sucked in a breath and opened her eyes. The warm body against hers shifted, and hot dog breath wafted over her face. "Bear, that's just gross." Her voice was a whisper in the living room. His living room.

Her shirt had been lifted up, exposing the skin on her side. She hadn't fallen asleep with her back to the room. She'd been moved into this position.

Victoria touched the bandage taped over it. He'd cleaned and redressed the wound.

She twisted on the couch and glanced around. The TV was still on, a 24-hour news show muted with the subtitles scrolling across the bottom of the screen. Not that the words being typed made any sense. But that was one problem she would never be able to solve, so she'd learned to let it go.

Victoria shoved at Bear so she could sit. He lifted up to standing on the couch and then hopped over her. He stretched out, then shook. Tags jangling against each other, hanging off his collar.

"Bear?" Mark sat up. Gun in one hand. He rubbed his face with the other.

Victoria shoved her shirt down and sat up. "Hey."

He stared at her without saying anything for a full minute. "That's it? Hey?"

"I'll make the coffee." She started to move and couldn't fight back the wince.

"You'll do no such thing." He scooted forward on his chair and flipped the switch on the lamp, but didn't stand. "Not with that wound."

"I didn't know she had a…spork, or whatever it was." She also hadn't known getting stabbed in the side would hurt so much. The doctor had even put a couple of stitches on the inside.

"It's only by the grace of God you don't have internal bleeding. Or something punctured."

Victoria wasn't awake enough to argue about God's grace that seemed to be available to everyone else except her. Not something she wanted to get into right now. "I'm here." She lifted both hands, then let them fall back to her sides. "I'm fine."

Mark shot her a look.

Victoria rubbed the skin of her forearm. Branded. Dumped in a South African prison. They should have just killed her rather than get rid of her like that. Now she wasn't going to quit trying to figure out who that faceless man was who haunted her dreams.

Who Oscar Langdon was.

When that was done, Mark could stop rescuing her. And she would stop letting him.

"Your grandfather is missing."

She nodded.

"I wasn't sure how much you knew. They think he was loaded into a black van, and they've looped local FBI agents into the search for him since it's becoming clear this is a kidnapping."

She would have to get their names and have the committee verify them. If they'd ever worked in Austria, she'd have them off the case.

"Did the police get anything from the suspect in the shed?"

One of his eyebrows rose. "He claimed no knowledge of it. They held him on breaking and entering until he made bail."

"Who was he?"

"An accountant from Virginia."

"And they believe that?"

Mark said, "Talia found something in his emails. She thinks he was paid to make your grandfather disappear and then wait for you. Leverage. I guess he's part of a crew, and they do this stuff in the Caribbean mostly."

"Kidnappers for hire?"

"I guess they do whatever someone will pay them for."

Victoria glanced around more, now that the lamp was on. "The place looks good."

"Couple more things, and I'll be done with this one. I'm thinking a gazebo. Though, it might be too late in the year to get one put together in good weather." Mark shrugged. "I have the house I'm going to flip next. I'll show you before you leave."

Victoria smiled. He liked giving her the full tour before he sold a house. The man hadn't lived in a place more than a year since she'd known him, constantly renovating houses. Selling them. Moving onto the next one.

He worked in the evenings and on weekends. As a result, she didn't think he'd worked out in a gym in his entire life. Because construction obviously built plenty of muscles, now outlined by his T-shirt. He even said he'd figured out sticky cases while patching drywall or putting tile in bathrooms, occupying his hands and giving his mind the space to work on a problematic investigation.

A good man. A man of faith, and honor. One whose family she had destroyed, and apparently, still wanted in his life.

It made no sense.

She stood, suddenly aware she was only in a skirt, blouse, and pantyhose. He'd taken her shoes off, or had she? She could barely remember stumbling in and falling asleep. "I'm going to fill a cup, and then get out of your hair."

"I'll make the coffee." He took her hand and walked into the kitchen, not quite dragging her with him. But it was close. "Sit. I'll tell you the latest on the search for your grandfather." He made a face on that last word, then turned and let Bear out the back door.

She sat. "I know you don't like him." Victoria smoothed down the edges of her blouse. "But he's my family."

"Took you in when no one else did, blah-blah. I know." He

turned away from her and filled the carafe at the sink. "Doesn't make him a nice guy."

"He's...mellowed with age."

"Way to choose your words."

"Doesn't mean it isn't true."

Mark hung his head, hands to the counter. His back muscles flexed.

"What?"

He turned around. Behind him the coffee pot started to sputter and trickle. "I just don't know why you go out of your way to spend time with him. And your friends, the people who care about you? They don't even know you're hurt, or where you are. You're pushing them away."

"I called Sal. He won't pick up the phone."

"And Dakota? Talia? Niall? Josh—"

"I get it."

"Me."

"What do you want from me?" She turned her hands over and showed him her palms.

Mark was silent for a long time. "You know what I want." He paused. "And at the same time, you also have no clue."

He set a full mug of black coffee in front of her. Some sloshed over the rim onto the quartz he'd installed as countertops.

What was she supposed to do with that? Victoria had tried to cut him off so many times. She thought she'd succeeded. Until he found her in South Africa. That had ended a three-year dry spell of not seeing each other and not talking. Lately they'd spent so much time together. She'd almost been able to believe they could make a relationship work between them.

But life got in the way. Like it always did.

"You should let me walk away this time."

Mark sipped his coffee. "You're going to leave me with this mess to clean up and just walk off into the sunset? What will you do now? Get another federal job somewhere else, start over with a new team?"

"I was thinking about going home."

He swallowed, coughed, and put down his mug. Opened his mouth. Closed it. "Why would you think that's a good idea?"

Victoria shrugged.

"You think he won't find you there?" His face changed, as realization hit. "You think going there will surround you with people trained to take care of themselves if it comes to that. As opposed to people you care about."

She said nothing.

He nodded. "Fine. I'll take vacation time and go with you."

"You can't do that." Besides the fact it would never get approved. Not at a time like this, when everyone in the FBI was in disaster cleanup mode.

"You're not going by yourself."

"I can take care of me."

"These people are trying to kill you, Victoria. How many times do you think it's going to take before they come at you and manage to put you in the ground?"

She shrugged. Her coffee wasn't finished, but it was time to go.

"Sit down."

"No." She turned back to him. "You aren't going to tell me what to do."

"Victoria."

She collected her purse.

He caught up to her at the front door. "You just got here."

"I got here hours ago. Thanks for letting me crash."

"I didn't let you. You broke in."

Victoria reached for the handle.

"You step out there, I can't protect you. Pacer thinks this has to do with Oscar Langdon. Tell me why he thinks that, and why these guys seem to all want to point the finger right back at you in the middle of an FBI corruption investigation?"

She stared at his shoulder.

"That mission. The one in Vienna?"

She nodded. "I said there were FBI agents involved. Now I've got them all scrambling to save face. Why wouldn't they try to turn some of the heat back on me?"

"But Oscar Langdon?"

"I thought it was FBI agents from the Austrian embassy who had betrayed me." She rubbed the skin inside her arm. Langdon's mark. She'd never told Mark about it.

"Stay here. Work this case with me, so we can figure out together who he is. Why he's so fixated on you." He touched her shoulder, his thumb skimming the skin on the side of her neck. "Help me keep you safe."

She shut her eyes. The image of him lying in that hospital bed, pale. Hooked up to machines. And she was supposed to stay here and let him stand between her and the next attacker that would come at her?

"You need to rest anyway."

He's strong, but we're not optimistic. You should prepare yourself for the fact he might not make it.

"I can't stay."

"Then why did you come here except to take a nap with my dog. This is the one place you *know* is safe. Why can't you let me keep it that way for you?"

"You know why."

He was already rolling his eyes before she'd even finished speaking. "Victoria."

"Obviously coming here was a mistake." She tugged the front door of his house open. "Thank you for the update about my grandfather."

His jaw clenched. She didn't look at his eyes.

She just walked out.

6

Mark let himself into his office and set his tumbler of coffee on the desk. He sat, then hit the power button on his computer before reaching above his head and stretching. He was too old to sleep in armchairs.

He wasn't too old to come home to his fixer upper—no matter that he'd now have to wait to make a profit on it—and find the woman he'd been in love with for years stretched out on his couch. With his dog. Bleeding.

Whoever she'd gotten to sew her up, he needed to find the person and punch them in the face for doing a hack job. If he thought she could reach that far, he wondered if she would've stitched it up herself.

Always walking away from him. In fact, the one time in his life that Victoria hadn't walked away—because he'd been the one to do it—was the worst day of his life. So it didn't bother him too much that she took that role. Unless she was walking away because she was determined to protect him.

He'd seen fear. From a woman who had been fearless since the day he'd met her in the fourth grade, and that didn't sit well with him. He knew where she'd been, and some of the things she'd done. The fact she was scared now? It wasn't all bad. No, it was actually good. It meant she understood the threat she was under. But if she was only scared for him, then it meant she didn't care what Langdon threw at her.

Was a man on the FBI's Most Wanted list really fixated on Victoria? There had to be a reason they'd both been brought up in the same conversation. Maybe it was well known among those corrupt FBI agents that Victoria was the one who'd exposed them. If Langdon was an FBI agent—or had been at one point—then they could be well aware of a threat to her.

It might not be misdirection.

He needed to do more interviews and put some serious pressure on if he was going to find out if Langdon really was gunning for Victoria in some kind of revenge plan.

He picked up his desk phone and called security. "Has Dennis Pacer checked in yet this morning?"

"No, Sir. We haven't seen him yet."

"Thanks." Mark hung up. Usually Pacer was here by now, ready to get to work routing out the corruption.

So where was he?

Mark's phone buzzed across the top of his desk. The number was local.

DID YOU REALLY PUT AGENTS ON ME?

His lip curled up at the corner and he texted back.

GIVING THEM THE RUNAROUND?

A second later, he got a reply.

THEY PROBABLY HAVE BETTER THINGS TO DO THAN WALK THROUGH THIS HOME DÉCOR STORE, TRYING TO FIGURE OUT WHERE I WENT.

Mark chuckled. Then he picked up the phone and called the senior agent of the two he'd assigned on his way home last night. He'd had them sit outside his house until Victoria left, and then stay on her.

Apparently she thought this was amusing. At least she wasn't somewhere wallowing. He was pretty good at brooding, but she won the prize for that every time. She was right. Those agents had better things to do.

JUST MAKING SURE YOU'RE SAFE.

She'd gotten into so many scrapes the last few days, he had a right to worry about her. Victoria's reply to that was a "greater than" sign and the number three. Took him a second, since he was a forty-something-year-old man, but he figured out it was a heart.

Mark stared at that heart for longer than was probably necessary.

Then he put his phone aside to read all the updates from last night and early this morning. He made a plan for his day. After he'd fulfilled those duties, he picked up his desk phone again. This time he called Salvador Alvarez.

Formerly on Victoria's task force, the man was a retired US Marshal. If anyone could find out where her grandfather had gone, it was him. Mark left the guy a long and detailed message. Then he took a minute to pray for Victoria's only living family. The man had treated her like any other piece of furniture in his house, barely acknowledging her existence until she became functional. Like if he'd run out of beer and chips, or if the bathroom needed cleaning.

He's mellowed with age.

The woman had a pathological need to see the good in everyone she cared about. She needed to be on the side of "right" so badly that she refused to believe they were capable of doing something bad. Even when she was treated like garbage, she still cared about people.

What that said about how she couldn't seem to return his affection? He didn't want to think much about it. He knew what the holdup was. But that didn't stop him from wishing about what could have been if things had been different that one pivotal afternoon. Hadn't life brought them far enough that the past shouldn't factor? Victoria didn't even want to entertain the idea, though.

But if he let her go, she would just float off like a released balloon. Who was going to catch her then?

His phone rang then. The same number he'd received the heart text from only a moment ago.

He swiped to answer. "Change your mind about that detail?"

"Dennis Pacer is dead."

The expression dropped from Mark's face. A moment of being alone and honest.

"Are you there?"

"Yeah." His voice sounded thick. "What happened?"

"I was supposed to meet him." Her voice didn't betray any emotion. It never did. "Showed up, saw him crossing the street. He was hit by a car that jumped the light and then rolled onto the sidewalk. He didn't see it coming until it was too late."

That was when a tiny portion of upset leaked into her tone. He said, "Are you okay?"

He heard her sigh. "They targeted him."

"But not you?" This time, at least. "Where are you? I'll come to you."

"I called in an anonymous tip." She gave him cross streets. "Hopefully it'll get to my team, and they will be the ones to investigate. Dennis deserves the best."

"Nothing wrong with local cops." Mark gathered up his keys. He sent a one-sentence email to two of his agents and then pocketed his wallet.

"I don't know them." She'd started walking.

Mark left the conversation about cops and moved on to another topic. "You shouldn't be on the street. It's not safe."

"I have somewhere to be."

His resolve slipped. "Will we ever get to a point in our lives where you fill me in on where that is *before* the fact, instead of after?" He pulled the door to his office open, more irritated than he had a right to be.

They had a friendship, but aside from that, certainly nothing resembling an agreement or any kind of consensus between them.

Victoria had already hung up.

Mark rode the elevator to his car, then drove to the scene. Uniformed police were on scene. He found the uniform with chevrons and stuck his hand out. "Mark Welvern." He told the guy who he was, and flashed his badge.

The cop just raised one eyebrow.

"I don't wanna take over. Just looking for information, okay? This guy was working with me on the investigation into our dirty agents." Mark had learned a long time ago that problems didn't get solved until you took ownership of them. This issue was an FBI one, and so as the ranking agent in this city, it was on him. The buck stopped with him.

"Hit and run. You think it was related?"

"I have a source who thinks it was, but she's suspicious of everything." Mark shrugged. "This guy was spearheading the cleanup. And I don't believe in coincidences."

The sergeant scratched his jaw and nodded. "Dark SUV. Could have had government plates, the witness wasn't sure. What they do know is that it barreled right for Pacer. No confusion, no mistake. They were aiming for him sure as they'd pointed a gun and pulled the trigger."

Which was the method Mark would have chosen. Clean. Less public. This was a brash message that had been received, loud and clear.

"One hit, and he was dead."

Mark blew out a breath. "Not an easy task. They couldn't have been sure they'd kill him, which means they were making a point and didn't mind coming back later if they needed to finish the job."

There were certainly cleaner ways to kill someone.

A car pulled up at the curb. Two people climbed out, a man and a woman both with federal badges displayed on their belts. It hit Mark that Josh and Dakota, an engaged couple, got to work together. Just as they were working to build a personal life together. Maybe some couples wouldn't survive both living and working together, but he always thought it'd be ideal.

They got to do it.

He got terse phone calls. Secrets. She never lied to him, but he knew there was a lot she didn't say. Because she thought he wouldn't want to know?

He sighed, then went to greet his friends. "Hey." He shook both their hands.

Dakota said, "Hey."

Josh looked him up and down. "You look terrible."

Mark wasn't going to get into all the ways that was true. "Has Victoria checked in with you?" He told them about the phone call, but not that she'd been at his house the night before. A couple that weren't planning to spend the night together until after their wedding wouldn't understand Victoria even just sleeping on his couch. With the added bonus that it would likely make them more frustrated.

Mark never wanted to carry the weight of stumbling someone he knew was a genuine believer trying to do the right thing.

Dakota folded her arms. "Don't you have more important things to do than worry about someone who can take care of herself?"

"If she carried a gun on her at all times I might not worry so much."

"She doesn't carry a *gun?*"

He shrugged. "Most spies don't, unless they think they need one."

"I always need one."

"It's a good thing you have that badge then."

She grinned. "It really is." Then she sobered. "Two agents still unaccounted for?"

Of course she was going to be all over him about that. "I have people on that." When she said nothing else, but continued to study him, he figured that meant she wanted an update. There were two stragglers who hadn't been picked up in the sweep. Two agents implicated in the dirty dealings.

He said, "One was scheduled for vacation the week of the arrests. He never showed up at his hotel."

"So he's on the lam?"

Mark nodded. "The other just disappeared. He had to have known we were going to conduct the operation and round them all up. Somehow he got wind of it and fled."

Josh glanced at the yellow tape, strung up around the spot where Pacer had died. "And in light of this?"

"I need to find out if either of them worked in Austria or anywhere in Europe five years ago when Victoria was there."

"So you have leads."

Mark nodded.

"Good," Dakota said, "When bodies drop around my friends, it's too close for comfort. She's being targeted isn't she?"

Mark understood the gravity of it, and her fear. Still, he said, "I don't think there's been a day in Victoria Bramlyn's life over the last thirty years when she wasn't in danger. It's all she knows."

"I don't have to like it."

Mark didn't either. And hadn't last night, when he'd been cleaning her bandage. "Doesn't mean there's anything we can do to change what is."

7

Victoria turned away from watching Josh and Dakota talk to Mark. She shouldn't have waited around to see who showed up. To watch the body of her colleague be scraped off the sidewalk and hauled away.

She cleared her throat and glanced up at the gray sky where the sun blazed valiantly behind.

He was dead. Now what she needed to do was focus on the next step. Langdon had known Pacer would be here, and yet he hadn't also targeted her. Not after her grandfather and the airport bathroom incident.

She glanced at the screen of her phone, then tucked it back into her purse. The police still hadn't found her grandfather. If he was being held against his will somewhere, it was a wonder he hadn't irritated his captors into releasing him. She could see that happening, and it made her smile. Better than the alternative. Victoria was a realist, but she also intentionally didn't feel things deeply. If she opened that dam, the whole ocean of her emotions would roll out like a tsunami.

And she would never get her work done.

Sure, it wasn't fair to Mark. He deserved more than the muted feelings she didn't want to acknowledge. He deserved what Josh and Dakota had. Which meant that if she was a better person, she'd have let him go a long time ago.

Apparently she just wasn't that good of a person. She was still stringing him along. Still claiming him as part of her life. Still calling. Still texting. Still thinking of him—more than she should.

He was the antidote to everything she didn't like about her life. A safe harbor. A place to go home. That two week beach vacation where you were supposed to forget about the stresses of life waiting for you back home, but you never really did. The dream of early retirement. The yearning for a life where she didn't have to glance over her shoulder all the time.

But that was all it was. A dream.

Her cell buzzed as she climbed into the driver's seat of her car. She swiped and read the text.

It's ready for you.

Victoria replied a quick, "Thanks," and drove to the Navy base at Bremerton, where Niall's desk was. The NCIS agent had been part of her task force. Now it was under a different umbrella because everyone said they needed "oversight." Like that had helped the FBI. Niall had elected to return to his traditional posting.

Niall met her in the lobby. As they walked up to the floor where his team worked, along with the assistant director of NCIS on the west coast, Niall shot her sideways glances.

Finally she said, "What?"

He worked his mouth side to side, then finally spat it out. "They told me what happened. Talia found video footage, so I know you were stabbed with plastic ware in an airport bathroom."

Victoria nearly laughed, because it was kind of funny…until she moved and it hurt.

"I can't even tell that you're injured." He tipped his head to the side. "Which makes me wonder how many other times you were hurt and I never even knew."

Victoria shrugged one shoulder. "It isn't that big of a deal."

"Don't do that." He stepped off the elevator first. "You're not a liar."

Victoria said nothing. She followed him around the outside of the office, aware of the glances shot her way. She'd long ago stopped worrying what people thought of her. But when they were good people, and hardworking, she had to put it somewhere. And that was getting more and more difficult.

"You have ten minutes." He looked at his watch. "That starts in two."

She glanced at the door to the MTAC room, a secure communication room and one of the few ways she could have a secure conference call with the committee without having to fly to Washington to meet with them in person.

"Thank you."

He shrugged. "The AD wants to talk to you before you leave."

"Copy that."

He shot her a slight smile. She didn't know any more than he did, what his boss might want with her. Maybe the assistant director just wanted to say hi to the State Department Director who was occupying his resources. Even if it was only for ten minutes.

Victoria had no authority though. Without the title, she had nothing. It gave her a lot of pull with the right people, but it was nothing more than a cover she used to fight against FBI corruption. To follow a hunch.

Sure, she'd turned out to be right. But that didn't mean she hadn't hurt her friends in the process.

"This'll be over soon."

The skin around his eyes narrowed. "That's what you want?"

She shrugged. She'd be out of their hair, then. The team could move on with their lives, and their relationships. Like Sal was doing.

The buzzer on the door sounded.

Niall pulled it open, and she stepped inside. "See you in a minute."

The door clicked shut in her face, and she turned to the Navy seaman who handed her a headset. "They're ready for you."

She muttered, "Thanks" and donned the headset. Victoria cleared her mind so she could focus on the call and stepped forward. On the screen were two images of men. One blank square, where Pacer's face should be. The fourth quarter of the screen read, STAND BY where a woman's face should have been.

There was no way she was late. "We're two down?"

The Secretary of Defense, Andrew Jakeman, nodded. "I have agents from NCIS in Arlington headed down to her house now. They should be checking in soon."

"Hurst?"

He looked scared. His bronze hair and the age lines on his face were stark against the rest of his pale skin. "The situation is dire." The older man wiped at his brow. "Steps must be taken to maintain security."

"General Hurst—"

Jakeman cut her off. "You gotta man up Hurst. We all knew this was going to happen. If that Army base of grunts can't keep you safe, what hope is there for the rest of us?"

Jakeman wasn't exactly swinging in the breeze either. He had security on him at all times. It had been part of their agreement when she'd presented him with the idea of forming a committee. Gathering evidence. Taking it to the US Attorney.

Finally finishing what was started five years ago.

Victoria wasn't going to allow Langdon to get away. Not this time.

Pacer was dead. Their fifth committee member was Supreme Court Justice Isabella Cellini. Victoria wanted to text Mark. Tell him to pray she was all right, that they'd find her safe and well and that she would be protected. But she'd left her phone outside the room, for security reasons. And besides, it wasn't like she really believed prayer worked. But...it felt better than doing nothing.

Hurst made a face. He first muttered something neither she nor Jakeman could hear, then, "Pacer is dead."

"I know," Victoria said. "I was there. I saw that SUV hit him."

The thud. The image of his body flying through the air before it landed on the pavement. She shut her eyes for a moment while Jakeman chastised Hurst.

That ever present cold in her soul was there. The dam that held her resolve where it should be, the place her feelings went to get absorbed by the numbness of it. It was like cryostasis, sitting there inside her. A good thing for a spy to have—or so they'd told her.

She used those same tools now, though it had occurred to her that maybe she didn't need them. No. That wave stood ready to crash down on her the moment she let her guard down.

Jakeman and Hurst were quiet for a few seconds. She figured what had blown through was gone now. "Pacer had Assistant Director Welvern mention Langdon in an interview."

Jakeman nodded. "And the next day, he's dead. Do you think Welvern is in danger?"

"The pains we took to keep Mark under suspicion have been working. He's a gray area to everyone in and around the investigation, so much so that Langdon is unlikely to target him. Even local police are taking the concept on board." She'd seen that with her own eyes.

Jakeman's expression changed. She'd never liked that face on him, the one where, in any other scenario, she'd have been his daughter doing something he disapproved of.

"It's for his own good."

"Mmm."

She shot him a look. "Hurst, do you have anything to add?"

"Just get the FBI there to work faster."

"They're already aware this needs to be done as quickly as possible. But if it's not done correctly, they'll find themselves under so much scrutiny they'll be paralyzed and unable to do their jobs."

Hurst made a face of his own. "Well, perhaps they can at least manage to find Langdon before we're all killed like Pacer."

He shifted in his seat right before his image on the screen switched to black.

Jakeman sighed. "His fear is not without justification."

Victoria didn't have an argument for that.

"Care to tell me what measures you've put in place for your own security?"

She shifted her stance and pain rippled through her middle. She winced. "Mr. Secretary—"

"Don't give me that…" He used an Italian word she was pretty sure meant poop, but it might have meant trash. "You and I both know what I'd have to deal with at home if you were killed. Especially when I knew you were in danger and didn't convince you to exercise a little good sense."

Victoria smiled. "They'd get over it."

"You know that's not true."

Her amusement faded. "I know." He started to argue more so she lifted her hands. "I know. Sorry. I do know that."

"Be safe. For goodness' sakes."

She said, "Langdon took my grandfather."

"Call Sal. He knows how to find people, right? You're the one who told me that."

"He won't help me." Ugh. Her voice made her sound like a teenager who couldn't get their best friend to forgive them. "You call him."

"Coward."

"It would work. He'd do it for you."

"He'd be doing it for you. Even responding to an order from the secretary of defense."

Not many people would turn that down, even someone who'd never worked for him. Victoria had known Andrew Jakeman for years—five years—since he was the US ambassador to Austria. She'd worked a mission in France a year before the job that led her to betrayal. His daughter had been kidnapped. Victoria had tracked her down in Czechoslovakia on a train, about to be shipped east to yet another country where she would be sold to the highest bidder.

That had given her the insight she'd needed only a few months ago when Talia had been sold into that same world. Skills she'd never wanted but had utilized to save people. To protect those who worked to keep America safe. To keep her secrets.

"What I want to know is why you're not the one down there finding him?"

Victoria bit her lips, then swallowed. "I can do more good here, finding Langdon. Rooting out the problem from the source."

"You don't think Langdon is in Florida?" Jakeman frowned. "Do you think your grandfather is dead already?"

"They haven't called with a ransom. They took him, then one doubled back to wait for me." She hadn't wanted to admit it to herself, but Jakeman deserved her honesty. That was the relationship they'd established. She'd saved his daughter's life, and he'd promised her anything she wanted.

After the other Austria job went so wrong and she'd woken up in a South African prison, Victoria had recuperated and then gone right back to his house. Together, they'd figured it out.

And made a plan to get Langdon for good.

To expose the corruption in the FBI.

That was all she'd worked for these past five years. All she'd done. All she'd thought about. Every move, every decision. Every case. It had been all about this.

The fallout would probably cost her everything, but she would be able to walk away with a clear conscience that she'd done the right thing.

She said, "Langdon wants me on edge. He doesn't care about making a trade or getting something from me." She took a breath. "And he knows I'm not going to stop. That's why he's continued his attempts to kill me, even with my grandfather in his grasp."

Jakeman was quiet for a moment. Then he said, "There's only one person who might know what he's got planned."

A deafening noise like thunder sounded throughout the room. The whole place shook.

Victoria stumbled and nearly went down.

"What's happenin—" Jakeman's image went black. Dust rained from the ceiling.

She turned to the uniformed seaman at the computer. "Are we under attack?"

8

" A research facility in Bremerton just blew up."
Mark looked up from the conference table of papers at the female agent who'd walked in. She had a tablet in her hands.

"There's more."

He motioned to her to go ahead.

"St. Petersburg Police Department got back to us about that case you asked about…" She paused, reaching for an explanation. He didn't give her one. "They've gone through surveillance footage from the neighborhood. Found a man driving a black van leaving the scene, he's their main suspect."

"And the man they took into custody?"

"That's why I came here. Florida police cut that guy loose before we could find out who he is." She frowned down at the tablet, then strode over and flipped it so he could see the screen. "Take a look for yourself."

"That's one of our AWOL agents." Mark pulled over a still photo from the file, the one he'd spread out on the conference table. "Tell me I'm not crazy."

She tipped her head to the side. "Maybe."

"So reassuring."

She chuckled. Then he realized how close she was standing and took a step back. This was his place of work, and Mark was the boss. The female agent pressed her lips together. "It could be Vance Davies. That certainly would be handy, a man we're looking for here. One of our dirty agents shows up as a suspect in a crime you asked about in Florida."

"Yes, it would." He blew out a breath. "I'd like to know about any and all developments at once."

She winced. "I'm not sure they're gonna agree, considering they only told us this much out of courtesy."

"Then tell them that guy—" He motioned to the tablet screen. "—is one of our dirty agents, and we'd appreciate their help bringing him in."

"That might work." She spun around and walked away.

"Tines."

She glanced back at him over her shoulder. "Sir?"

"The explosion."

She looked down at the tablet. "It was a research facility, close to the Navy base. They're responding to the scene. Initial reports say it was some kind of incident, but they're holding off on what actually happened. Word is, ATF is headed over as well."

The time was past when he'd have sent a handful of agents over in order to assist. Thanks to the dirty ones, the whole FBI had been tarred with the same brush. The Navy would close ranks even tighter than they normally did, not wanting any help from feds they didn't know they could trust.

Mark didn't blame them. But they had to carry on regardless, because they couldn't just all pack up and go home. Call it quits. The good agents had to stay on the job. Do the right thing.

They'd all been vetted. But that didn't matter now that they had a reputation. Other agencies, the police and the military, only concentrated on the fact they'd operated with bad seeds among the good.

Mark went back to his files.

Had the man in Florida, the one Victoria questioned about her grandfather's kidnapping, really been the man he was looking for now? The FBI agent had worked in Portland for the past three years. Before that he'd been in Quantico on extended training. Prior to that he had been in Berlin, Germany.

Close enough to Austria. It also fit the time frame.

This agent was the one who'd never showed up to his vacation. His wife and two children were at his house. The man had rented an apartment two years ago, leaving his wife for a string of broken relationships. She'd eventually moved to Seattle, where her parents lived.

Mark had already interviewed her once.

Maybe he needed to do it again. Drop the name Oscar Langdon, and see how she reacts. She might know more about her husband's history than what she told him—particularly the time they'd lived in Europe.

"Sir?"

He didn't look up. "Yeah, Tines."

"You have a visitor."

He glanced over to where she pointed to the far end of the office. Victoria strode through the open plan area to where he stood beyond a wall of glass windows. Wide eyes. Brittle smile.

He met her in the doorway and walked her straight to his office where he shut the door and closed the blinds.

"What—"

She bent double and sucked in breaths, dropping her purse on the floor.

"Oh, honey."

"Don't." She shook her head, her long blonde hair hanging down by her knees. "Don't be sweet. You'll make it worse."

"You want me to be a jerk."

She lifted up, immediately turning so he couldn't see her face. "It would make things easier."

Now why would he ever want to make things easier for her?

Mark said, "Did he try to hurt you again?" Or was it her grandfather? Had she already heard news that he hadn't?

"The explosion."

"The one in Bremerton? That was you?"

"I was on the phone in Niall's office. MTAC?" When he nodded, she continued, "I thought we were under attack." Her whole body shuddered. "I thought there were going to be hundreds of deaths. Because of me. Because he was destroying a building, just to get to me."

His whole body relaxed, releasing the tension. He moved to her and held his arms out. She walked into the hug, holding his waist while the tremors worked through her.

He rubbed his hand up and down her back, thanking God in silence that she'd sought him out. She hadn't gone anywhere else but had come to see him when she needed someone. A friend, but still. It meant something.

He didn't bother asking her if she was all right. It was obvious she wasn't, but she'd never appreciated her weaknesses being pointed out.

The door opened and someone cleared their throat. He turned to find the Director of the FBI, his boss from Washington D.C. Victoria turned the other direction. Probably to compose herself.

The director had no hair, just a shiny, bald head. His face was lined—stress from work, laughter shared with his grandchildren and every experience between. His tie was red, and his suit pure black. Well cut. Nicer than what Mark could afford, by far. Then again, that was what the D.C. federal culture stood for—good impressions. Politicking. Something he'd never appreciated, which was why he was clear across the country doing investigative work and not sitting behind his desk like so many assistant directors.

"I should be going." Her voice was soft. Unsure. He'd heard that tone before, and he'd never liked it.

The last thing he wanted was for Victoria to disappear again.

Especially with the current threat. But holding onto her was like trying to catch a cloud.

"Victoria Bramlyn, yes? That is who you are?" The FBI Director held out his hand.

Mark tensed. It was automatic, given how much scrutiny he and all the other agents on the West Coast were under right now.

She shook his hand. "Director Bramlyn. That's right."

"We've had a development on the search for the two unaccounted for agents."

He realized after he said it that he sounded like a kid trying to impress their parent.

The director nodded. "I've decided to take a personal interest going forward. Too many things are happening, and we need to get all this straightened out."

"We would appreciate your assistance, sir."

"I've also brought Pacer's replacement with me."

"You can't replace a man like that." Victoria lifted her chin, daring him to challenge her assessment.

"Nevertheless." The director eyed her. "Duty demands that we do our best."

"True." She nodded her head.

"I can walk you through what I have, if you'd like."

The director strode to Mark's desk, rounded it and set his briefcase on the surface. "I'd like all updates in email."

"Yes, sir." Mark motioned for Victoria to go with him, and they stepped out. He shut the door, leaving his boss in his office occupying his desk.

She stopped and looked up at him.

Mark read everything he needed to know on her face. He smiled. "It's fine."

She chuckled, shaking her head. It had been cute when she was twelve, and it was still cute now.

With a whoosh, the director yanked the blinds cord so it raised all the way to the top of the door. He stared at them through the glass. Caught again, having a personal moment in the office. During work hours.

Victoria turned away. Probably so he wouldn't be able to see her face. "I'm going to leave now."

Mark followed her to the elevator. "I'd rather you stayed here."

"Like your boss is going to be okay with that?"

They walked past Special Agent Tines, who shot Victoria a side glance. Whatever that was about. But she didn't know what Victoria had been through.

When he didn't say anything, she hit the button to go down. "I'm not going to be standing next to you when the next car comes barreling down the sidewalk."

Despite the bravado in her tone, he'd known her long enough to read between the lines. "Where do you think I *want* to be when your life is being threatened?"

The elevator doors opened. She got on and it was empty, so he did as well. No way would he pass up the chance for a few more minutes of quiet conversation with her.

Victoria shot him a look, but there was the edge of a smile on her face. "Are you going to pull the emergency button and make the elevator stop between floors so you can get in my face?"

"That wouldn't be what I'd do." He shot her a look and let her figure out what he meant by that.

Victoria's cheeks flushed. A former spy, a woman who'd seen probably everything and hadn't been left unscathed by the horrors of the world. Still, there was a slash of innocence that hung in the air between them. Like a secret shared by only the two of them.

"Please let me keep you safe."

Her gaze drifted to the side. "I don't want you getting hurt."

He took a step closer, but didn't touch her. "Can you see how I'd think the same about you?"

She scrunched up her nose.

"So what aren't you telling me?"

She opened her mouth, but hesitated first. "We need to find

Langdon." A shutter fell over her eyes, blocking him from reading any expression. "He put me in that prison. I think he's one of these FBI agents."

"Only one left. The other one was in Florida, but not the guy from the shed."

She nodded.

"Are you going to draw him out?" Though he wouldn't assume she'd lose that fight, it would likely cost her dearly.

"I'm going to do what it takes to bring him down."

"And then?"

She shrugged, not meeting his gaze.

"So there's no future for us?" When she didn't answer, he said, "I know the worst about you, and you can say the same about me. What could be so bad?"

She inhaled and he saw her entire body shudder. Fear. That was all this was. *God, give her Your love that casts out fear.* He didn't have any answer for her, aside from faith.

The elevator dipped. She moved to him, kissed his cheek, and then strode out into the lobby while he stared after her.

9

T he car door opened. There was a breath of fear, and then Victoria smelled food. "Please tell me that's Pad Thai."

Mark slid into the passenger seat with a white grocery bag on his lap. "I got your text."

All she'd told him was where she'd parked. The dinner was all him. He handed her one of two cartons and a plastic fork. She flipped the lid and the smell wafted up. "Yum."

Mark chuckled.

"Good day at the office, dear?"

He shot her a sideways look. She knew what that meant. Yes, she was happy. And why not? She got to spend time with him, and the lighter she could make it the better. Even though what they were doing had huge implications, she needed the banter. The sharing of a meal and friendship.

As much as she loved their quiet "moments" where feelings swelled and words were shared, she knew it wasn't helpful for either of them.

"The director told me to show up tomorrow with movement on the case."

"Or what?"

"I don't know." He shoved a forkful of sticky beef in his mouth.

Victoria stared out the front windshield, watching the house down the street. The wife and her kids had come home an hour ago, the little girl dressed like she'd been at dance class.

Her phone rang in the cup holder. The screen read, *Talia,* but she didn't answer it. Nor did she explain the reason to Mark. Even though he shot her another look.

"Are you wearing *jeans?*"

"What?" She swallowed the bite before attempting to speak around it again.

"Have I seen you in jeans since high school?"

"I don't know? Have you?"

Mark didn't comment on her sneakers, though maybe he couldn't see them in the dark. He ate, then pulled the paper file she'd stashed between the seat and the center console, the spot where everything disappeared down under the seat. He flipped through the pages. "Is there a reason why you want to sit on the ex-spouse's house of a man last seen in Florida?"

It didn't sound as accusatory as it probably could have.

She wanted to retort, ask why she couldn't simply have wanted an excuse to have dinner with him. But she didn't. That man had been in her grasp, and she'd left him in that shed. One of their missing corrupt agents.

"I got word he was seen at the Denver airport, on security cameras. We think Vance Davies made his way back here after the police in Florida let him go."

"To come after you again?" He sounded like he might think that was a bad thing.

"I want him to," she said. "This is the only place I can think of that he'd go."

"Better than you standing on a street corner wearing a sign that says, *Come get me.*"

"Please." She grinned, still watching the house. "I'd be more eloquent than that. I might even craft a haiku for such an occasion."

Mark laughed. He reached over and squeezed her knee. "I'll be there to help."

"Bear already did." Dog snuggles cured basically everything.

"You saw him?"

She nodded. "I let him out at lunch and then took a quick nap." He was quiet long enough that she finally glanced over for a second. "What?"

"Not that I mind you helping take care of my dog, but your place doesn't work?"

"Too obvious."

"I thought you wanted to draw him out?"

"On my terms." She bit her lip. "I don't like the idea of being surprised in the shower."

"So you're using mine instead?"

"What can I say? I appreciate your handyman skills." The tile he'd put in the master upstairs was better than anything she'd seen on Pinterest.

Mark went quiet again. She didn't disturb him. Neither felt the need to fill the silence with more awkward conversation.

She needed the man from the surveillance in Florida—the one who had likely kidnapped her grandfather—to show up here. She wanted to sit him down so he could explain everything. He had to know about Langdon, among several other things she needed answers to.

The second file Mark pulled out was thicker. "This is the agent we think is Oscar Langdon."

She nodded, though he probably didn't need her to confirm that.

"Colin Pinton. Forty-nine, with more than twenty years on the job as an FBI agent. Stationed in Europe for most of that, working with Interpol and local agencies. Racked up some commendations. Closed a lot of cases and only got one mark on his record when an artifact was lost in transit and unaccounted for."

Victoria huffed out a breath as she looked at the picture; fighting the urge to wince. The man from that office in Austria? She still couldn't remember.

"We can't prove that Colin Pinton is Oscar Langdon, right?"

"If we could, I wouldn't be sitting here," she bit out. Of course, that would be the answer she was looking for. The thing she'd been trying to figure out for years. "And Pacer wouldn't be dead."

It was past time to admit the truth to herself.

Colin Pinton was Oscar Langdon.

"No, you'd probably *all* be dead. Every single one of your committee. A guy like this doesn't go down easily."

"Yeah," she said. "I know that. I have the scars to prove it." Not to mention stitches that didn't feel good right now. She'd raided his medicine cabinet for over-the-counter pain killers, but they were wearing off now.

"Maybe I should have brought ice cream."

She whipped her head around to face him. "Get some if you must, but don't even think about touching my Pad Thai."

Mark chuckled. "Anything?" He motioned to the window.

"Not yet. Maybe he won't show up." She blew out a breath. "Maybe he's watching my condo. Or sitting in *his* car watching *us.*"

"Or he's got a rocket launcher, and we're about to be blown up."

She narrowed her eyes. "Any last words?"

"Depends on whether you'll say them back."

Victoria didn't move. She stared out the window so long her eyes burned, and she had to blink. He had too much hope. That was the problem. Too much faith that "God would work things out in the end," or whatever. There was no point in admitting that what he wanted might also be what she wanted. It would never change.

"I don't care about this guy." She needed this conversation steered back around and on track. "I mean, he and I need to finish that conversation we started in the shed in Florida, but my focus here is Langdon."

"And we have no idea where he is."

She shrugged one shoulder. "Doesn't matter. I'll find him eventually. He's covered his tracks for years." She did appreciate a formidable opponent much more than a stupid one who made mistakes enough to land him effortlessly in her lap. "But he's the one who put me in that prison in South Africa. For that alone, he's going to answer."

Mark didn't move, and he didn't touch her. "That's always been a mystery to me. He could have killed you right then and there."

"He'd have had to explain a body." And the ambassador would never have let her death go unanswered.

"He could have dumped it."

"My disappearance would have caused an international event when Andrew heard of it. No one in law enforcement across three continents would be able to rest until he found out what happened to me."

She heard him shift. "Andrew?"

"Jakeman." She glanced at him. "The secretary of defense."

"That's how you did it. The Sec-Def is on your committee."

It wasn't a question, but she nodded anyway.

"Why am I not surprised? I wondered who was sending me those emails. The ones that led me to South Africa. I'd have never found that lead if not for him." Mark said, "There still has to be a reason why Langdon didn't kill you."

Victoria knew exactly what the reason was. She just had no intention of telling Mark.

She changed the subject again. "Does Talia have all that information on Colin Pinton, a.k.a. Oscar Langdon?"

"You didn't send it to her?"

Victoria didn't answer that. "Their boss doesn't like it when I contact them. He gets all butt-hurt, like I think they still work for me."

"So you've been cut loose."

"I still get paid. Technically the secretary of state is my boss, but I don't think he likes me anymore after all that business with his psycho-terrorist son. I don't think I'll get my next pay raise."

"I can see how pointing out the fact he wasn't helping anyone by covering up the issue might have been a problem for him."

"He should take a leaf out of the FBI's book," she said. "Press conference. Full transparency. Efficient cleanup of the situation, with your best assistant director on the case."

He chuckled. "We try."

Mark barely got the words out before she had the door open and was climbing out of the car. The dark figure up the street approaching the wife's house might be the man who'd kidnapped her grandfather. She was going to find out.

Victoria snuck along the outside of the cars, running down the street with her head ducked. The man walked under a streetlight and a breath escaped her. She sucked in another and held her breath so she didn't have to cough.

She could hear Mark's muted footsteps coming up behind her but kept watch on the man. They needed to intercept him before he—

Something had to have spooked him. He looked in her direction. She ducked down, but wasn't convinced she was fast enough.

Then he turned and ran.

Victoria groaned and raced after him. The stitches in her side pulled, but she'd maintained a decent fitness level for years now. She could hold her own. Which hopefully was more than this guy from Florida could say.

"Left."

Mark broke off, taking a side street. It was a gamble, trying to cut the person off, but she hoped it would pay off for him.

Victoria pumped her legs and tried not to swing her arms too much. She didn't want to rip her stitches.

The man turned the corner left, up ahead. She breathed a thank you to whoever was listening. It seemed natural to offer gratitude to someone other than herself for something that benefited her but that was completely out of her control. She wasn't going to tell Mark that, though. He'd get all excited and think she wanted him to explain his beliefs again.

She darted around the corner at a full run. Every step she gained on him. When the man stumbled to turn again, she covered even more ground.

At the last second, it occurred to her that it might not be a good idea, but it was too late. Victoria tackled the guy, and they fell to the ground in a tangle of limbs.

His elbow jabbed into the exact spot where her stitches were. Victoria cried out and kicked him away from her.

"FBI! Freeze!"

She lay there, staring up at the cloudy night sky, just trying to breathe and not throw up.

Vance Davies lifted both hands.

"Don't move." Mark kept his gun aimed on the guy, but said, "What was it you said about not needing me?"

"I never said I didn't need you."

She realized what she'd said and studied his expression since he wasn't looking at her. Then she focused and got to her feet. This was about finding Langdon. Being this close to Mark, and spending this time with him, was an anomaly. Soon enough things would go back to normal. Sure, she'd have to move again, but that was no big deal. She didn't care about her apartments. They weren't home.

She faced off the guy on the ground. "Where is my grandfather?"

10

Mark's heart clenched. Not normally a sensitive type or to take cases personally, Victoria was the one person who brought that out in him. Her grandfather's fate was going to haunt her. Whether he lived or died—because of her actions and choices—would be something she lived with for the rest of her life.

Davies said nothing and didn't seem inclined to do much right now but lie there on the ground looking up at them both like all of this was amusing to him.

Mark handed her a set of cuffs and held aim on the man while she flipped him and put the bracelets on.

If this guy made one move to harm her again, Mark would shoot him. No matter that he could be their star witness against the FBI agent they thought was Oscar Langdon.

It should stun him to realize that all along an agent had been working for himself, causing mayhem. Murdering people. But given all that had happened recently, he just couldn't bring himself to be surprised. So much corruption had been revealed. The FBI needed a culture change now, and he intended to spearhead that as the head of the Seattle office.

That promotion had been a surprise in itself. Not that he'd argued it. He'd been seriously flattered that the director had appointed him. That a man who didn't seem to like him had respected him enough to know he'd do a good job and had invited Mark to apply.

Now he was doing the best job he could. Just as he had all along.

He hauled Vance Davies up, and they walked him to the car. Victoria followed, but he couldn't gauge her expression in the dark of the evening. She'd mentioned her grandfather before Langdon —the person he'd thought she was going to ask Davies about. A reflex.

Out of the abundance of the heart, the mouth speaks.

He knew she hurt for her grandfather and the suffering he might be enduring right now. Regardless of how Mark felt about how the guy had treated Victoria, she cared for him. Some people just never experience what a healthy family relationship feels like. He'd seen her try to keep that toxic relationship because it was all the "family" she had.

When he caught a look at her in the streetlamp, over the roof of the car, she seemed embarrassed. Because she was concerned for her grandfather?

Mark called out, "Can you call the local police in St. Petersburg and find out if they have any new leads? They might want to talk to this guy."

"Tomorrow." She nodded. "Let's just get this guy back to your office."

Mark nodded. He drove, giving her his gun to hold. Not pointing it at the guy. She didn't need to risk Vance Davies grabbing it and causing harm. Just in case.

He kept an eye out for tails. Davies had been the one in the SUV who'd killed Pacer. "Why'd you do it?"

He had a whole lot more questions than just that but needed to start somewhere. He said, "Why did you kidnap an old man in

Florida? Why did you run down the assistant US attorney with an SUV."

Mark couldn't see his face. Not while he was driving. Neither could he ask the guy to scoot across the backseat so he'd be able to get a look in the rearview.

"I'm not talking without a lawyer."

"Smart move." Not that he'd expect anything less from an agent with years on the job. But confession wasn't something they could base a case on. Not like the police could. They needed evidence, which they'd have to gather if they were going to make charges stick. The surveillance video was good but might not be enough.

Victoria shifted in her seat. She hadn't put her seatbelt on, which made him nervous. But she was angled to watch for any move Davies might make. Probably to protect Mark, even knowing he would object to that. Victoria had always done what she believed to be right no matter what. Not a popular standpoint, given the lengths she would go to safeguard those she loved. Or to get the result she desperately wanted. Thankfully she worked for good and for justice, instead of for her own selfish motives like Oscar Langdon did.

"I just don't get it," she said. "You could have easily walked up to Pacer and shot him. Yet you chose to hit him with your car. That was big, brash, and public. You also didn't guarantee you'd actually kill him. Were you really only trying to maim him, or what?"

Mark heard Davies give a low chuckle. "He said you were coldhearted, but I didn't believe him."

"Because I'm not all torn up about my grandfather? Who says I'm not? Just because Langdon thinks I'm coldhearted doesn't mean it's true."

"I guess it's all that spy training. You'll do whatever it takes to get the guy, even betray everything you stand for and everyone you know." Davies paused for second. "After all, that's exactly what you're doing right now."

"You're a late addition, right? I don't remember your face from Europe. That means you joined up after you met Langdon here." It was her turn to pause for effect. "You really wanted to lose your wife and kids over him? Why?"

Davies didn't answer.

Mark had his own ideas about why that was. It was possible that the marital problems that led to their divorce didn't have anything to do with his signing on as one of Langdon's crew. Then again, it might easily be a symptom of the bigger problem. His wife could have seen the change in him when Langdon started working on Davies to get him to turn against his oath.

Considering all the psychological testing they went through before and during their training at Quantico, Mark still had a hard time believing any of them malleable. Yet Langdon had managed to form a crew of men who'd gone to great lengths to do his work.

It had to have been money. He'd never met Langdon, as Colin Pinton had worked out of the San Francisco office. Perhaps he was one of those people who could persuade anyone to buy his line. Then there were the people more susceptible to taking it on board than others.

Agents with gambling problems. Secret affairs. Those who had taken bribes before.

No agency or department was completely free of those who might second guess their choice to do the right thing. People not so steady in their resolve.

It was the antithesis of everything Victoria was and everything she stood for. Of exactly the person she had been since the day he'd met her. Mark wasn't entirely sure anything would ever change that.

But if there was one thing he could ask God to do, it was that He might change her heart toward Him, the God who made heaven and earth.

Davies spoke again. "I guess you guys are gonna offer me some sweet deal for testifying, right?"

"No," Victoria said. "We're going to do something else."

Mark knew exactly where she was going. He said, "We're going to spread it far and wide that you sang like a canary." He paused. "Do canaries sing? I've never understood that expression. But whatever it means, Langdon is going to hear that you told us everything in exchange for special treatment."

"You wouldn't—"

"If you want to live," Victoria cut him off. "Then you'll give us enough that we can get the US attorney to guarantee you protection. Good enough that we'll get your family into witness security."

Davies roared. He whacked the back of the driver's seat to let out his frustration.

Victoria tensed in the passenger seat. Those protective instincts leading her to be all the more cautious about what Davies was prepared to do. "If you don't want Langdon to find out that you spilled everything to us, you are gonna tell us where to find him right now."

He could hear the anxiousness in her tone. She wanted to interrogate him until he told her everything he knew about her grandfather and where the man had been taken.

Davies let out another frustrated cry. "You think I know where he is? It's not like he checks in with me on his whereabouts."

"How do you two communicate?" Mark gripped the wheel and turned a corner onto the street where the office was located. "How did he tell you where to go in Florida and what the plan was?"

He pulled into a space and put the car in park. He got out and pulled Davies to his feet, despite the man's reluctance to be brought in. Then again, the man should've thought of that before he made the decision to betray his oath.

He started to walk, holding Davies's elbow. The man didn't move. When Mark looked back at him, Davies said, "I want my family protected."

"Tell me where Langdon is."

Davies shook his head. "Not until I get your guarantee that they are in witness security."

"That's going to take time, considering you murdered the previous US attorney working on this. The new one is going to have to be read in, probably after we rouse him from his hotel bed considering what time it is. Might not make him super amenable to giving you whatever you ask for."

Mark moved closer to the man, aware that Victoria had come closer around the hood of the car in order to hear what they were saying over the moving traffic. Even this late at night, the surrounding area droned with activity. "So whatever it is you have to say, it had better be good."

Davies worked his jaw side to side. "He's up to something. That's what the explosion in Bremerton was about. He needed something from the lab."

Mark sucked in a breath. That had been a military research lab. A place where they made electronics that went into all kinds of weapons. Computers. Communications equipment. The possible implications ran like one of those old school calculators that spit the numbers out on a long paper receipt.

Victoria shifted closer to Davies. "What does he have, and what is he going to do with it?"

A muscle in Davies' jaw twitched.

"You can either tell us," she said, "or you go to prison knowing your family is directly in the line of fire."

Davies shook his head, a defiant look in his eyes. "There's nothing you can do to stop it. No one can get in the way when Langdon wants something."

"What does he want?" Victoria seemed prepared to push him until he broke.

Mark was the one with the final authority here. He needed to bring this guy in with no bruises. He hoped that Victoria understood the tight rope he was walking right now. And yet, they both wanted the same result.

He had never before been open to the idea of deliberately

going against what he had been trained to do. There were lines no one was supposed to cross. Despite what all these agents had done. Langdon was a guy who did what he wanted, no matter the fallout. There were some who thought the ends always justified the means. But Mark wasn't one of them. Procedure was there for a reason.

Victoria said, "Answer the question, Davies. Or I ask assistant director Welvern to step inside without us for a minute so we can chat in private."

Mark was about to object to that when Davies shifted. The decision had been made. He shoved at both of them, and before Mark could grab him, the man ran flat out toward the street.

Vance Davies ran out in front of the truck coming head on.

The collision flipped his body into the air much like Pacer's had done when Davies hit the guy with that SUV.

And also like Pacer, Vance Davies was dead when he hit the pavement.

11

Somewhere over the Atlantic, Thursday 12.42p.m.

S he had turned away. At the last second, right before that car hit Vance Davies, Victoria had turned away.

Paperback tucked against her stomach, blanket covering her legs, Victoria held her eyes closed behind the sleep mask. Underneath her, the drone of the airplane engine provided white noise. She had a hard time at home if there was too much quiet. Sometimes she played those tracks that were coffee shop noises and conversation, just so she could sleep.

Her phone buzzed, tucked into her back pocket. She'd logged onto the airplane Wi-Fi so she'd have email during the flight. She pulled it out and looked, then stowed it into her backpack tucked under the seat in front.

EVERYTHING IS IN PLACE.

Andrew Jakeman, the Secretary of Defense, didn't often coordinate directly with the guys whose boots were on the ground overseas. Unless it was a time like this. Unless it meant finding out what Langdon was up to.

Her friend had pulled strings. It didn't sit right with her that she'd asked for a favor, but she was cut off from a lot of resources right now, and the asset she needed to speak to was hard to reach.

Cut off, the way she'd done with Mark.

It all played back through her mind. That sickening thud. Knowing what Davies had done, how he'd ended his life by his own choice rather than Langdon making that choice for him when he found out Davies was "cooperating."

Her fault? Maybe, but she wasn't going to spend energy regretting her choices. If she did that, she'd never be able to move forward.

Like regretting her choice to disappear the moment Mark had turned away to make his phone call and get help for the Davies' situation. She hadn't looked back. Just walked away from the scene, trying to pretend she hadn't been there.

A tear gathered under the sleep mask, wetting the material with a single drop.

She knew herself well enough to have come to terms with simple facts about herself long ago. She was an ex-spy who didn't like death. Didn't want to see death. Didn't want to be around death. Certainly couldn't actually kill someone.

Even being responsible for someone's death was bothering her. Wrong line of work? She hadn't thought so. The ways Victoria had used her spy skills over the years had little to with all the ways she could kill someone…yes, most of her skills required only her bare hands.

The airplane lights came on. Flight attendants brought a light breakfast, and she drank the coffee. Black. She'd probably start heaving if she ate anything, and it was easier to get over jet lag in the fasted state as opposed to having a disoriented stomach full of food.

The guy beside her looked like he wanted to talk, but she just ignored him. What was the point? Plane was going to land in twenty minutes, according to the pilot's garbled French, relayed over the intercom. Besides, he'd be just one more person she'd disappoint with all the ways she fell short.

Victoria appeared as any other business woman going through immigration at Charles De Gaulle airport in Paris, and she produced papers for the university symposium she was attending. Supposedly.

She walked to baggage claim, smiling to herself about supposedly being at the symposium. By the time she was pulling her rolling case out the doors, her amusement had faded.

Then she saw who was at the curb.

He held both arms wide and yelled, "Babydoll!"

Victoria stopped. She cocked one hip and set her free hand there. "I told you to stop callin' me that." She used her favorite accent—raised in Georgia, went to school in Tennessee.

"Was told you needed a care package." He patted the hood of the ugly old family car he was partly sitting on.

Two Asian ladies walked between them. As soon as they'd passed, Victoria crossed the distance. Three guys piled out of the backseat of the car, and the driver's door opened. The five of them circled her.

"They let you guys out of your cage, just for me?"

The sergeant grinned. "Just for you."

They might not be in uniform, but that didn't mean there wasn't a sense of it in the way they all wore jeans, boots, and T-shirts. Couple ball caps...including one on the new guy.

She gave him a side glance, but no one introduced them. "Welp. Better get going, I guess."

The sergeant didn't move, so neither did the rest of them. "Need some help?"

"Y'all authorized for that?" She glanced around the team. They weren't. "I figure the brass won't be too happy if you guys go off script. The Sec-Def might owe me, but I'm not gonna push it like that."

"I don't like it." The sergeant folded his huge arms across the bigger expanse of his chest. "It doesn't sit right with me that a woman swings out there alone."

"Some missions require...finesse."

He snorted.

"Not your bull-in-a-china-shop tactics. Even if they are fun to watch."

"More fun when they let us blow stuff up."

She tipped her head to the side. "Like I said, fun to watch." Someone chuckled. She didn't glance around to find out who it was. "I'll be fine. But thanks."

"If I see your body on the ten o'clock news, I'm gonna be seriously pissed."

Victoria leaned up and kissed his cheek. "Now you know how I feel."

He tossed her the keys, and the team broke off. Victoria climbed in the front seat of the car and watched as Delta Force's finest disappeared into the Paris airport crowd. It wasn't the spy way to have a team for backup. Her job really was more about finesse than about brute force, as she'd told them. Both had applications, which was why both existed.

Besides, she already owed them for saving her once early on in the Sergeant's career. Back when he'd been the new guy on the team, and she had been a green spy in big trouble.

Victoria didn't want to owe him double.

Two hours later she was winding through countryside hill roads, sunglasses on. She'd stopped to check out the arsenal they'd stuffed in the trunk and found some interesting things that would likely come in handy.

Victoria checked her watch and pulled off to the side. She parked the car behind cover so that it would be disguised from the street and pulled the spike strip out. She pocketed a stun gun, along with a pistol she didn't want to use. She strapped on a bullet proof vest and grabbed a baton.

It didn't take long until the information she was given proved true.

A white van. No escort. No markings.

Victoria tossed the spike strip in front of it. The van tires blew.

It veered to the side and off the hard shoulder, into a ditch where it landed on the passenger side.

Victoria pulled the stun gun out and raced to the driver's door. She climbed up and saw that both the men upfront—full gear, their helmets off—were unconscious. She zip tied one hand each to the steering wheel and then moved to the back door.

Inside she could hear movement. Then gunshots. Muffled, given the insulation that had been added to the side panels, the roof, and the doors.

Victoria stood off to the side as she opened the door. A man raced out, uniformed but unarmed. She zapped him.

He fell to the grass, still twitching.

Victoria watched the open door and listened. Slowly she moved until she could see. Three men in uniform, all dead.

A woman lay sprawled on one, gun in her hands. A hood was placed over her head, secured to the overalls she wore. She held the gun up. Aimed toward the back door despite the fact she couldn't see anything.

Victoria moved. She made a sound, but the woman didn't react to it. After a couple of steps, making sure she was out of the gun's aim, she knelt on one of the dead men and reached over to tap the woman twice on the shoulder.

The front of the hood puffed out on an exhale and the gun lowered an inch. Victoria touched the woman's elbow while she detached the hood from the snaps on the overalls. Then she tugged it over the woman's head. After that, she pulled out the earplugs that had been stuffed into her ears.

Not total sensory deprivation, but close to it.

The woman had dark hair, now threaded with some gray. No makeup. She was a few years older than Victoria, and still as thin as she had been when Victoria first infiltrated her circle and befriended the woman.

"Took you long enough." Her accent was thick, east London. Not the speech pattern she'd used when Victoria had first met her.

Victoria shifted, ready to climb out of the stuffy van. "You think I'm rescuing you?"

"Then get out of the way." The woman shifted and handcuffs clinked.

Victoria shot her a look, then she found a key on one of the men and uncuffed her. Victoria let her keep the gun.

They climbed out of the van. "Tell me why I shouldn't shoot you and find whatever car you drove here in?"

She was no less aristocratic Europe, even with the overalls and the London accent. The woman was in desperate need of a salon visit, followed by a shopping trip. Victoria figure that would be the first thing Genevieve Moran would do when she left here. Before she went on a grifting spree across the Mediterranean, conning old rich guys and then probably poisoning them. Though, no one could prove that part.

Victoria stared her down. "Because shooting me would be poor gratitude in exchange for setting you free." Even though she had no intention of setting the woman free.

"What do you want, *cher*?"

"Information." She paused. "You're a hard woman to track down."

"That happens when one is the guest of a corrupt prison system." Something flashed in her gaze, and her accent held a British upper-crust lilt to it for a second. A product of the fancy boarding school she'd gone to before she cut loose and headed for Monte Carlo with her boyfriend.

Multiple countries had bartered for the chance to question her about unsolved crimes. There were a lot of disgruntled heirs and heiresses out there, all wondering where their inheritance had gone. Rich people pulling strings—making deals with governments and police departments. Money talked.

"Tell me what I want to know, and I'll take you wherever you want to go."

"You always were soft."

Victoria shot her a look.

"Okay, softer than me." She swung her arm around Victoria's shoulders and kissed her cheek like she still considered them old friends. "We made a good team."

"I'm in a…different place now."

Genevieve laughed, high pitched like they were dressed in those hats at a horse race in the English countryside, and Victoria had just told her that they should ride the train home instead of having a car service pick them up.

"Can't blame me," Genevieve said, waving that gun around. "I've just been set free. I'm allowed to be happy about it." She studied Victoria, then tipped her head to the side. "I'm not going to be happy when you tell me what you want, am I?" She blew out a breath. "Are you sure we can't drive to Rome and talk about it over a glass of wine?"

Victoria set off, heading for her car.

Genevieve's white sneakers made barely any sound on the asphalt. "Wow, I'm really not going to like this."

She stopped close to the hood. "Give me the gun." Genevieve started to argue. Victoria said, "Tell me what I need to know, and I'll make sure you're set up with a whole new identity. You can start a new life wherever you want."

"You think I know something."

Victoria didn't comment on that. If she thought not, why would she have come here?

The first shot pinged off the hood of the car.

"Get in!" Victoria raced to the driver's door, digging keys out as she moved.

12

Bremerton, WA. Thursday, 9.41a.m.

M ark shut the car door and strode over to the door, file in hand, and signed in to the NCIS office on the Naval base where the research facility had exploded.

He rode the elevator up to the floor where the Director's office, along with Niall's desk, was located. He found them in the conference room, though. With another man Mark only knew from press clippings.

"Mr. Secretary."

Andrew Jakeman turned. But it was the NCIS Director who said, "Assistant Director Welvern." As though pointing out that he was only an *assistant* and not the FBI *director* was important to him. Putting other people in their place, as usual.

"Director." Mark nodded. He stood in the doorway, with no intention of entering unless it was requested.

"Thank you for coming." That was Jakeman, who strode over and held out his hand. "Welvern."

"Mr. Secretary."

"Please, call me Andrew." He gave Mark a knowing look,

which communicated much. This was a man who knew Victoria well. A man she had helped, who meant something to her.

He gripped Jakeman's hand. "Mark."

They turned together, back to the table where the director stood. The NCIS agent in charge was an older man with silver hair and a suit that looked more like it should be worn by a mob boss. In fact, his skin was a little too tan and he had a ring on his little finger. He would probably be great at one of those murder mystery birthday parties.

"What have you brought us?"

Mark waved the file in front of him and answered Jakeman's question saying, "A statement of what was said between myself and Vance Davies."

There was a tiny shift in the skin around Jakeman's eyes. He knew what Mark wasn't saying, that Victoria had been there.

Mark continued, "I believe it has something to do with the explosion at the research facility."

"The explosion," the NCIS director said, "*and* the theft."

"What was stolen?"

The director's eyebrows rose.

Mark figured now was the time to plead his case. "I've got two dead men and reason to believe that a third man was responsible for what happened here. I believe he's up to something, and needed whatever he stole at that research facility to enact a plan he's working on." Mark flipped open the file and handed him a page about Oscar Langdon. "This man is clever, and very dangerous."

Langdon was an FBI agent and a criminal. He would be one step ahead of them. He would likely know every move they were going to make. And he hadn't gone this far without being exposed, or captured, because he took unnecessary risks. He was careful.

"This is not an FBI case."

"You're right." Mark nodded. "That's why I'm here, handing over everything I have on this man and letting you know I'll lend any assistance I can."

After all, there wasn't much point going back to his own office when it was currently occupied by the FBI director. Probably for the foreseeable future. Mark might as well be here, actually working to find Langdon; the last FBI agent they needed to bring down as part of this whole corruption thing.

That was the only reason the director had signed off on him coming here.

Jakeman said, "Let's step out and let Assistant Director Welvern get Special Agent O'Caran up to speed."

Mark realized then that Niall was in the room. As soon as they moved toward the door, Niall grinned at him. Mark was about to make a comment when Jakeman added, "I'll also put in a call to Homeland and rustle up some extra resources."

The door clicked shut behind the two men.

"I guess that means Hurricane Dakota is going to make land-fall before lunch."

Mark held his hand out and Niall shook it. "Sorry I didn't see you before."

Niall shrugged. "Jakeman called me in here. I don't think the director liked it overly much."

"My director is currently occupying the chair at my desk."

Niall winced. "Why don't you fill me in on what you have?"

Mark spread out the file on the table and explained everything.

"And you think Langdon is behind this attack?"

Mark said, "What did the research facility have? What was stolen?"

Niall studied him. Not sure if he should share? Mark had to wait for the other man. He might be senior, but they worked for totally different branches of government. The secretary of defense had final call over this office, which probably chapped the NCIS director's sensibilities, but Mark worked under the Department of Justice.

Still, at the core they were both cops. And Mark figured they both cared about Victoria.

"Chips."

Mark waited.

"Guidance chips."

"Like for weapons?"

"Very specific weapons. The ones in the megaton range."

Fear prickled like cold at the edges of Mark's senses. With all the technological advances in weaponry—computers and biological and chemical warfare—there was some seriously scary stuff in the world right now. Threats had many different faces. But the threat of a nuclear bomb was a mental picture everyone could muster up.

"Langdon has a nuke."

Niall pressed his lips together. "Perhaps the pieces of one. It could take time to assemble."

"Or he could be ready, and he could use it tomorrow."

"Any idea where?"

Mark blew out a breath and sat on the edge of the table. "He's been trying to kill Victoria, the way he had Pacer killed. So far it's been through Vance Davies, but he's dead now. Langdon has been hands off for a lot of it." Mark glanced in the direction the secretary of defense had gone, but couldn't see him or Niall's boss. "Langdon could be planning to go after the committee as a whole, or make a big splash. Use a city to get his point across. Maximum destruction to keep us busy while he makes a break for it."

Except that they had no idea where he was.

Oscar Langdon, or Colin Pinton as the FBI knew him, had outsmarted so many people.

Now that Mark was sure the last missing FBI agent was Langdon, he realized the man was so much more than his FBI personnel file. He'd worked both sides under the radar for years. Victoria was the only one who'd pointed a finger at the FBI, and even she seemed to have been unaware of the extent of what had been going on.

She'd never thought Langdon himself was an agent.

Though, honestly, he didn't know what she'd known. And he

still wasn't clear on what made her suspect the FBI as having been involved in what had happened to her in Austria and her need of rescuing from a South African prison. She hadn't explained much after he brought her home. In fact, she'd taken two whole days to say anything at all.

She had kissed him, though.

Gratitude and relief and their history all wrapped up in one lip touch he wasn't ever going to forget.

"Where is Victoria now?"

"Honestly, I have no idea." Not that he'd have lied if he did know. Maybe he just didn't want to admit that she'd so readily given him the slip. "Davies stepped in front of that car. I turned, couldn't see her. By the time I hung up from calling the local PD, she was gone."

"You think she didn't want to have to make a statement?"

Mark shrugged. "Some of us don't have that luxury, we have to work within the boundaries of the law."

"Good. Considering."

Mark said, "I'm not bitter or anything. She's always been a law unto herself, a force of nature. And yet..." Did he really want to get into this with a man he considered a friend but actually didn't know all that well?

Victoria had a deep well of emotion in her. She was one of those sensitive personalities, though she'd learned how to bury that part of her deeply. From a really young age.

He knew she felt a lot, and often that ability to feel was a hindrance that had to be buried. Though not with Jakeman's daughter. Victoria's empathy had caused her to work twice as long and twice as hard as anyone else looking for her. She'd told Mark later that she hadn't quit. In the end she had found the girl after most people had given up. It was the foundation of the bond between her and Jakeman now.

She might be in her forties, but Jakeman considered her like one of his own kids now. He knew the kind of person she was, and it had bonded them. She'd brought him back his child.

Now the secretary of defense had formed this committee, and they'd exposed so much corruption. How far would Jakeman go to give her what she needed in this? He'd want her to have what she wanted, which was Langdon in prison. Or dead. Between Mark and Jakeman, they could probably keep her from doing something that got her hurt in her quest to find Langdon. Mark knew she didn't care what the fallout was for her personally. She just couldn't bear for anyone else to be hurt.

He didn't understand how someone could work so selflessly for other people, care so little about her own wellbeing, make so many choices that strained the boundaries of honor, and yet feel so deeply for those she cared about.

Then again, if he had an answer to that, it would be the end of his lifetime search for understanding Victoria Bramlyn.

And then what would he do?

The door flung open. Talia strode in, followed by Dakota and Josh. Haley, who was Niall's fiancé and who worked at a bank, carried three white paper bags.

She gave the man she loved a quick kiss. "We brought lunch."

"Ready to find Langdon?"

Mark spun and lifted his brows at Josh's question. "I'm more concerned with where Victoria is right now."

Dakota glanced at Talia. "GPS?"

Talia looked at her tablet. She tapped and swiped the screen. "Offline, which means she's on a mission."

"Doing what?" Did they know? Had she ditched him and then checked in with her old team? He'd thought she wasn't doing that. More concerned with keeping them safe right now, when bodies were dropping. Most of them in front of Victoria.

They glanced at each other.

"Did she order you not to tell me?"

Talia was the first to object. "It's just that—"

"Don't bother making excuses for her. Langdon might have a nuke—" He heard someone gasp, but ignored it. "—but if Victoria wants to shut me out, then I guess I'll go back to my office and find Langdon like an actual cop would do, instead of this renegade spy thing she has going on."

He strode to the door, already regretting taking his frustration out on good people. They didn't need his added to their own. He was doing the same job, though he had to prove himself in a way he hadn't needed to before. They had a new office, a new boss, and the team had been—at least in part—broken up.

The only thing he could do that would actually help was exactly what he'd told them. Find Langdon and take him out. End this threat against Victoria and countless others.

He strode through the office. The director's door was open. Mark figured telling them he was leaving would be the polite thing to do. Politics didn't play much into the kind of FBI agent he was, but given the current situation, he figured observing the niceties would be a good idea.

Jakeman wasn't in the office, however. He was standing outside of it, pacing.

"I understand, sergeant." Jakeman's expression was hard as he gripped the phone to his ear. Not upset, but seriously frustrated. "Keep me apprised. And you keep *her* alive."

13

North of Le Mans, France. Thursday 5.00p.m.

Victoria peeled out, the tires spewing dirt and gravel behind the car. Genevieve gripped the handle on the passenger side, the gun still in one hand.

Gunshots splintered the back windshield.

Genevieve ducked her head. She glanced out the back. "These guys trying to kill you, or me?"

Victoria gripped the wheel, concentrating on not spinning off the side of the road. Should she have Genevieve get her phone? If she did that, who would she call? It wasn't like she had the sergeant's number. Talia couldn't help her, though she'd probably break some protocol trying to rouse local police here in France or the US military close by.

Victoria bit her lip. "Just one car?" She glanced in the side mirror but couldn't see it as they'd just rounded a bend. When the road straightened, the van came into view. White. Side panels with no decals that she could see from this distance.

"Just one." Genevieve turned to her. "What's the plan?"

"Why am I the one who always has to come up with a plan?"

"How about because you're the spy who pretended to be my friend just so she could sell me out to Interpol?"

Victoria wanted to deny it. "Just doing my job. And it wasn't me who handed that information over. I was still compiling everything."

"Which means I'd have been convicted publicly of *everything* instead of passed back and forth between European governments who all want answers to their own stack of unsolved cases where I'm the prime suspect." Genevieve paused. When she continued, her voice had a hard tone to it. "Trying to do me a favor, in your own way?"

Victoria couldn't get into all that right now. The van was gaining on them.

It got close enough to bump them, both vehicles going sixty-five on winding country roads. She needed to get on the highway back to Le Mans, or head toward Paris. A little visibility and some other cars meant they'd have the police there soon enough. She could hand Genevieve back over, and they'd be safe. She didn't like the idea of putting regular folks in danger, but she'd do what she could to minimize the fallout.

Genevieve hissed. Victoria fought the swerve.

"If they want to kill us, they should just do it." Victoria's fingers were starting to cramp. "Otherwise they're just playing with us."

She had to think on that idea for a minute. Either she'd been betrayed by someone on the committee—the only people who knew she was here—or Langdon had people following her. She figured the latter option was the right one. Especially considering her grandfather's disappearance and the two attacks.

"Maybe they're here to kill you because they think you're trying to kill me," Genevieve suggested.

"Is that more likely than any of the other scenarios?" Victoria figured either way they still had to get out of this alive.

Another gunshot hit the back corner. She caught sight of a

guy hanging out of the front passenger window, holding a shotgun.

"You wanna take care of that?"

Genevieve hit the button to roll down the window. She twisted and knelt on the seat, firing left handed out the window.

Victoria took the next corner. Genevieve had to pause firing. The van's gunman hit the left side this time. She pressed her foot harder down on the gas pedal.

Behind the van, Victoria spotted a little gray car with multiple passengers closing in fast. They'd brought friends? Or were they friendlies?

Except right now she had to admit—if only to herself—she'd have appreciated Mark being here.

He'd been a figure in her life for years, though mostly from a distance.

Did she want to change that? Of course. She'd always wanted things between them to be different. Now it was like this holding pattern had existed for so long they would just continue to circle each other, and the concept of a different kind of relationship, for…ever.

Because the alternative was that she tell him the truth.

After that, she wouldn't even have the measure of Mark in her life that she had now. Because he would push her away for good.

Done.

Over.

The van bumped them again.

Maybe it was better that she die here. Then he would never find out.

Genevieve shoved at her shoulder. "Focus."

Victoria realized another car was heading toward them. A silver compact. It, too, had multiple passengers. "They're crowding us in."

The compact burned rubber on the road, then flipped around. A J-turn. "Sarge."

"What?"

She ignored Genevieve's question. "The cavalry."

"Is he worth this?"

Mark was worth anything, and everything. He was certainly worth her telling him the truth. She just didn't want to see the look on his face when he found out. She'd made a lot of choices in her life. He would question whether they were the right ones, even given the evidence of what she'd accomplished.

The good *always* outweighed the means.

Her priority was to keep him safe and alive, despite herself, and always over her own romantic entanglements. They both knew that. He might hate it if he found out she was protecting him. Probably he figured he didn't need her to do that. But she wasn't about to put him in danger any more than he would want *her* to be in danger.

"Langdon is obviously pissed and lashing out."

"And he's going to have you killed?" Victoria glanced at a woman she still considered a friend. A woman she'd tried to do right by, even while she still worked to maintain her integrity.

"How do I know what Langdon has planned?"

The two cars got in front and behind the van. Victoria let the silver vehicle get between her and her pursuers. They were going to take care of this for her?

"He's hiding out. Biding his time." Victoria spoke her thought process as it formed. "He isn't running, he's fighting back and no one knows what he's capable of, not like you do."

Genevieve shifted in her seat. The two cars had slowed, forcing the van to pull back with them.

The other woman said, "I've always tried to…minimize the damage. Rein him in a little." She glanced at Victoria, who couldn't look at the expression on her face to see what that meant.

She navigated the switchback while she thought it over. "That was you."

"What?"

"South Africa."

Genevieve shifted again, muttering under her breath.

"You got him to put me in prison instead of killing me, didn't you?" Victoria wanted to pull over. To look this woman in the eyes and get the truth. Finally. "He wouldn't have left me. He'd have dumped my body after I figured out it was the FBI. I fingered them, and the next thing I know, it's all gone wrong and I'm waking up in South Africa. With a tattoo." Of course, it made total sense. "It's his insurance. In case you double cross him, or I come back to get him again."

"Tattoo?"

"UV." She shifted her elbow to flash the skin of her forearm. "Not normally visible. He put it there. It has to be his insurance policy. A way to implicate me if it goes wrong."

She needed to have the medical examiner look at Davies's body under black light. See if he was part of the same group of thieves and con men. Bad guys masquerading as good.

A group she would be at risk of being associated with anytime Langdon felt like throwing her under the bus in retaliation.

Victoria wanted to think this through more, but there wasn't time. There was just one thing she wasn't clear on. One thing she needed an answer to now. "You were already in prison when it all happened. How is it that he came to make you this promise?"

She didn't really need Genevieve to answer the question.

Victoria said, "He knows how to get in contact with you. Or you with him."

The fact they'd pulled it off was a credit to their skill and tenacity and might be commendable, if it wasn't also seriously illegal subterfuge. The kind of custody Genevieve was in. Even those prison guards back there hadn't known her real name.

Genevieve held the gun loose on her lap, but her intention was clear. She was prepared to shoot Victoria. "There's a guy. I do him…favors. He passes along messages."

Victoria shook her head. "Do the people interrogating you about their missing money know Langdon can still get to you?"

She certainly hadn't, considering she'd never have come here if she'd known.

Genevieve shrugged one shoulder. "We all have to live with our choices. It's not like it can ever get washed away."

Another gunshot blasted. Victoria ducked her head on a reflex. The two cars had engaged the van. It swerved to avoid the one in front, slowing down. They were trying to get the driver to pull over.

She kept up her speed, winding around the bends in the road like she was on a British country road with their high speed limits instead of in France, like she was.

The van collided with the car in front and seemed to push it aside. Victoria watched as the car spun out, careening across the road and off the side into a ditch. It blew through a fence into some pasture.

Genevieve watched it go. While she was distracted, Victoria grabbed for the gun. She wound up with both hands on it, her knees lifted to hold the wheel straight. Feet off the pedals.

She elbowed Genevieve in the nose and got the gun, then grabbed the wheel and hit the gas again. "You're not going to shoot me."

"Guess not."

She didn't want to know what this woman would have done if pressed into a corner. Victoria was going to ensure she went back into police custody. The lives she'd taken might not have been innocent, but murder was murder. Regardless of the quality of the person whose life had been lost, justice still needed to be served.

A gunshot rang out.

Before Victoria could figure out what had been hit, the car swerved. The steering got really sloppy. She couldn't straighten out, no matter how hard she fought. A tire. They had to have shot out a tire.

The second she realized this, they were already off the road. She narrowly avoided a sign post but couldn't get back onto the street. Not without a miracle. She wasn't someone those worked for, so she gritted her teeth and tried to minimize the damage.

They bumped up an incline and into rows of wheat. The dirt was rutted, shifting the gun around in her lap. Genevieve's head hit the ceiling and she grunted. Victoria hit the brake, but they kept going anyway. The smell of burning rubber filled the car.

Genevieve grabbed the gun.

The car stopped.

Victoria blew out a breath, acknowledging that though dying might feel like a better alternative at the moment, the reality was she liked being alive. And she appreciated every day she got.

"I didn't want Langdon to kill you because I wanted to do it myself."

Victoria turned to look at her.

The gun was pointed right at her face.

"My life is already over. What do I have to lose by killing a spy no one but that sad-sack FBI guy will care is dead?"

To be fair, Bear would probably miss her as well. Not just Mark.

Then there was her former team. They'd care if she was killed, right? She thought so. At least Talia would show up at her funeral. She'd probably stand a distance away with a black umbrella so it would seem like Victoria was just mysterious—not lacking in the friend department.

A bullet hit Genevieve's right shoulder the second the glass of the passenger window splintered.

She cried out and slumped in the seat.

Victoria grabbed the gun from her. Then she realized it wasn't Genevieve's shoulder that had been hit. It was the side of her neck. Victoria pulled off her jacket and balled it against the woman's neck. "What does Langdon have? What is he going to do?"

Genevieve's skin was pale, the blood coming too fast.

"I'll get you a doctor. Just tell me." The door opened. She saw the sergeant, but kept her attention on Genevieve. "Tell me."

She gasped. Formed a couple of words with her mouth, no sound emerging from her lips. Until the last word. One that sent cold through Victoria's whole being, straight to her soul.

"Uranium."

She made a run for it.

14

J akeman walked into the conference room, stowing his cell phone in the inside pocket of his suit jacket. "She's on her way home."

A good thing. Too bad Mark caught sight of the look on Jakeman's face. The look of a worried father, concerned about where his daughter had been and what she'd been doing, never mind that she was safe.

The man was at least fifteen years her senior. Mark appreciated the fact this guy cared about her, but it still kind of irritated him that Jakeman knew more about what was going on with Victoria than he did.

"Thanks." Josh nodded. Beside him, Dakota looked relieved.

Talia sat in the corner, head bent over her laptop. Niall had disappeared to sit at his desk for a while.

No one was ready to clock out for the day.

"What was she doing?" The question came out far more irritated than he intended. Everyone looked at him, even Talia. He wanted to squirm but forced his body to remain still.

Jakeman reached back and shut the door. "I know you're her

friends, but I have to temper that knowledge with the fact Victoria did not share any of this with you. She did not share her case with you. Nor did she share with you what happened to her in Austria."

"No, but without me," Mark argued, "she'd still be in that South African prison."

Jakeman didn't like that much.

Dakota made a noise—like news of a prison was something she hadn't known. Josh set his hand over hers on the table.

Mark said, "I get that you need to keep this committee under wraps for security reasons, but he knows how to get to her. Langdon is like a trapped animal trying to claw his way out. He doesn't care who is hurt in the process. So you need to read us in. That way we can keep Victoria *and* the people we care about safe."

Out the corner of his eye, Mark saw Josh nod.

Jakeman turned to Talia. "You're the NSA one, right?"

"Yes."

He gave her a name to look up. Talia got her computer hooked up to the TV on the wall, and a photo came on screen.

Dakota said, "Who is she?"

"European socialite. Except that she upped her game from stealing from boutiques in Monaco to grifting on old, rich guys. Bankers. Businessmen. Last estimate is that she got at least five million in the span of eight months."

"Says here she's in prison." Talia clicked on her keyboard and brought up a report of the charges. "Twenty years for murder."

"The last guy. They're still looking for his body."

Mark frowned. "She was convicted for murder, yet no one is certain the guy is actually dead?"

Jakeman shrugged. "Europe has different rules, I guess. Anyway, Victoria had an assignment. Genevieve Moran was Langdon's intermediary with buyers. She was the face of his operation for months, and the key to figuring out his identity."

Several people over the last few decades, high on the ten most wanted list, were only a persona, no photo. It wasn't common, but it also wasn't unheard of.

Jakeman continued, "She got close to Genevieve. Made friends with her. Two socialites out on the town. Victoria was gathering her case together when Genevieve was busted by Interpol. She never told Victoria who Langdon really was. After that, we heard he was selling artifacts. Victoria got what she needed, went to the event, and the rest is history." He pushed out a breath. "Near as we can tell, now that we know the FBI had serious corruption issues, is that it got back to Langdon that the CIA was running a mission. He took her out of play."

"And dumped her in a South African prison?" Dakota looked like she wanted to start throwing punches to make herself feel better.

Josh said, "Who is this Langdon guy you think is your missing FBI agent?"

Mark moved to his file, still thinking about what Victoria was doing in Europe right now. Meeting with that woman, getting herself into trouble. She might be okay right now, and heading home, but he couldn't let this feeling fester. When it came, as it often did when he heard what she'd been doing, he had to process the retroactive fear and then set it aside. She wasn't in danger now. She had been. She was fine.

Until the next time.

He flipped the file open and slid the photo of Langdon— Colin Pinton—toward the couple. "This is who we need to find. The man we now believe is Langdon."

Josh's jaw muscle flexed.

"Uh…" Dakota paused. "This is Oscar Langdon?"

"Yes."

Josh looked at her and nodded.

"What?" Mark folded his arms across his chest.

Dakota said, "We've met this guy."

"I remember thinking he had a civil veneer, but it was pretty thin." Josh scratched at his jaw. Mark waited, as did the rest of them, for him to explain. Josh said, "Earlier this year, in the course of our investigation into the source of some VX gas, we came upon a biker compound."

Talia said, "Wasn't that when you guys met?"

He nodded. "This guy—" He poked at the photo with his index finger. "—was one in a community of bikers who assisted us with escaped convicts from a local prison."

Mark nodded. They didn't need every detail of what had been going on back then. He knew a lot about Clare Norton and the VX gas and the person she'd gotten it from—Malcom Kennowich. "Tell me about him."

"He seemed to be in charge," Josh said. "The leader of this group of bikers. Helped us out, seemed to care about the rest of them being in danger. Determined to protect his family."

Mark flipped through papers in the file. "Colin Pinton worked undercover in a biker gang out of northern California two years ago."

"So, post Austria, pre-now."

Mark nodded to Jakeman. "He worked out of San Francisco, as did most of our corrupt agents. But Colin Pinton never turned anything up on the bikers. The undercover activity was shut down when it was clear he wasn't going to come up with evidence."

Josh said, "So he formed a bond, got in as their leader, and then told his SAIC that he got nothing."

Mark shrugged. "That would be my guess. The special agent in charge probably wrote up a report. I'll have to see what he said, but the guy in charge of the San Francisco office is one of our agents in jail now along with the others. He's as corrupt as Pinton."

Josh blew out a breath. "So it was a cover up? A whole lot of work on paper but not much in the way of results."

Mark nodded. "Pinton had the freedom to work as Langdon behind the scenes. To keep both sides of his business going—working as an agent, and being a bad guy—because his boss covered for him."

"That explains how he's been able to stay under the radar." Dakota skimmed the pages. "He's got a built in persona he can fall back on at any time. Playing both sides, though this would be a third one. The FBI, the world he inhabits as Langdon, and now this biker community."

"But you saw him in Washington, right? Not northern California." Mark wasn't sure it made sense how the guy could have been working out of San Francisco while living in the backwoods of Washington state.

Dakota tipped her head to the side. "He had to have hooked up with them, and maybe the undercover work took him all the way up here."

"I can look at the file from his undercover work and compare dates. Though, this whole thing was covered up so it's not like it'll be in the actual report of where he was and when." Mark blew out a breath. "If you say it's him, then it's a good place to start looking."

"The compound is a fortress. We'll never get eyes inside unless they invite us in," Josh said.

Dakota said, "I could—"

"No."

She frowned, shifting in her seat.

Mark figured she was willing to take a risk for the case. For Victoria.

"Are you marrying me next month?" Josh kept his tone low.

Dakota made a face. "I hope so."

"Then I need you to get there in one piece."

"Maybe I'll just quit and be a stay-at-home dog mom."

"I'll buy you an apron," Josh said. "It'll be nice. Not too many ruffles."

She chuckled, cracking a smile. "You do that, you'll lose your partner."

"Deal."

Mark realized then that there was a whole lot more to what they were saying than the exchanged words. It seemed both of them were willing to take each other as they came. Faults, foibles, and fears.

They had stuff to work through if they wanted a strong relationship but were willing to put in the effort to do it.

Together.

"Let's go." Dakota stood, pulling on her jacket.

Josh shook Mark's hand. "We'll find out if he's there, and if he isn't, see if they know where Langdon might have gone."

Mark nodded.

Dakota gave him a wave, and they moved past Jakeman out of the office. Josh followed to do whatever the secretary of defense did on a Thursday night at dinnertime. It would take most of the night to get that information, considering the drive out to where this compound was located. The two of them were dedicated to their jobs, and each other, in a way that seemed to incorporate a good balance of each.

Partners in life, and work. After they were married, that bond would be even closer. Even stronger.

Mark's stomach rumbled. He needed to go home and make sure Bear was okay. He'd been working longer hours than usual lately, but that normally happened in the thick of a case. Especially one where every eye was on his office, making sure it was all above board.

"You love her, don't you?"

He turned to Talia, already shaking his head. Victoria was safe. They had a way to find Langdon. What was the point in talking about things any further? "I—"

"Don't bother denying it."

He closed his mouth. She was really going to do this? Talia was a sweet lady, but people in relationships always thought single people should also be hooked up. Like it was the ultimate end goal.

"Have you told her?"

"She knows how I feel."

Maybe they hadn't said it out loud for a while but nothing had changed. And nothing ever would. So what was the point in making their lives more painful than they already were?

What was the point in dragging it out with someone who wouldn't understand?

He said, "I made Victoria a promise a long time ago, and I'm sticking to it."

She wasn't going to disappear forever, but she would always come back. Eventually. He wasn't going to push her into what he thought they should be.

"And what do you get in return for that promise?"

15

Somewhere over the Midwest. Thursday, 11.22p.m.

"Hog tying me was hardly necessary." Victoria rubbed at her wrists. Not that it had been uncomfortable or left any marks.

The sergeant grinned at her from across the military transport plane. "You ran, we caught you. Doesn't matter how much you're gonna complain. What's done won't change."

"Isn't that the truth."

"For whatever reason he didn't feel like explaining to me, the secretary of defense wants you back in Washington state in one piece."

"Sorry you had to take the detour."

He shrugged one shoulder. "The team is headed to a training exercise nearby right after, so it wasn't too far out of our way."

"The training exercise. It doesn't happen to be in a place called Last Chance County, does it?"

His eyes flashed in surprise. "How'd you know that?"

"Lucky guess. Which is what I'd have named the town."

He barked a laugh.

"I grew up there." She wasn't sure why she said it. Maybe

because she wanted to talk instead of see Genevieve take her last breath all over again every time she shut her eyes. Maybe she wanted the connection after such a loss.

"For real?"

She nodded. "It started as a safe haven for veterans. Right after Vietnam, I guess." Her grandfather had been one of the first residents of that small mountain town. The place was a lot bigger now. Hundreds of families, schools, and a shopping mall. Churches, two libraries. All the amenities of a big town.

"And now it's a training center."

"Started out as a place for washed up grunts to go. Somewhere they could blow off steam, no questions asked." Her grandfather had been one of them, and her father had grown up under a cloud of alcohol and fists flying, gotten her mother pregnant, and then split. Her mom had died young. Alcohol again. "For decades, it was a rough place to live. Then a new sheriff showed up, sometime in the late eighties. Straightened a lot of things out and allowed the whole town to just…breathe. Mellow out a little."

He studied her, not saying anything.

"A few years ago, a group of Marines showed up. They revamped an old school that'd been shut down. Set up a whole training facility, which they later added to. Now they contract it out. Private parties. Military units."

He nodded then.

"Brought some much needed income to the town. Established jobs."

"You ever go back?"

She shrugged. "My grandfather signed his house over to me when he moved into a retirement home in Florida." Not exactly the truth, but it was close enough. "I go back from time to time and clean out the place after renters leave." Also not entirely true. It was used more as a safe house than a regular rental home.

"Small world."

She shrugged. Small world, given it was the town the sergeant and his team were headed to. But maybe not. Especially considering his line of work and the place she'd lived until the day she moved away to go to college. That was where she'd been recruited into the CIA. Mark had been a senior when she'd been a freshman in college. Enough distance there might have been a universe between them. But still, they'd made time to email each other from two states away. Kept in touch.

As they'd done since.

Part of each other's lives, but not in the way either of them actually wanted to be. That meant talking about what'd happened, though. How their lives had changed since he'd come home to find her waiting for him.

She bit the inside of her lip and looked away so the sergeant didn't see something on her face she had no intention of revealing.

One of his guys came over to talk to him. She was tempted to thank God for that small concession.

Mark's role in her life had been cemented that day. Her protector, but nothing more than that. He had saved her and she would be forever grateful for it. She would grieve the rest of her life for the way it had colored what was between them, causing it to go bad.

Victoria was destined to go through life never having what she actually wanted.

Her father had been the same. Her grandfather.

Maybe it was genetic. Something coded on her DNA meant she would never realize her dreams. Life would always get in the way and prevent her from having what she longed for.

Family. Love.

Dumb things that didn't mean anything and yet, at the same time, meant everything.

Seeing each of her team members fall for the person they wanted to spend their life with had only made it all worse. Mark had been shot because of her investigation. Sitting with him in the hospital, she realized how much better she needed to be at segmenting parts of her life. Otherwise Langdon would get

Mark on his radar. He would be hurt. There would be no stopping it.

The sergeant's teammate wandered off and he turned his attention back to her again. "Are you going to let me in on why the secretary of defense suddenly has my personal phone number and is calling me directly?"

Victoria shook her head. "You know who Oscar Langdon is?"

"No. Should I?"

She said, "Are you personally acquainted with any FBI agents?"

He shook his head.

"Then don't get in the middle of this." She didn't want the blood of another person on her hands.

First Pacer. Now Genevieve. Her grandfather was missing, possibly also dead. Entirely possible. She didn't figure Langdon was keeping him around as leverage. What would be the point when he was also actively trying to kill her?

Victoria rubbed her breastbone with the heel of her hand and looked away. She might be a former spy, but guys like him—special forces types—were trained to spot changes in body language.

"It's okay to grieve for your friend."

Apparently he was good at it. "Crying isn't something that I do." As much as she might want to sometimes, that wasn't a dam she intended to break.

Genevieve was gone. But she'd been gone long before that, although to be fair she had been in prison. Her change in status didn't make much difference to Victoria though. *Keep telling yourself that, maybe you'll believe it.* Death was a different kind of prison. One Genevieve would never come back from.

"Are you going to be safe in Washington?" He tipped his head to the side. "Jakeman's assistance notwithstanding."

She made a face. "The old man refuses to take no for an answer." The committee had been her idea, but the day she'd floated it as something she wanted to do, he'd jumped in. Both feet. And decided he was going to head the whole thing, leaving her free to do the ground work.

The sergeant chuckled. "I can tell. His voicemails?" He winced. "Though I'd imagine he's a good one to have in your corner when you need it."

She nodded, thinking more of Mark than Jakeman just then. The secretary of defense was her friend, and a man who had her respect. The person she wanted back-to-back with her, fighting to keep each other safe...was Mark.

No change, then.

She glanced aside, realizing she needed to get over this. Despite wanting Mark in her life, and having him, she just wasn't satisfied. Not completely. And in a way, she never would be... unless the situation changed.

The airplane began its descent. Victoria shifted in her seat. She had to bite the inside of her lip to hide the wince. Her side hurt. She'd probably torn a couple of stitches loose. A trip to the hospital would likely be expedient, when all she really wanted to do was go see Bear. Curl up on the couch again so she could sleep away the burn behind her eyes.

Would Mark change her bandages again? Normally she tried to space out the times she needed him like that. Though they seemed to have become more frequent lately. Maybe he would decide it was too much. Tell her he couldn't help her because he had to concentrate on work right now.

She sucked in a choppy breath and shut her eyes. The airplane hit the tarmac. She swayed in her seat as the pilot pulled back the flaps and they began to slow.

Mark's face filled her vision. Standing close as he had in the doorway of his home the last time she'd left. His fingers on her face.

It had to be enough.

The click of seatbelts echoed throughout the plane. Victoria was among the first to disembark, quickly realizing they were at an Army base in Washington state. Not too far to drive to Seattle from here, though she wasn't sure how she would get there. Jakeman must have figured out a plan. Unless she was supposed to stay here for the night.

The moment she stepped off the bottom of the stairs and onto the pavement, she realized what the plan was.

"Mark."

"Alternatively," he said, moving toward her. "You could pretend to be happy to see me."

Relieved was what she was. Not that she'd tell him that. His presence overwhelmed her. It washed over her like a sunrise in Hawaii. Jeans. A T-shirt. He had to have gone home, changed, and then driven out here to pick her up. Was Bear in the car?

It was like she'd always imagined coming home should be. A family waiting. Bone tired, but back with the people you love.

She'd never experienced it. Until now.

The sergeant and his team wandered away. She watched them go, shooting her backward glances, and waving to her. Then she turned back to Mark, not really sure what to say. "You're here."

With a sardonic shake of his head, he pulled her close and gave her a hug. Loose enough he didn't hurt her side, but strong enough she rested into it. "Nowhere else I'd rather be."

He spoke the words close to her ear. For her, and no one else to hear. Victoria squeezed his waist and held on. "Thank you."

He seemed about to say something, then didn't. Instead he pulled away and said, "Rough day at the office."

She was about to fire a quip back. Nothing came out of her mouth. Then, to her consternation, a sob worked its way up her throat.

"Vic—"

She stepped back, lifting her hand. "No." She cleared her throat. "Let's just go."

Disappointment washed over his face. He walked her to his car, neither of them saying anything. When he shut her door, he rounded the hood to the driver's side and slid in. He inserted the key, then before turning on the engine, he turned to her. "You know what? No." He tossed the key in the cup holder. "I know your friend died."

It was on the tip of her tongue to say, "So?" But this was Mark. The one person she didn't pretend with.

Except you're pretending with every breath.

They hadn't been friends. Then again, maybe considering who she was and the kind of woman Genevieve had been, it was possible they'd been the closest thing to friends that each other had back then.

Now she had her team. For all she'd spoken to them the past few weeks.

She had Mark.

"I'm sorry."

She barely let him finish before she was moving. Victoria touched the sides of his face with shaky hands, leaned in and pressed her lips to his.

Things were just getting interesting when his phone rang. He shifted, enough she was left just breathing. Feeling more bereft than she was comfortable with.

He looked at his watch. "It's Talia."

She shifted, moving away. He had to have seen what she couldn't hide from him on her face, because he said, "Hold that thought for a second, okay?"

She didn't answer.

His smile said all she needed to know.

16

Joint base Lewis-McChord, Washington. Friday 01.30a.m.

There wasn't time to explain to Victoria that he'd pulled back figuring it was Jakeman on the phone. The secretary had been calling every half hour since he'd told Mark to drive here and pick up Victoria. As in, ordered him to do it. Mark had refused to give the man access to the GPS on his phone, despite him asking for it over and over again.

Mark slid to answer the phone. "Welvern."

"It's Talia."

"Pulling an all-nighter?"

She blew out a breath, audible over the phone connection. "I hadn't planned to, but I guess."

"And Mason?"

"He's here. Asleep on one of the chairs so he can drive me home when I'm done."

"Good." That was exactly where Mark would be in the same situation, had it been him and Victoria. When it was the right person, you pulled out all the stops.

Like allowing Victoria to kiss him even though it went against all his resolve. All that determination to keep her in his life, but partitioned, so it didn't affect everything else. Thereby making him worthless at work and everywhere else. Probably it had been a bad idea, but he was way too tired to figure that out right now. Later he would unpack it and draw his own conclusions.

She hated when he did that, preferring to make her mind up on the fly as she'd been trained to do. But it wasn't his way.

Mark had to think things through. He needed to figure out how this changed things.

"Anyway, Josh and Dakota checked in a few hours ago," Talia continued. "I tried to call you, but it didn't go through."

"No signal for a while."

Mark would much rather be still kissing Victoria than having this conversation. He should have ignored the potentially important phone call and just stayed right where he was, even though it would be testing his resolve to stay honorable. Maybe getting interrupted was God's mercy. A way to remind Mark of what he'd promised.

They both had things that held them back. And not ones that could be solved by a single kiss—even if it had been a very nice one.

"That's what I figured." She was quiet for a moment, and he could hear her typing. "They reported Langdon not present at the biker compound. Apparently, the club members are all away at a rally in Oregon. All that was left were one guy and a couple of girls they'd met before. Josh reported they were excited to see Dakota. I guess she saved one of their lives."

Victoria shifted in her seat. He saw amusement and a twinge of pain on her face in the low light of the car interior. "You think that's where he is? At this rally?"

"Maybe," Talia said. "Also, uh…hey."

Victoria's face softened. "Hey, Talia."

"You okay?"

She was quiet long enough Mark wasn't sure she would reply. Then at the last minute before he could break the silence she said, "I lost an old friend today."

Mark wanted to kiss her for that. Since they were doing that kind of thing now.

Instead, he reached over and squeezed her hand. She turned hers over and grasped his fingers, not letting go. She looked at the window. "That seems to be happening a lot lately."

Mark wanted to cry for her.

She was scared. He was realizing it more each time he was with her. More and more of what she did was characterized by stark fear.

She wanted to bring Langdon down. Herself, without the fallout. Was she likely to keep the intel to herself, shut them all out, and then take off to find Langdon alone? Absolutely.

Mark was beginning to better understand Jakeman's methodology of keeping her close but still allowing her to do what she thought she needed to do.

"Tell us what else you have, Talia." He figured she hadn't only called them because she wanted to make sure they got an update from Josh and Dakota. That could have been sent in an email.

Mostly he figured she was still awake and working because she'd wanted to know the minute Victoria set foot back on American soil, safe and sound.

Mark started the car and began the drive back to Seattle. He figured Victoria would fall asleep on the way. Then he might pull a Jakeman—who'd told a Delta Force team to bring Victoria home *by any means necessary*—and just drive Victoria to where he thought she should be. It could work.

"Well, instead of following the *man*, I decided to follow the stuff. It's different than following the money, but it works sometimes."

Victoria was the one who said, "And?"

"The explosion at the research facility, there was a microchip stolen. It's pretty benign tech. Unless…" She went quiet for a second. "You have the know-how to reconfigure its primary functions. In which case it can be made into a weapons guidance chip. GPS to the target. Explosion. Catastrophe."

"Uranium."

"No, just a chip."

Victoria shook her head, even though Talia couldn't see her. "Genevieve. Before she died, she told me Langdon has uranium."

Mark nearly pulled the car over. From sixty to a dead stop, in mere seconds. It took all his determination to stay on the road. "He's making a nuke?"

"Calm down."

Seriously? "You can't tell me to calm down." He glanced at her in the passenger seat. "He could kill *thousands*, and we have no idea where he's going to use it. Unless *you* know."

"Of course I don't know," she cried loudly in the car. Loud enough his ears rang. "How would I know? I've never seen his face in person or even had a conversation with him. I barely know the man, and yet he's determined to kill me and a bunch of other people." She let out a frustrated sound.

Mark shook his head, gripping the wheel as he followed the highway toward home.

"You two fight like a married couple." There was a measure of humor in Talia's voice. "It would be cute if you weren't talking about mass murder." Her tone had switched to being sardonic.

He gritted his teeth. "So that explosion in Bremerton was, for sure, all Langdon then."

"Well," Talia said. "Not exactly."

Mark waited for her to explain.

Victoria said, "Middle man?"

"The surveillance shot we got of who we *think* stole the chip and caused the explosion is a man with a long rap sheet. He just got out of prison a matter of months ago, off a stint serving time for aggravated assault and burglary."

Victoria said, "So he's going to take it to Langdon, get the balance of the money he's owed."

Mark saw an opportunity there. "Can we find out where? Get in, and get the chip back...before Langdon gets his hands on it?"

"If he didn't already." Victoria didn't sound quite so hopeful now.

Talia chimed in. "To save all the back and forth, I did find out where I think he might be going. It's an art auction in Portland. Right up both of their alleys, considering it's uh…off book sales."

"Black market art auction?" Mark would need to meet with the special agent in charge of the FBI office in Portland. Form a joint sting operation. They'd need to get in there incognito, get the chip, and then take down the whole auction. Arrest all those participating.

Not just one chip. This was now a full-blown operation that would take people and time.

"Mark will let you know when he's figured out what the plan is."

"Copy that," Talia said, humor in her voice. "I'll send everything I have on this guy."

"When is the auction?" Mark slowed the car for a red light, not far from his house.

"Tomorrow night."

"Of course it is." Victoria shot him a look. Mark saw what she tried to hide below the humor.

Mark said, "Thanks, Talia," and hung up the phone. "Do you need a doctor?"

"Why would I need a doctor?"

"You know, for a spy, you're kind of bad at lying."

"It's not that." She shook her head. "It's you—you've always been able to tell when I was up to something. Whether I liked it or not."

"Lot of good that did me."

She said nothing.

The worst day of both their lives. A day that cemented everything going forward. One where she'd kept something from him, and he'd let her. The consequences…

She said, "Maybe it's that when I did keep a secret, things

went so terribly wrong. I think I've just never tried with you since then. Because it could go badly again."

Mark reached over and squeezed her hand again. An hour later, after a detour to a 24-hour emergency room for Victoria to get restitched, he pulled into his driveway. The lamp in the front window was on, illuminating Bear, sitting there, waiting.

The dog barked. Mark couldn't hear it, but he saw the lift of the snout.

"He sees you."

Victoria climbed out and waited at the front door for him to unlock it. Bear came trotting over, tail wagging. His whole body shifted and wiggled. "Hey, buddy." She stroked his sides as he leaned his head into the side of her leg.

Mark's chest ached watching them. The knowledge that they could have this very thing every day…along with the rest of what a relationship could be. Marriage. Kids. He knew she wanted both.

He'd been married for two years in his late twenties—a mistake from start to finish.

"Get me a blanket?"

"I'll get one for myself," he said, heading for the linen closet. "Since I'll be taking the couch."

"Mark—"

"Nope." He wasn't even going to talk about her being between him and whoever could break in. "I'm the one with the gun, remember?"

"I'm the one trained not to need one," she fired back. "Remember?"

He nearly laughed, but figured she didn't need to be encouraged.

"Come on, Bear. Let's go get some sleep."

Of course, she was going to take his dog with her. "We're not even going to talk about that kiss?"

She turned back, one hand on the stair rail. Bear went to the landing midway up the stairs and turned to wait for her. He shouldn't be doing this. She was hurt and tired. She'd had a long day. Sure, they both had, but he hadn't been on a mission. He'd been in the NCIS office working the case.

Was she going to deny that their kiss was a big deal? Maybe she didn't think it was anything worth talking about.

"I don't want to ruin it."

"What do you mean?"

Victoria shrugged. "I mean, overanalyze it until it's less than what it was."

He nodded slowly. "I can get on board with that, I guess. If you tell me what it was."

"A very nice kiss."

"It was. Very nice."

"And maybe…when the case is over…we can talk about doing that more."

Mark had to know. Otherwise he would lay awake until breakfast wondering what she meant. "You want things to change?"

He saw her bite her lip. "I at least want to talk about it."

Hope swelled in him. "Okay." She looked about ready to fall asleep standing there. "Good night, Victoria."

She gave him a soft smile and turned to the stairs. Mark fell asleep quickly, knowing everything he cared about in the world was right here under this roof.

Two hours later he woke up.

He knew immediately something was wrong and reached for his gun under the couch cushion before he was even fully awake. But it wasn't a threat he could fight with his weapon.

Smoke filled the downstairs.

His house was on fire.

17

Seattle, Washington Friday 4.45a.m.

Victoria sucked in a breath. Panic was an elusive friend. She'd been trained to process things entirely differently. To assess and *then* react, instead of simply reacting. Usually without the full picture as to what was happening.

Bear clambered to his feet onto the bed. He came close to her, and she heard a low whine.

Victoria ran her hand through the fur on the side of his neck. "Okay. Let's figure this out." Though, she'd already gotten most of it. House fire.

The room was full of smoke.

She could hear Mark yelling her name.

Victoria shoved back the covers and moved to the door, the dog running alongside her leg. He stuck with her like the best-trained canine companion. A fact, for which, she was extremely grateful. As though someone, somewhere, knew that Bear was exactly what she needed and had given him to her. A gift.

Moving tugged at the skin on her' side and the new stitches she'd been given last night. She felt like she'd slept for just ten minutes even though the alarm clock said it'd been a few hours.

"Hang on Bear." She waved him off. No way did a dog need to go first. Especially one as protective as Bear.

Victoria rotated her hand and touched the back of her index finger to the door handle. Warm, but not so much that she would be burned.

She lifted the hem of the T-shirt she'd "borrowed" from Mark and covered her mouth. The door was hot. Mark still yelled, probably at the bottom of the step. If he wasn't up here already, that meant he couldn't get up here.

She twisted the handle and gingerly pulled the door open.

Flames roared up the stairs, licking the walls. A wave of warm, smoky air wafted toward her and breezed at her hair.

She lowered the T-shirt for a second. "Mark!"

"Victoria! I can't get to you!"

"Just get out!" She wanted to ask what had happened, and if the fire department was on their way. But neither would get her out of this situation. Instead, the minutes spent on conversation would probably cost her safety. Maybe even her life.

She looked back at the bedroom and then raced to the window to see if there was a way down where she wouldn't wind up breaking her leg. The world outside was dark and quiet. A light came on at the house belonging to a neighbor across the street. The front door opened, and the porch illuminated a man standing there. Phone to his ear.

She looked at the ground. Whatever instinct that drove her to protect herself at all costs, it fired then. She glanced up the street.

At the edge of what she could see, a man stood beside a pickup truck. His body was in shadow, but light shone from a street lamp onto the blonde of his hair.

Langdon.

She raced back to the hall. "Mark, Langdon is outside! White pickup, he's west...up the street on the other side!"

"How are you going to get out?"

"I'll figure it out, go get him."

She couldn't climb out his bedroom window. Bear wasn't

going to be able to jump that far, and she didn't especially want to either. No, the window across the hall would be better. She yelled, "Patio!" and then ran for the spare room.

Bear followed her in, working his way around paint cans and drop sheets. Buckets of rollers and brushes. At the window, she jimmied the lock and had to shove at the pane to get it to raise.

Another gift, the pergola over the patio was wood covered with regular roofing tiles. Mark had paid a guy to redo them so they matched the new roof.

Victoria climbed out, wincing as her foot touched the scratchy tile. Abrasions were never fun. But she was alive to care, which was a good thing.

"Tori!" He hadn't called her that in a long time. She saw him on the grass, looking up at her.

"Go get Langdon!" Why was he back here? He needed to go out front with his gun and a pair of handcuffs and get the guy. The one who'd probably set this fire.

Victoria called Bear out. He hopped onto the tile and surveyed the pergola roof. She crouch walked to the edge and looked down.

"I'll catch you."

"No," she yelled back down. That was a disaster waiting to happen. "Get out of the way, I'm going to jump." She looked at the dog. "Call Bear first."

Talking made her need to cough. The air was better out here but still laced with smoke that smelled funny. Not just burning wood like a bonfire, there was an added tang in the air.

Too bad she couldn't call Sal or Allyson. ATF agents were either trained to work fire scenes, or they had people on their teams who were fire investigation experts. They were the ones you wanted working the scene of any bombing or explosion.

Was that what this was?

Victoria half expected Langdon to walk into the backyard any second, brandishing a gun, and shoot them both. *Bear.* "Call him."

"Bear, come." Mark waved at him.

The dog took one look at the distance and jumped down onto

the grass. His leg gave out. Victoria held her breath while he took a couple of steps. He favored his back left leg for a second, and then seemed to recover. He trotted off to do some business on the grass like this was any other night.

"Come on."

Victoria moved to the edge. "You need to turn around, or you'll get an eyeful when I climb down."

He turned his body to the side, but looked back.

"Aren't you supposed to be a gentleman federal agent?"

"We all know the two aren't mutually exclusive." He even folded his arms.

Victoria shot him a look. "Go get Langdon."

"That's not my priority right now. You are." He pulled one hand free and waved his phone. "I've got agents on the way. Langdon is *their* priority."

Victoria tried to figure out how to hang, and then drop. In the end, she just hopped down. Breath escaped her lungs in a whoosh. She rolled to displace the force and came to a stop pretty much on Mark's feet. Bear trotted over to lick her face.

"I'm okay." She pushed the dog away and sat up. Which hurt.

"Did you pull out all your stitches again?"

"No. Now go get Langdon."

He snagged her hand and started walking to the front of the house. They were doing it together? "I don't have shoes."

He kept tugging all the way to the front lawn. A fire truck pulled up at the curb and the firefighters got to work.

Victoria pointed. "He was over there." The truck was gone now.

"You and I, and Bear, are alive and mostly unscathed. We'll get Langdon."

She spun to him. "Mostly unscathed?"

He swallowed, mouth closed, not hiding his attempt to keep from wincing.

"Smoke?"

Mark shrugged. "Ambulance is—" He coughed. "—on its way."

Victoria turned back to the street. The need to double check that Langdon wasn't still standing there watching them was powerful. She would have jumped in her car and taken off after him, looping Talia in on the search...if she wasn't in just a T-shirt with no shoes. But then, she didn't even have her car keys, so she couldn't have taken off even if she wanted to. No, she wasn't going anywhere.

Had Langdon heard that Genevieve was dead? He had likely done this for revenge, if that was the case.

Langdon might have hired those men in France to get Genevieve and kill Victoria in the process, or kill them both. Victoria didn't know which it was. But that hadn't worked, and now Genevieve was dead. Langdon was probably tying up loose ends, getting rid of whoever still knew he was the last corrupt FBI agent still out there evading capture.

Buying himself time to enact whatever plan he had going on.

But why do that himself, when at every point in this process so far he had sent someone else to do the deed?

Two SUVs passed them on the street. Mark lifted a hand to wave. "There's my guys."

"They'll get him?"

"They'll do their best. That's all anyone can ask of anyone."

Victoria pressed her lips together. Mark tugged her elbow, moving to face her even as he pulled her to face him. He tipped his head close. "Are you okay?"

She made a face. Her throat hurt. "I could use water."

Mark leaned in and kissed her forehead. Apparently that wasn't enough, because he pulled her into a hug and held her against him.

The chattering voices penetrated. Firefighters. A couple of uniformed cops had shown up in their black and white car.

She twisted to look at the people around them. "Are you *staking a claim* right now?"

Mark didn't let her go. He still held her in that loose hold, but she spotted the curl of his lips.

"You are." She pushed at his shoulders. "Let go."

"You need a blanket." He glanced down at her legs.

"Am I showing more skin than if I was at the pool, or the beach?"

"We aren't at the pool, or the beach. And it's cold out here."

She shook her head, turning to look at the house. Mark walked her over to an ambulance as it pulled up.

They were still there when the sun started to come up.

She'd been checked out but had refused transport to the hospital. Mark's breathing seemed worse than hers anyway. Though it occurred to her that the two of them were simply trying to out-stubborn each other in their attempt to prove they were fine.

Mark hung up his phone and strode over. "They saw the pickup, but lost Langdon."

"So we have no idea where he is?" He was here, though. Not a pleasant thought considering the man was responsible for hauling her unconscious to South Africa and dumping her into a prison with no ID, taking months for Mark to find her.

"We'll find him."

She shot him a look, holding a blanket around her that the paramedic had given her. Probably she didn't look as threatening as she was trying to. But Mark had always seen that kid he'd known so many years ago, even now. Just like she often saw the teenage boy he'd been, that old-soul kid with too much on his shoulders. He laughed more now than he ever had then.

Time healing old wounds, and all that.

"Together."

Like she was planning on leaving? She had no actionable intelligence. No leads she could run down—by herself. "I'll have to get a change of clothes." She glanced down at her bare feet, then shot him a pointed look. "You have things to do here. Paperwork, and phone calls. Your stuff is ruined."

Plus there was likely going to be an operation tonight. A

mission to go get Langdon before he could purchase that guidance chip. Take him down before he hurt a lot of people.

His eyes flashed with humor. "Nice try. But Langdon burned my house down, which means he knows who I am." Mark crossed his arms over his chest. "That means I'm in danger. He could come back at any time and try to kill me, so you'll need to protect me. The FBI doesn't have the additional resources to waste on a detail at a time like this." He actually grinned, the rat. "You'll have to make sure I'm safe. *Personally.*"

She glared at him.

"My life is on the line."

18

Portland, Oregon. Friday 9.14p.m.

M ark walked into the art gallery opening, Victoria on his arm. Not that anyone would recognize her in that glittery black dress and the short, black bob wig. She even had serious heels on, so that she was four-inches taller than normal. It was a wonder she could walk in them.

Mark handed over their embossed invitation and Victoria allowed a security attendant to give a cursory inspection of her purse. Her hand slid around his forearm and they moved to the three steps that led up to the main gallery area. A wide, open room with display pillars the height of the ceiling, under a balcony that ran around the room. The whole place was white. Ceiling, walls, and floor.

"I should have brought sunglasses."

Victoria gave him a tiny squeeze as they ascended the steps. The crowd in the room was thick. Mark spotted a few people he'd seen on the local ten o'clock news, and saw a lot of flashy money. Manicures, diamonds. Victoria looked like one of them, not a girl he'd walked barefoot with in the summer, down to the lake to fish. Though, after they'd found that anthill, they'd always worn shoes.

"You seem like you fit in a place like this."

Victoria lifted a glass of bubbly liquid from a tray carried by a waiter and scanned the room. "I'd rather be at home with Bear."

Mark's earpiece came to life. "Who is Bear?" Talia's voice was loud and clear, as it had been when they did their comms check.

A second voice came through his earpiece. "Mark has a dog?" Much to Dakota's consternation, she'd been stationed in the van with her teammate. Josh was inside the gala, having managed to infiltrate the security team.

Victoria smiled, taking a sip of her drink.

Mark lifted his hand to scratch his nose and said into his sleeve. "I have a dog." Then he shoved the glasses he wore up his nose.

Talia said, "Aww, he's so cute."

Victoria lifted Mark's hand and kissed his palm. "Did you just hack Mark's phone?"

He sucked in a breath but it got stuck.

She let go of his hand. "How's your throat?" She frowned at him from eye level, those heels making her a match for his height.

"Fine."

"You caught a lot of smoke last night."

"No more than you did."

"What about Bear? Shouldn't he go to the vet and get checked out?"

He wanted to tug her close and give her a hug. "He'll be fine. And if he isn't, then the neighbor whose house he's at will take him to the 24-hour vet."

She didn't look appeased.

"Everything is going to be fine." He touched her cheek, swiping his thumb across it. Then he moved to scratch the side of his neck, turning his head closer to his sleeve. "Any sign of our guy?"

The man who'd set the explosion at the research facility and stole the guidance chip was the one they were looking for. Mark turned and scanned the crowd.

Victoria chuckled. "Don't give up your day job, okay?"

He turned to ask her what she was talking about, but she'd already turned away. She set her glass down, then tugged on his hand. "Let's dance."

A small dance floor had been set up in one corner where an older man sat playing the piano. The tails of the tux he wore flapped over the bench behind him, and on occasion his glossy black shoes reflected the light.

Victoria spun in Mark's arms and they settled into a slow waltz.

Talia reported in. "No sign of him on surveillance. I've gone through all the images for everyone who checked in, and he's not here. Nor is he one of the wait staff, or in the kitchen."

Victoria grinned up at him. "No sense in not having fun while we're waiting."

Mark wasn't so sure about that. Except that it was her, so how was he supposed to resist? His entire body was tense wondering what was about to happen. How he could keep Victoria safe *and* confiscate the chip. Maybe they would even get Langdon as well. She was right about the dancing. It was helping him relax.

"I'm a little more used to kicking in doors and telling everyone to get their hands in the air." He grinned. His next inhale got stuck again, and he had to cover a cough so he didn't draw anyone's attention. "Which is probably why you look fabulous, and I look like Clark Kent's more nerdy brother."

Glasses. Gelled hair, parted on one side. Even the suit was cut differently than he liked.

Someone on the other end of the radio chuckled. Victoria had a tiny earpiece under her wig, but no transmitter. The only one between them was in his sleeve. She'd claimed she had nowhere to put hers, which was valid since that dress had no sleeves and only part of a back. He was in no way complaining about that, or the fact it meant they had to stay together.

"So smug."

He twirled her around. "I have no idea what you're talking about."

She chuckled. He was feeling pretty happy with himself. They were dancing, he was relaxing, and the danger hadn't happened yet. Plus she wasn't here by herself, which she would absolutely have been...if he hadn't essentially manipulated her into staying with him.

Since she would have been here with or without him, he had no guilt. He was in danger, potentially. She needed to keep him safe.

Sure, it played on her need for him to be all right and remain that way. She had a mile-wide protective streak and the training to back it up. So did he. And he could take care of himself. But that didn't negate the fact he wanted her *with him*. No matter what.

"I'm not sure I'd be so happy if my house burned down. I'm upset enough that my grandfather is missing and the investigating detectives *still* have no leads on where he is."

"Most of the damage is superficial. When he threw the bottle through the window by the front door, the hall rug took most of the spray from the alcohol." He swallowed and had to cough again. "A lot of smell and smoke but not much damage."

Victoria made a face.

"It's just a house. I have insurance, and I'm fixing it up anyway." He shrugged one shoulder.

"I still don't get it. It's your home right now."

"Not forever." He knew what home was for him.

Or rather, who.

If he had Victoria—and yes Bear, too—in his life, then what did he care about charred drywall and the smell of smoke?

"Sorry to interrupt," Talia didn't sound sorry, just focused. "But I've spotted our guy headed for a back hall."

"Copy that," Josh replied. "Time to get to work boys and girls."

Mark went to move, but Victoria held onto him. She gave him a tiny shake of her head. "Where?"

Mark said, "Direction?" into his sleeve. He stayed with Victoria, still swaying to the melodic piano chords and notes. He would be able to appreciate it more if they didn't have a man to catch and a buy to intercept.

Was Langdon really going to be here, or would he send another intermediary?

He almost didn't believe Victoria that she'd seen him outside Mark's house last night…except for the fact it was she who saw him. Was Langdon really in Seattle, or was he hiding out with his biker friends? They had more leads now but still nothing additional, as far as results go. The FBI director had only authorized Mark's participation in this operation because Mark had all but promised him a result. Of the "case-closed" variety.

"Got him." Josh continued a second later. "North hallway, leads to the offices and an exit door. He took the third door on the right. Knew exactly where he was going."

Like he'd been here before? That was interesting. The alternative was that the guy who'd stolen the chip had been given very specific instructions on where to bring it.

"Shall we?" She was calm as anything, totally cool. Like she was asking him if he wanted popcorn at the movies.

Mark wrapped her arm in his, and they wound through meandering people in the crowd, heading for the north hallway.

Josh stepped out, just as they approached the door. He blocked the security guard's view of them and shifted the back of his suit jacket. He handed off a Glock to Mark, behind his back. They slipped through the door while Josh struck up a conversation, his laugh overly loud. As soon as the door clicked shut, Mark looked for the third room. The one where the man had gone.

"Inside that room," Talia said, "I have no eyes. I cannot see anything or anyone, and if you get into danger, I'm not going to know."

"That's what the radios are for." Mark knew Talia had to say it though. She had to voice aloud the fact she was trusting them to keep each other safe.

Victoria stopped at the door. "We're going in."

To an empty room, or one that was full of people? Mark palmed the gun, with its attached silencer, checked that it was loaded and ready to go. "Handle?"

She nodded, then twisted it and pulled the door open. Victoria kept her body covered by the door. Mostly out of sight. Mark entered first, praying the vest he wore under his shirt would provide necessary protection. Or that his body would protect Victoria from taking a hit. He'd rather neither of them got hurt, but he knew who he'd want to get shot if it came down to a choice.

His weeks-old wound twinged with an ache of pain. Gun up, he scanned the room. "Hands. Let me see your hands." His feet clipped the floor across to where the man turned, awareness on his face.

Younger than them. Eyes like Mark had seen many times on the faces of death row inmates. Serial murderers, and the worst of the worst. "He said you'd be here."

"Hands." Mark raised his tone a little, using his fed voice.

The man smirked, but lifted both hands. His coat jacket splayed wide, revealing a gun under his shoulder. Not the most efficient place to holster a weapon, it was more about the cool factor than function. Mark preferred his on his hip, where he could have it up and firing in fractions of a second. Not fighting to aim as he drew his gun and swiped it left to right to reach the target.

"Where's the chip?"

The man didn't answer.

This time it was Victoria who asked the question, "Where is Langdon?"

Mark said, "We could use Josh's assistance."

"Copy that," came back over the radio from the man himself. "Ten seconds."

The suspect moved. Mark fired off a shot, throwing the man

back two steps as the bullet picked off a chunk of his coat sleeve and the outside of his arm.

The man fired. The action had already begun before Mark even fired. The suspect's shot discharged in Victoria's direction. Mark raced to him and tackled the guy, slamming his wrist to the floor.

He slammed it repeatedly until he let go.

The door opened. "Don't wait for me or anything," Josh bit off.

Mark didn't have time for that. He flipped the guy to his face and pulled his arms back. "Victoria?"

"I'm okay." She sighed. "I can't say the same for this painting, though." He heard movement and looked over to see her pull it back. A wall safe had been hidden behind it. "Well, hello there."

"We have no reason to believe that has anything to do with what he's doing here."

Victoria shot him a look. "Sometimes you're *such* a cop."

"Yeah. Me and everyone else wrapped up in this that you call 'friend'." He secured the man's wrists with the zip ties Josh had given him and hauled the guy to his feet.

"Could be a dead drop."

"In a safe?"

She turned to survey the safe. "I'm opening it. I want to see what's inside."

19

Portland, Oregon. Friday 10.32p.m.

Victoria turned away from the two men and the suspect. She didn't want any of them to see how shaken she was. After everything they'd been through, she'd have thought a couple of gunshots—only one aimed in her direction—wouldn't bother her that much.

Apparently not.

Her hand shook as she lifted it to the keypad on the safe. She ran her index finger around the edges, thinking through how she was going to get inside.

Did she really think this was why the suspect had come in here? Maybe. It could have been about meeting with Langdon out of sight…or a million other reasons. There might be nothing in here. Or there could be serious evidence.

She glanced over her shoulder at the suspect. He seemed just like all the rest, a man who had lived hard. Seen too much. Now he was bleeding down his arm and in custody. She tried to assess what he was thinking, namely about her move to break into the safe.

His jaw hardened.

"I'll call the Portland FBI office." Mark slid his phone from his pocket. "Get some backup here."

Josh shifted his stance, Victoria wasn't looking at him, but she heard the rustle of his clothing. "Sure about that?"

"We have to trust them at some point. Let them prove the agents that remain are the good ones."

"Okay," Josh conceded. "I'll call in as well, get Homeland over here. It can't hurt to have some interagency cooperation on this."

She heard more shuffling and looked over to see Josh pat down the suspect. Hadn't he checked the guy for weapons already? The man's gun was discarded. What was...

Mark pulled a phone from the guy's jacket pocket. "Talia?"

The reply came in her earpiece. "Go ahead."

"I've got a phone from our suspect. Can you see what you're able to get from it?"

"Sure," she said. "Call me from the phone and I'll dump the contents to my computer."

The suspect hadn't heard Talia's reply, but he still shifted. Nervous. For what they were going to get from his phone?

Victoria wandered over and took the phone from Mark. She called Talia's number. When Talia answered, Victoria left the call open and navigated back to his call history. A string of numbers he hadn't labeled in contacts. She went to the messages and scrolled through the couple of conversations. Definitely a burner phone, he hadn't used it much except for business. To make an arrangement with someone who'd brought him here.

She showed it to Mark who said, "You seeing this?"

"Yep." Talia sounded distracted in her reply, the way she did when she was doing a deep dive into someone's life. "I'll run these numbers and see if any of them is Langdon."

"Copy that." Victoria handed Josh the phone. He was on his own cell.

Josh nodded, then headed out into the hallway with his badge now prominently displayed on his belt. She glanced at Mark again.

He nodded. "Good guy."

"I know." As if she would handpick someone for her team who wasn't? She'd known of Josh even back in his days as a Marine, working alongside Neema. A dog Victoria had met as a puppy. Of course, she couldn't tell anyone she knew the details of any of that. It was all classified and would probably be as long as she was alive.

Now she had no team. But what remained were friendships forged by fire. A group of people settling down for the most joyous years of their lives, something Victoria would get to be part of.

She walked over to the suspect and got in his face. The safe wasn't going anywhere, she could get to it in a minute. She faced off with him. "Where's Langdon? You were supposed to meet him here, right?"

He sneered at her.

Victoria grabbed his arm, right where he'd been winged by Mark's gunshot.

He battled the pain, but it wasn't more than a few seconds before his lips parted and he cried out.

"Victoria." Mark's point was clear, though he only said her name.

"I'm not a cop. I'm not bound by the same rules, or procedure." She glanced at Mark, refusing to back down. "If you don't want to be a party to my…questioning of this man, then step out into the hallway. I'll let you know in a few minutes everything he has to say about Langdon's whereabouts. And the chip."

Mark knew what she was doing. She saw the moment he realized this was—mostly—for show. So the suspect thought she was unhinged and prepared to seriously hurt him to get answers. It was a variation of the old good cop/bad cop scenario. Mark would bluster, then he'd tell the suspect he should just cooperate instead of having to face her. The suspect would bond with Mark, getting the same result. But without the bother of her having to figure out what to do that would work to get the information she needed.

"Okay." The suspect cried out again.

Victoria realized that she'd been squeezing his arm for a minute. She let go.

The suspect let out a long breath. "I'll tell you what you want to know, but I want protection. Langdon will kill me if he finds out I talked."

"Yeah," she said. "He probably will."

Mark shifted. Fine, she might not have needed to say that. Langdon would do whatever he wanted—as evidenced by the fire damage at Mark's house. Among other things.

"Tell me what he did with my grandfather."

The suspect frowned. "There was an old guy, a few days ago. Langdon said they hit a bar and got drunk first. I'm pretty sure they tore the place up." He shrugged. "I don't know where he dumped the body. How would I? Florida had nothing to do with me."

Victoria stepped back. It was like receiving a blow.

Her grandfather was dead.

She bit the inside of her lip and turned away to the safe. At the last second, she saw him smirk. He knew that hurt. He took satisfaction in telling her that her grandfather was deceased, dumped at an unknown location.

As she got to work on the lock mechanism, it occurred to her again to call Sal. The US Marshal was the best at finding people, especially ones he cared about or someone he knew cared about. He'd found Allyson, hadn't he? That had been next to impossible, but her entire plan had been contingent on him locating her. And he had. Too bad now he was mad at Victoria for putting Allyson on the line in the first place.

She'd done it willingly. Just as she'd visited her grandfather after every mission, also willingly. Exposing them to danger. Putting them on a map, like targets to be taken out.

That was the job. She was supposed to feel guilty about it? If she was, then that would mean she'd be more focused on her emotions than on getting the job done.

Life was about many things, and unavoidable regrets were one of them. A bad thing among so many good.

Give and take.

Push and pull.

It wasn't like she could change that.

But she could make sure her grandfather was found. She could lay him to rest properly, or get him help if he needed it. Knowing him, the story about tearing up some bar was probably right. Though, why Langdon would do that was anyone's guess. Had he been trying to gather intel on her? Given what happened the last day, from the fire to the meeting here, that was likely the reason.

Victoria twisted the handle and pulled the door open, half expecting to find an envelope of money. "What? No payout? I figured you'd leave the chip and he would leave money."

"He has the chip. I get the rest of what he owes me." The suspect frowned. "It's not in there?"

"There's nothing in here." She turned back. "You already gave him the chip?" That meant the deal was done. They were too late.

They had missed it.

Langdon wasn't coming.

Mark had that assessing look on his face. He turned to the suspect. "You were here to get paid?"

"Where's the chip?" She folded her arms.

"Langdon took it yesterday." The suspect made a face. "And he didn't pay me, did he?" The guy broke off into a hurried spew of muttering that included some choice language that made Victoria want to wince.

"All right." Mark tugged on his uninjured arm and shook the guy once, just to get him out of his head. "What kind of mood was he in, what did he say?"

"He was furious. Some chick killed his girlfriend and he's on the warpath. Said he was going from the meet up to start his plan of revenge."

"Burning your house down." Victoria pointed out to Mark.

The suspect blanched at Victoria. "It's *you?*" He turned to Mark. "Get me out of here. Dude, do it *now.* We can't be around her."

"Calm down." Mark shook his head. "You said he was furious. Where is he staying?"

The suspect shrugged his shoulders, then winced and cried out. "How am I supposed to know?"

"What kind of car did he show up in?"

"None. He was walking." He blew out a breath. "I can't be around here, man. She's bad news. He's on a rampage."

"I know. My house has serious fire damage because of Langdon." But Mark walked him to the door and pulled it open.

"Fire? He's going to *kill us.*"

"Maybe."

Victoria checked the contents of the safe, which was only business papers for the gallery. They continued their conversation, the suspect pleading his case while Mark talked him down. Her team, or the FBI, would need to look into this art gallery's business. Find out how Langdon got a contact here that was solid enough he could use their safe for a dead drop.

That, or he'd never planned on leaving anything. Maybe it was all this suspect's idea. Maybe Langdon only drew him here for another reason altogether. Perhaps in order to draw her out.

Was this all part of his plan, and they'd fallen for it?

Maybe the suspect was right, and she needed to get out. Keep them safe by drawing Langdon away to a place where she could face him down. It would be the right thing to do, except that she'd promised to stay and help Mark be safe. If she left, and that caused Mark to be targeted, she would never forgive herself.

That was one regret Victoria wouldn't be able to survive.

"Done?"

She followed him out into the hall where Josh talked on his phone, occasionally glancing up at the camera. It sounded like he was reassuring Dakota.

"They good?"

He shifted the phone away from his mouth. "Yeah. Nothing on the surveillance."

Mark said, "Let's get this guy out of here."

Through her comms, Victoria heard Talia say, "Good idea. I have a bad feeling."

Victoria glanced at Mark, but he already had the suspect halfway to the EXIT door at the end of the hall.

She hung back, waiting for Josh to go with her so they all left together. There was an infinitesimal tingle. Some latent instinct that sensed a coming disaster two fractions of a second before a detonation.

Josh grabbed her before she could even react. A testament to his own instincts, being in the line of fire.

Talia's voice screamed across the radio.

Victoria couldn't make out the words. She hit the floor and the weight of Josh's body landed on hers.

Flames erupted around them as the hallway exploded.

20

Portland, OR. Saturday 1.07a.m.

"Mark!" Heels clacked on the tile floor of the hospital waiting area. "Mark!"

He blinked and lifted his gaze from his shoes. "Talia." He got up and moved to her, across the waiting area. His eyes strayed to the clock and he winced at the time, even while his entire body processed aches and pains with each step.

She didn't stop, just opened her arms and stepped into his hug. Her gold purse slammed against his hip.

Mark ignored it.

"Mason is going to come down first thing, after he checks in at the office. He'll be here by lunch. Niall and Haley, too."

"Good."

Even in the middle of the night, her hair and makeup were professional. Her clothes had considerably fewer wrinkles than his. Talia looked like she'd worked the day, and clocked out. Not that it had been an entire day that lasted until midnight.

She shook her head, a sheen of tears in her eyes. "We found it."

"The rocket launcher?"

Talia sniffed, nodding. "Dakota made me stay in the van. She wouldn't let me get out and go with her to make sure you were all right."

He wasn't going to tell her that was the right call. Dakota had done her job and kept Talia safe.

"So I wound back the video feed. I watched from the outside angle. The building exploded and you and the suspect were blown out the door."

He winced. His hip smarted, and the old wound in his abdomen, where he'd been shot by a sniper, didn't feel much better. "The suspect was treated for the head wound and the gun shot he had. He's been taken to the FBI office here."

That was the least of their problems right now, the easiest one to solve. Mark had simply required the wherewithal to coordinate that. He'd grabbed an ice pack from the first EMT and then coordinated with local police and the feds that'd shown up.

He blew out a breath, just thinking about the burst of energy that had taken. He was so far past drained right now, he didn't know how he was still functioning. Maybe he was delirious. Or making no sense at all.

"Sit down." Talia led him to a chair. He planted his backside in it and leaned his head against the wall. Artwork hung there. His head collided with the gilded frame and he frowned.

"I'm okay." Irritated, and tired, but that was all. He wasn't the one hurt. Or, more accurately one of the *ones* who'd been hurt.

"Victoria?"

He rubbed his hands down the legs of his jeans, to his knees. "Still unconscious."

"She hit the floor pretty hard." Talia's voice broke on the last word.

He looked at her.

"I watched it. On the feed. I wound it back and watched." She pressed her lips together, and he spotted a quiver. "The wall exploded. They reacted almost at the exact same time, fast enough it looked like they moved before the blast even happened."

"I've seen it with law enforcement. Military. Peace officers. If you know you have to react the second something happens, in order to minimize the fallout, then you develop those instincts. You know what it feels like when something is about to kick off."

"You?"

Mark shook his head. "My grandfather was a prison guard. He was so fast it was instantaneous." He didn't have to tell her it involved him getting back handed on too many occasions. She probably knew.

She studied him, out the corner of his eye he saw her. But Mark didn't want to know what was on her face. Pity? Compassion? It didn't matter. The past was the past, and he couldn't change it. No matter how much he wanted to. What he'd done was break the cycle. He hadn't turned into a drunk with an explosive temper. First generation sober, full-time job. He'd never been fired in his life. Stable.

Just not the rest of it that he wanted—the part where he had love in his life, and a family.

How long, God?

He'd been told so many times to be thankful for what he had, and for him it was instinctive to apologize when he was tempted to ask for what he wanted.

But what about those verses about trusting God, about asking for the desires of his heart? The part where God gave him every good and perfect blessing.

Well, he had that in part with Victoria in his life. But not the full realization of it.

The abundance that he wanted.

It could be because she hadn't yet put her trust in Him. Maybe Mark was holding back, knowing she wasn't there yet. But he couldn't ignore that niggling question of whether she pushed him off on the togetherness stuff because she couldn't fully trust him. Maybe she was protecting herself.

From him—and the fact that if she accepted Mark, then she

would need to accept God as well. The two were synonymous, at least as much as he'd figured out.

"What is *with* the two of you?" Talia asked. "I just don't get it."

Mark shook his head. Protecting himself, in a way. Keeping Victoria's confidence in the pact they had made.

"Just seems like there's a whole lot more going on than a few months of working together and developing a friendship."

"We grew up in the same town. We've known each other for years."

"You've—"

He got up before she could say more, moving to Dakota who had wandered in. "Hey." He touched her elbow.

"Hey." She didn't hug him. Pretty typical for Dakota, though he hadn't spent much time with her. She connected with Victoria on a level that was particular to the two of them. He couldn't begin to understand it.

Talia came to stand by him. "How is Josh?"

Dakota rolled her eyes. "They told me to get out. They're running tests, so they politely told me to get lost. I mean, *go get a cup of coffee*. Like I need a break."

"Do you want to sit?"

"Not when I'm waiting for my fiancé to wake up."

That seemed to be going around. At least Dakota had Josh's ring on her finger. Mark wasn't even allowed into the room, since he wasn't family. Like Victoria had an abundance of that in her life—it was all her friends and coworkers. Not to mention Bear, who she'd latched onto when Mark had first brought the puppy home. The feeling was mutual there, and he was hardly going to complain that she spent too much time at his house.

He didn't want it to end. And he'd been dealing with the frustration pretty well, considering he was the root cause of all of it.

Dakota ran her hands through her hair, then retied her pony-tail. Mark glanced at Talia, who didn't seem alarmed by this withdrawal. A moment Dakota needed to compose herself. At least, that was what he figured.

Why were women so hard to figure out?

Dakota said, "They're concerned about a spine injury, but they have to wait for the swelling to go down."

"He took the blast to his back," Talia said. Something all three of them knew. "He was protecting Victoria, shielding her with his body."

Dakota nodded.

Mark tugged Talia against his side, hugging her shoulder with one arm. Josh was going to recover, but the lingering question was over whether he'd be able to walk. If he'd have to retire from federal work. And in the meantime, Dakota had to hang out here with her whole future in the balance. They would be together, but no one knew yet what that together would look like.

"I sent my mom a text," Talia said. "She's got her whole Bible study group praying."

"Thanks." Dakota gave her a small smile.

"In the meantime, I've been finding out all about how Mark and Victoria *grew up together*."

He started to back away, before she'd even finished. "No—"

Dakota took a step toward him. "I can only sit around waiting for the doctor to tell me that my fiancé will walk out of here instead of leaving with a medical retirement paper. I need a distraction."

He shot her a look to tell her how he felt about that. The expression Dakota gave him back indicated she felt zero remorse about manipulating him like this.

"What's said in a hospital room at two in the morning," Talia said, "stays in the hospital room."

Mark walked a couple of steps away and then turned. He scratched at the growth of stubble on his jaw. "I should be asking her if it's all right that I tell you guys."

Dakota folded her arms. "I'll tell her it was her fault for being unconscious."

Mark slumped into a chair.

"None of us have anything to do." Talia sat opposite him. "So spill. Regale us with tales of Victoria and Mark as kids, running around that small town in bare feet with fishing poles. Getting up to trouble."

Dakota grinned, stretching her arms above her head.

Mark squeezed the bridge of his nose. "It wasn't like that."

"So what was it like?"

"We wore shoes."

Talia cracked a smile. "I knew it."

"She was..." Mark didn't even know where to start. "Exactly like she is now. She's just always been like that, and I don't think there was ever a time in her life where she was...naive." But she had lost something that day.

"What day?"

He blinked. "What?" He'd said that part out loud?

Dakota leaned forward, arms on her knees. "What did she lose?"

"You're interrogating me."

She flipped one hand over, palm up. "Tell me you don't have something to hide."

"Everything I've ever had to hide came out during FBI training at Quantico. The bureau has full knowledge of every secret I've ever kept."

"Because they train to spot inconsistencies in people's stories by having you investigate each other."

It worked. "I'm just saying."

"What?"

She was interrogating him. Mark shook his head. At two in the morning he was off his game, but apparently Dakota never was. "Victoria... You know what? No. She'd have told you if she wanted you to know."

"What makes you think she hasn't told me?"

"Because I'd know. She would have told me, you know."

Dakota tipped her head to the side. "Maybe. What did you do?"

He opened his mouth, then realized he'd been about to tell her.

"Confession is good for the soul."

He stood. "I don't have to tell you anything."

"Sit down, Mark." Talia pointed a manicured finger at the chair he'd vacated. "What did she do?"

He shook his head.

"Why do you two dance around each other?" Dakota asked.

"I'm not—"

"Why aren't you together?"

"It's not—"

"You love her."

"Yes." That wasn't even up for debate. It was the easiest question he'd ever had to answer.

"She loves you."

Maybe.

"So why not—"

"Because I killed my father."

"And it was her fault."

He spun around. "No!" He blew out a breath and tried to get some control.

Talia sat, staring at him. She said quietly, "You killed someone?"

Mark sat in the chair.

"Start talking." Dakota's tone didn't invite argument. She'd gone from pushing him over why they didn't have a relationship, to wanting the whole story so she could decide whether he was even worthy of being in Victoria's life.

"It was an accident."

"I'll be the judge of that."

"No," he said. "You won't. Because the case is closed." Two could use that tone. "She was waiting for me at my house. My father was there, and he was drunk. As usual. He got handsy with her, and there was no one around to put a stop to it. I came in the front door, home late from football practice. He was on top of her on the couch."

Talia looked like she wanted to throw up. Dakota looked like she wanted to resurrect his father so she could punch him.

"They both had their clothes on, but still." Neither argued his point. "I hauled him off. He lost balance and fell, clipped his head on the coffee table. I left him there, and we ran out. Didn't see how much blood there was until I got home and the sheriff had already had his body hauled out of the house by the coroner. He told me a neighbor found my father, and that there had been an accident."

"There's a reason why no one's ever convicted you over it, and that's because it wasn't your fault," Dakota said in a matter-of-fact tone. "How old were you?"

"Seventeen."

"And it's colored everything between you and Victoria—"

A nurse said, "Mark Welvern?"

He turned.

"Ms. Bramlyn is awake. She's asking for you."

He started to move, but she held up a hand.

"She wants you to call a 'Jakeman' for her. Do you know who that is?"

21

Portland, OR. Saturday 2.49a.m.

"He killed his father for you?"

Victoria turned to the door, not finding the person she'd been expecting. The man she wanted to see. Dakota stood there, hands on her hips. She shut the door while Victoria sat in the hospital bed, not moving.

Dakota hauled the chair back a foot and plunked herself down in it. "Well?"

"He told you?"

Dakota said, "I get there was a situation and all. But the man killed his father for you. And you've got him in the friend zone over it. Like it was his fault."

Victoria touched the bandage over her eyebrow and shut her eyes for a second.

"And let me tell you," Dakota continued, "I know a thing or two about killing fathers—"

"Too soon," Victoria snapped.

"For who?"

"Uh… how about everyone?" She looked at Dakota with a raised brow.

No one's father was perfect, but Dakota's hadn't just hurt her. He'd also hurt a lot of other people. He'd actually murdered her stepmother in front of her. Yes, he'd been a bad guy, and in resisting arrest and attempting to kill her, she'd been forced to discharge her weapon. She'd killed him. That had literally only been a few months ago.

Dakota shrugged her shoulders. She looked so tense it probably hurt.

Victoria sighed. "He really told you?"

"Pin a man down at two in the morning and interrogate him, things tend to come out of his mouth that he wasn't intending to say."

Victoria blinked. "Please tell me this isn't how you plan on having a good marriage."

Dakota actually cracked a smile. It was short lived. "He might not walk." She blew out a breath. "Josh might be paralyzed."

"What did they say?"

"There's so much swelling around his spine they literally have no idea. We have to wait and see."

Victoria wasn't going to placate her with some pithy comment that sounded nice but didn't mean anything. Dakota was processing her fear.

By coming in here, mad at Victoria.

Anger was easier to handle than fear.

"Meanwhile you and *Mark* are banished to the friend zone because, what? He saved you. You should be grateful."

"You think I'm not?"

"I think you don't like being vulnerable." Dakota raised one eyebrow. "Which is why you never told anyone about that. So don't get all mad because he told me and Talia—"

"Talia knows?" Never mind the fact that this woman was the epitome of that "pot calling the kettle black" saying, telling Victoria that she didn't like being vulnerable. Like Dakota ever did herself.

Dakota's lips twitched.

"You shouldn't find other people's struggles hilarious. It's not nice."

"You know we didn't give him any choice. Anyway, now it's out. You can move on and get together." Dakota shrugged. "You love his dog, apparently. So what's the problem?"

Victoria glanced at the tiny sink in the corner. The blank gray screen of the TV.

There was so much to say, and yet she was having a hard time voicing any of it. She rested her head back on the pillow and shut her eyes. Maybe she'd be more on her game if she hadn't been in that hallway right when Langdon had someone fire a grenade at the outside wall. Talia had filled her in on what happened, right before the cops had shown up to take her statement.

Thankfully, no one except her and Josh were seriously hurt. The suspect and Mark both had minor injuries, not counting the suspect's gunshot wound.

Now they just had to heal.

And find Langdon.

"Strategic retreat. A classic technique."

Victoria shook her head, not opening her eyes yet. Mark had told them. They knew the guilt he lived with, despite the ruling. By the time he'd gotten home that day, the sheriff had been there. A neighbor had come over and found his father dead. Everyone just assumed he was drunk—confirmed by the autopsy—and had fallen and hit his head.

No one knew she'd have to live with the memory of his hot breath on her neck. His hands.

Or the realization that Mark had been there. That he'd *seen it*. That alone was worse than knowing he felt so guilty over his father's death and knowing he'd only done it for her.

"I don't need this." She'd just been blown up but that attack had hurt Dakota's fiancé far worse than it did Victoria, so she exercised a little restraint and didn't say all she wanted to say.

"Deflecting with an attack. Another classic technique."

She glanced at Dakota. "What are you, a shrink?"

"If I was, I'd stick with one client. You. And you'd be a lifetime case study."

Victoria wasn't going to dignify that with a response. It was all out now. The whole team would know the worst about her, the fact she was to blame for Mark killing his father.

She vividly remembered the day he told her he would have to explain it all to the FBI. He'd known the secret would come out somehow, and he'd been determined to be upfront about it. Fear like that, she didn't like it. Never had and never would. Fear for the person she loved most in the world. That he would lose his dream.

"Things are getting worse, not better." The words were out before Victoria could pull them back.

"With Mark, or Langdon?"

Victoria shrugged one shoulder. "Jakeman should be here soon." She glanced at the clock on the wall. "You should probably go check on Josh."

"You think they're not going to let me know when I can see him again?" She didn't move from the seat.

It hadn't worked.

Dakota said, "I want to know what Jakeman says. Whatever plan you guys come up with, I want in. This guy hurt the man I'm marrying, and he might not be able to walk down the aisle—" Her voice broke on the last word.

"Dakota."

She lowered her head, then lifted her hand as she shook it. Victoria waited. When she had composed herself, Dakota said, "I have to believe he'll be okay. And if he's not, then we'll deal. It's not like either of us is going to walk away."

"I've been doing that, 'dealing' for years. It sucks, being stuck in the friend zone. Sometimes I just want to scream. But you can find the strength to carry on." Victoria shrugged one shoulder. "Because what's the alternative? You give up on what you want."

"I'm going to find somewhere to pray."

Victoria nodded. "That's a good idea."

Dakota paused at the door. "Not because it'll make me feel better, even though it probably will. It also moves the heart of God. Prayer can literally change a situation."

Victoria didn't know what to say.

"Maybe you should try it."

"Subtle."

Dakota tipped her head to the side. "It's a gift." She turned to leave with a smile, but someone was coming in at the same time. She started, then stepped around them.

Jakeman walked in, shaking his head. "Nice friends. I think that one's scared of me."

"I doubt it." She knew Dakota better than that. "Her fiancé is the other one who was injured last night."

"And that man of yours…Mark? He didn't seem happy I was coming in here while he was stuck out in the hallway." He settled into the chair Dakota had just vacated.

"I don't really want to talk about Mark." There was far too much to talk about, and she needed about a week of quiet time to process everything that had to do with him. She might have asked for him earlier, but that was to call in Jakeman. And now that the story was out, how was she going to face him? Everything was so close to the surface.

Jakeman said, "Langdon, then."

She nodded. He'd tried to kill her. That meant everyone on the committee didn't make a move without protection until he was behind bars, or dead. It meant the suspect knew something of value. Otherwise, Langdon wouldn't have waited until she was in there with him to then open fire.

"I'm shutting you down." He leaned back in the chair like they were talking about the weather. "I have a team, they've been reassigned to get Langdon. You need to stand down now."

She sat up in the bed. "You're benching me?"

"They'll find Langdon. You don't need to worry about it anymore."

"Don't need…" She sputtered, unable to say anything else

when he was stripping away everything she had. Her team all worked for other people now. She couldn't handle whatever was happening with Mark. At least until she figured out what she was going to do with it. How on earth was she supposed to deal with being taken off the case on top of everything else?

It niggled at her to admit it, but right now she could kind of appreciate how Allyson must have felt. Victoria had been more than prepared to absorb Allyson's search for her missing friend into her own FBI corruption case. She'd gotten the result she wanted, regardless.

Which was exactly what Jakeman was doing right now.

"Turnabout's fair play and all that?" Jakeman lifted his chin. "Don't even worry about it. I have the entire defense department behind me, and I'm going to employ every resource I have to find this guy before anyone else gets hurt." He folded his arms. "End of story."

Victoria pressed her lips together and shook her head. "This is a federal case."

"I'll clear it with the department of justice. When my guys find Langdon, no one will complain about a military operation on military soil. No one trusts the FBI right now. They can't be left to bring in one of their own. A man who went unnoticed for *years*."

"Don't do that. It's not fair."

"You were leading the charge. Now's not the time to change your tune."

Victoria said, "I'm not going to sit back."

"You will if you want to come out of this alive."

"Let Mark help. He needs to give Langdon to his boss, to make this right for the FBI."

"You know, when you told me to push for him as the new assistant director of Seattle FBI, I wasn't sure. Now I know he's good. Why else would you keep him around for so long?"

"It isn't—"

"Has there ever been anyone else?"

Victoria didn't answer.

"You know he was married."

"I sat in the back row." That had been one of the worst days of her life. She didn't count the day of Mark's divorce on her "best days" list. That wouldn't be fair. But she could admit she'd been relieved. Now they had each other again.

What if things between them changed?

What if Langdon was no longer a threat, she gave up her fear and they both got everything they'd ever wanted?

"You need protection as much as I do."

He spread his hands out, palms facing her. "secretary of defense. Protection comes with the job. You, on the other hand… Is this guy going to keep you safe?"

"I keep myself safe. Proof, I'm still alive aren't I?"

"You've got good friends."

"I know." After all, Josh had thrown himself on her, weeks before his wedding, not knowing what would happen to him. Willing to give his life for her.

"Drop this. Leave Langdon to me and get some rest."

Victoria lifted her chin and lied to his face. "Okay."

22

Seattle, Washington. Saturday 2.23p.m.

"R eady?"

The FBI director looked over, blank-faced from his study of the computer monitor at Mark's desk.

"We're all set."

The director stood. He smoothed down his tie and lifted his suit jacket from the hook, shrugging it on. Mark led him to the interrogation room where the suspect had been brought up from Portland for questioning.

He didn't like the fact Victoria hadn't been released, and he'd had to leave. She was due to be checked out of the hospital later today, and Niall had strict orders to bring her up to Seattle to his house when she got out.

Mark had figured making it sound like a direct order increased the chance they would all do what he said. It was worth a try, at least.

They stepped into the viewing room. Through the glass, two men were settling into chairs across from their suspect. One was Mason, Talia's fiancé and the head of the Secret Service in Seattle. The other was the US attorney.

"Mr. Bakemeister, I'm Assistant Director Mason Anderson with the Secret Service. This is William Zane, he's the US attorney who will ultimately decide what charges are brought against you."

Trevor Bakemeister. That was his name? Mark studied the man they'd found in the art gallery, heading for the safe that had held nothing. He looked considerably more worn than he had last night. Pale-faced, dark circles under his eyes. His arm was now in a sling, taking the weight off the gunshot wound in his arm. Tiny strips of white held the edges of the gash on his temple together.

He looked like Mark honestly felt, even with the few hours of sleep he'd managed to snatch up before coming here.

"FBI?"

Mark shook his head at the director's question. "The first one we've brought in who is connected to Langdon, but not an agent."

He made a "huh" sound but went quiet as Mason began the interrogation. Considering all the FBI had gone through recently, they figured it was better to outsource this. They were chasing one of their own. Making it an interagency investigation was better for PR. They weren't afraid of what shook loose in the course of things. They wanted transparency.

Trevor shrugged. "Whatcha want from me?"

"The issue here," Mason said, "is what *you* want. To spend your whole life in federal prison for all kinds of conspiracy to commit "this" and attempted "that"? Or the alternative."

Mark almost smiled. Mason wasn't the kind of federal agent who investigated criminal activity. Mark had brushed him up on a few things, as had the US attorney. Mark wasn't worried that he wouldn't be able to pull this off. It wasn't his fault he was only a Secret Service agent.

The US attorney, William Zane, opened a file on the table. He slid a photo across the surface so Trevor could look at it. "This is Colin Pinton. You might know him as Oscar Langdon. He's someone we're very interested in finding."

"You think I know him?" Trevor shrugged.

"This man blew up a hallway you were standing in," Mason pointed out. "He holds no loyalty to you. It's in your best interest, here and now, that you return that favor."

Trevor's expression didn't change. He seemed determined to hold whatever he knew close, as Mark had seen many suspects do for years. Whether that was the right thing to do wasn't something they usually considered. Nor was the fact that a lawyer was likely a better idea than not. This man would hold his own counsel.

"I tell you what I know, I go free?"

Zane shifted in his seat. "The break you receive on these considerable charges you've managed to rack up will depend on the extent of the information you give us."

The director said, "You think he knows where Langdon is right now?"

Mark shrugged one shoulder while he watched Trevor think it through. "We got nothing from his phone so far, right?" Talia hadn't found much of anything that would get them a location on Langdon. The man was the most slippery criminal he'd ever gone after. "We don't have a lot unless Trevor here gives it to us. Langdon has a nuke, or at least has all the parts to put one together, and we have no idea where he'll use it or what the time frame might be."

A thought occurred to him. Before he could voice it, the director said, "A scientist."

Mark pulled out his phone and unlocked it. "Someone who knows how to put it all together and get it set up so Langdon can use it." He typed out an email to Talia that necessitated he copy several people who needed to be part of the loop. Then he stowed his phone and focused back on what Trevor and Mason were talking about.

"...idea where he is."

"Maybe," Mason said. "But you might know something you don't know that you know. So run it all down for us, everything Langdon said and did, and we'll tell you if we think it's important."

Trevor made a face. "I'm not one of your crooked FBI agents."

Zane said, "No, you're a wanted thief, suspected in the murder of a museum security guard in Washington D.C."

Trevor worked his jaw side to side.

"Didn't think we knew about that, did you?" Zane probably had a smug look on his face, but Mark could only see the back of his head through the window. "It won't go well for you, getting tied up with a ten-most-wanted terrorist. You think being associated with Langdon is something you want to leave a jury to wonder about? You're better off bringing everything out into the light."

Mark agreed with that. If Trevor offered conclusive proof he'd done a job for Langdon, but had no ongoing association with him, then it would be hard for the US attorney to make a case over his involvement in the man's organization, or group of associates and friends. He needed to distance himself from Langdon and the fallout of whatever he had planned.

Mason said, "You sold Oscar Langdon a chip. He's going to use that chip to set off a nuclear device that will kill thousands, if not more. Care to be an accessory to a terrorist attack, or you want to stick with the burglary and whatever you get for setting off an explosion at the research facility?"

Trevor sputtered. "It's a *guidance* chip. It's—" His face washed pale. "Oh, God."

"I find in these situations that prayer is an excellent idea." Mason said, "However, we are running out of time. Where is Langdon, and where is he going to set off that bomb?"

Trevor leaned back in his chair, head tipped back, and ran his hands down his face. "You can't think I have something to do with this. I'm not *part* of it, I have nothing to do with Langdon."

"So tell me how to find him," Mason suggested. "Get this guy out of your life before he ruins it even further."

Trevor blew out a breath. "You think I know where he is? I

have an email. I get requests, and I respond to what I want. I do the jobs I want."

"And you wanted to do Langdon's?"

"It was good money."

Mason said, "You're going to destroy the rest of your life over a paycheck?"

"I've got one skill, okay?"

Zane motioned to the file. "We know. Your rap sheet clearly indicates your drive to steal whatever you want for that paycheck. But it's not good money, and it never will be."

Trevor mashed his lips together.

Mason said, "There are ways to be one of the good guys, even if this is your skill set." He paused a moment so that could sink in, then continued, "We need access to your email account."

It would be a miracle if Talia could get a location on Langdon, or anything that could lead them to one, from an email address. He'd gone on for this long, active under the radar—he had to have a way to distance himself from communications that could potentially expose him.

Langdon had been an FBI agent until recently. He knew how they thought. He knew what they looked for, and how they undertook investigations.

Which was exactly why it had taken Victoria, and an entire committee, to finally identify Oscar Langdon as the FBI agent Colin Pinton.

Mark needed to get her take on this.

He pulled out his phone and checked the screen. All the notifications were FBI related, no personal ones. Especially not the one he was waiting for, telling him Victoria would be at home when he got there.

As though that was normal, and this was another life entirely.

One where she wore her ring. He wore his. She lived at his house.

The director headed for the door and Mark followed. Out in

the hall, his boss said, "Not much. Let's hope it leads us to something."

Mark nodded. There wasn't much to say, considering all that was swirling in his head right now.

"You don't work anything else until Langdon is caught." The director stopped at the elevator and turned. "I'll be giving you back your office, but I'm not going far."

Mark knew he had a meeting scheduled for tonight with the director of Homeland Security as well as other branches of the federal government, local and state police. There was no time to lose making preparations for an imminent attack. They needed all hands on deck and every eye open and peeled, watching for Langdon.

The director said, "I want half-hourly updates."

"Yes, sir. And I'll let you know if we get anything from either the email or the scientist angle."

"Very well." He hit the button for the elevator. "I'm trusting you. This is bigger than the limb I went out on by promoting you simply on the recommendation of a few key people who seem to enjoy having their noses in this investigation. You've proven your-self thus far, but we're all under a microscope on this. Don't let me down."

Mark frowned. "Who recommended me for this job?"

The director said, "Enough people I didn't have a choice, even though it was made clear I should have one. I don't like that kind of pressure, Welvern. And I intend for it not to happen again."

The doors slid open. The director stepped in.

Mark slammed his hand to the side, forcing the door to remain open. "Who specifically recommended me for the assistant director position?"

He'd been a controversial choice. Untested, a choice that had surprised a lot of people when he'd been offered it. He relished the chance to prove himself and figured he'd done that to the extent he deserved a straight answer to his question.

"The secretary of defense, for one." The director frowned.

"Don't get all hung up on this. So you have friends in high places, so what? It's done now, isn't it? We all have to live with the choices we've made. Thankfully some of us didn't betray every oath we swore like these scum bags."

Mark let go of the elevator door.

"Find Langdon."

The doors slid shut, leaving Mark alone in the hallway. For a second, until Mason and the US attorney walked out of the interrogation room.

Mason frowned. "Everything okay?"

He opened his mouth, ready to say something, then shook his head.

"Okay." Mason handed him a piece of paper that he'd made notes on. "I already sent it all to Talia."

Mark nodded.

Zane muttered something about the Secret Service assistant director being old school. Mason shot him a look. "Can't hack a piece of paper." He glanced at Mark. "Sure you're okay?"

Mark turned and headed for the stairs. He took them two at a time up to his office, calling Victoria's phone on the way.

She never picked up.

23

Seattle, WA. Saturday 4.40p.m.

"It's freezing out here." Victoria tucked her coat tighter around her and dipped her chin behind the buttoned collar at her throat.

The reply came through the comms earbud. "It was your idea." Niall was quiet for a second. "Want me to hand off a cup of coffee?"

Like he would be able to do that without it being completely obvious what they were doing? Victoria shook her head. Sitting alone on a park bench, only occasionally passed by someone walking the path with a stroller, or a dog. A couple jogged by her. The man gave her a sideways glance the woman didn't like.

She wanted to toss a clump of dirt at him. Where she grew up, people said "hi" to each other. They didn't invite trouble, mostly because they had enough in their lives already.

Her mom might have split before she turned four, leaving Victoria with her grandfather to begrudgingly taking care of her. And that was putting it nicely. She wanted to know where he was and if he was all right, but she wouldn't pretend he cared about her. Or that he would pick up the phone and call if he *was* all right.

Don't be dead.

As much as Mark was right about the way her grandfather had treated her, she would mourn him. Of course she would. He might be hard and cold, but he was her family. Maybe the kind of person he was made her the kind of spy she had been, able to detach herself from her emotions and make the best choice to get the results she needed. Had Mark ever considered that? Probably he only thought that her being a spy meant she maybe wasn't a good person.

Considering he was the *best* kind of person, she gave him a little leeway on that stuff. He just assumed everyone else would be as good as he was in spite of reality. Not that he was naïve, he simply preferred to believe the best of people until they proved otherwise. Well, life didn't work like that and he'd figure it out sooner or later when he'd been slapped in the face with reality enough times.

"Helloooo," Niall sang over the comms. "Earth to Victoria."

"What?" She glanced around like Langdon was going to be right in front of her. As though he'd shown up while she was daydreaming.

Niall chuckled in her ear. "Are you sure you don't have a concussion?"

No, she wasn't. "I'm fine. Just thinking."

"You were pretty deep in there. I was beginning to get worried."

She wasn't going to tell him that she got like that when she thought about Mark. Enough that she'd started to trick her brain into forgetting about him altogether when she was on a mission. But that was before they'd kissed.

Everything was different now, and she was looking forward to seeing how that would work out as soon as Langdon was caught.

"You don't need to worry." She didn't tell him that he just

needed to do his job. Niall knew that. As soon as Langdon showed up, they would arrest him.

Victoria just hoped she was sufficient enough bait to get him to come in person. To try and kill her, up close. Probably with his hands.

She shivered, and not just from the cold.

"Mmm. Tell that to Haley," Niall said. "And Talia. Dakota. Jakeman sent two teams of NCIS agents, like they don't have other cases."

"This is highest priority."

"Sitting in a park waiting for Langdon to not show up?"

"If you didn't think there was a shot," Victoria reminded him, "you wouldn't be here."

"I'm here because you'd do it without backup if I refused." Niall's tone hardened. "And I'd rather not explain to everyone that you got killed because I decided to have a 'tude."

Victoria had to smother a smile. "Did Jakeman really send them?"

"He signed off on it, if anyone asks."

"So you fumbled the paperwork in the hopes no one would notice?"

Niall sighed. "Like I'm going to *not* bring an army?"

Victoria wasn't sure she was worth all that, especially considering the flack Niall could receive if he was called on it. Jakeman couldn't know she was hanging herself out here to try and catch Langdon. If he did, he'd throw her in protective custody she didn't even want to think about. He wasn't over any law enforcement, and she didn't want to know what the military would consider "protection." It made her think about secret bunkers on ships, and prisoners with no names.

She hoped Jakeman did come up with Langdon's whereabouts. It seemed everyone was looking, and no one could find...

Victoria's body froze, though it wouldn't have appeared to have done so from a casual observer's point of view.

She glanced up at a couple of birds. As she did that, her gaze drifted over a man walking at the edge of her peripheral vision.

"Red jacket. Blue ball cap." They were generic, no labels. He had a medium build. Not someone you'd notice in a crowd; he blended in.

The face shape was too far away for her to see. "Anyone got an angle?"

Several people radioed in that they couldn't see him well enough. One could, but wasn't sure if it was Langdon or not.

Stood to reason he was a master of disguise, considering his resume. Both as a criminal mastermind in international arms and antiquities dealings, and as a decorated FBI agent. She'd read everything. She'd put them side-by-side once she knew who he was, and tracked Langdon's activities over the last decade. Then she'd read his FBI psychological profile.

No one had missed anything.

There hadn't been anything to miss.

Either the man was the best actor in the world, and a complete sociopath to pull this off under everyone's noses, or... she didn't know what the alternative was.

Someone asked. "Should we intercept?"

Niall replied, "Hold until my signal."

She'd given him control of this operation, making it clear to the others that he was in charge. Victoria couldn't command the operation from behind the collar of her jacket while innocent people wandered within earshot of what she was saying.

Deep in the pocket of her coat, Victoria's phone rang.

She lifted her hand and glanced at her wrist, and the smart-watch she'd dug out of her suitcase this morning. She hadn't worn it since before she went on that mission to talk to Genevieve. It felt foreign. As did the name *Mark* on the display. He was calling her.

For an update, or for another reason?

Either way, she couldn't talk right now. She couldn't even spare a moment to think about him, considering how distracting he was to her.

The man in the red jacket wandered a path headed for her, in a roundabout way. Not direct. Not obviously intending to go away from her. The view was obscured by bushes and trash cans. A tree.

His whole body flashed into view.

The guy held a dog leash for a small beagle. The dog trotted along behind him on a doggy adventure in the park.

Victoria dipped her chin. "It's not him."

Niall's reply was immediate. "Are you sure?"

She rolled her eyes, shaking her head at the same time. She could tell him she was sure, but then he would want her to explain *how* she knew. She'd only seen him from Mark's bedroom window, other than that he'd been a specter in her life. A ghost she knew was flesh and bone, but hadn't managed to prove yet. They had his picture, but this guy could be using a disguise. He could be good, as good as she was with latex and glue on facial hair. A wig.

"It's not him."

She'd been trained to be observant, down to the smallest detail. The ears. The walk. The way a person carried themselves, and what they did with their hands. Natural things that couldn't be augmented, no matter how much the façade was changed.

"All positions, stand down." Then Niall said, "Victoria, we're getting a call. I'm patching it through."

"Hello? Hello? Anyone?"

Victoria pulled out her phone and held it to her ear over the comms earbud, as though she was on the phone. "Hi, Talia." Victoria smiled, still not all the way recovered from thinking she'd seen Langdon.

"I heard you're swinging on the line, trying to be bait."

"Not trying. Just bait." Now Langdon just had to take it.

"Couple things." She spoke in a singsong voice Victoria refused to allow her friend to distract her with.

"Go ahead. Just be quick."

"Copy that, boss. Nothing on the email, Langdon's address originated with a dark web email server. Untraceable, and not just like it's hard but I manage to figure it out anyway. I mean impossible."

"Right." Victoria kept scanning the park. "Anything else?"

"Mark had an idea about a scientist, someone Langdon could use to put together the bomb. I'm looking into it, and I've got Homeland agents knocking on doors."

"Okay. Keep me posted." It was a long shot, but it could pay off. "Gotta go."

Another man had entered her peripheral vision. Before she could alert Niall, the man stopped in front of her. "Victoria Bramlyn?"

She blinked. This was how he was going to play it? "So he sends someone else."

Skin around his eyes flexed. He wore the hard features of someone who had seen a lot. He worked out. His suit was nice. He almost looked like…

"Please answer the question."

"Yes, I'm Victoria Bramlyn." Anytime now the NCIS agents would move in, and this guy would get a clue about what was happening here.

"Wow, the rest of the squad is never going to believe this."

Her instincts had been right. He was a cop, a detective if she wasn't mistaken. Victoria shifted to put her cold hands in her coat pockets.

"Hands where I can see them." He even reached toward his gun. Then he produced a shield which he slid onto his belt so she could see it. Yep. Seattle Police Department.

"Is there something wrong, detective?"

"I need you to stand up and turn around, hands behind your back."

"I'm being arrested?" The comms had gone completely quiet.

He tugged on her elbow, and she had no choice but to stand. Victoria bit her lip to distract her from the instinct to struggle. She fought back. It was what she'd been trained to do her whole life.

"What is this about?"

"There's a BOLO out for you. Came across the wires yester-day. Something about a guy missing from a retirement home in St. Petersburg. That's in Florida."

"Yes, I know."

"So you know about the man?" He slid the cuffs over her wrists.

"He's my grandfather." She wasn't going to stoop so low as to try and defend herself to this man who had no idea who she was, and probably didn't care whether she'd actually committed the crime or not. He wasn't investigating it, just doing his duty.

"You're under arrest. You'll be transported back to Florida for questioning."

"Hang on a second."

NCIS agents approached from all sides.

"Easy fellas." The detective held up one hand, the other on her elbow.

They flashed badges, Niall at the center. "You're not taking her."

"You can fight about that with my captain. She's coming with me."

Victoria stumbled as he tugged her away from the bench. "You're ruining a perfectly good operation, you know."

"Is that right?" He didn't sound like he believed her, or cared.

The hair on the back of her neck tingled. Victoria spun around, assessing all angles as to where the threat was coming from.

"Easy."

She glanced at him, long enough to see the red dot on his chest.

Victoria slammed into him, and they hit the ground just as the shot rang out.

24

Seattle, Washington. Saturday 9.37p.m.

M ark saw the moment they walked Victoria into the FBI office. He got up from his desk and moved to the door, watching her get escorted through the sea of desks toward the conference room. Two plain clothes detectives and their captain. Niall, and his director.

He wondered how long it would take Jakeman to show up. Whenever Victoria's life or her future were being discussed, it seemed like he was always there. In the middle of it.

Mark's coworker, Special Agent Tines, moved to stand beside him. She said, "My brother is an NCIS agent. I heard she was on an operation trying to catch Langdon when the cop spotted her. Apparently the police got the BOLO from the PD in St. Petersburg who were investigating the grandfather's disappearance."

It was on the tip of his tongue to defend Victoria. He was about to tell Tines that Victoria didn't have anything to do with her grandfather's disappearance. Then he realized that he didn't know that to be unequivocally true, did he? All Mark had was her word. As though he should trust that, because she'd proved herself to him. As though their years of friendship—or whatever they had —meant he could trust her.

Maybe he did. Maybe he didn't.

Maybe it was just Jakeman that Mark didn't trust as far as he'd be able to throw the guy.

Victoria spotted him right before she stepped into the conference room with his director and the group.

She opened her mouth. To call his name? Didn't matter, she had to have read the look on his face because she frowned.

Then she disappeared into the room, swept in there with no choice. She had to explain herself. No one who'd been anywhere near this FBI corruption would be content taking anyone's word for it now. Even if previously they'd have been afforded a whole lot of leeway.

"How did we not know about the BOLO?"

Tines shrugged. "Must have been missed somehow." There was a look on her face, one Mark didn't like and would have to follow up on later as her boss.

Right now, he said, "Find out how. I won't stand for slip ups, not when we need to be on our A-game these days." None of them could handle another scandal. The FBI's reputation barely survived the breaking news of so many corrupt agents in the West Coast offices.

Tines flinched like he'd reprimanded her and wandered off.

Mark made his way to the conference room where the group had settled around the table. They weren't going to interrogate her in a room? Maybe they would, but first there would be the usual bureaucratic back and forth. He wondered how long it would be before Jakeman showed up to throw his weight around.

He slipped in the door and sat at the far end of the table. The director glanced over at him, but none of the rest of them understood the significance of him being here. They probably thought he was just observing as the normal course of his job.

The police captain set a voice recorder in the center of the table and everyone introduced themselves so it would be on record. If Mark hadn't been the assistant director of this office, he probably wouldn't have been allowed to stay.

He looked up from his notepad, resisting the urge to tap his pen on the paper, and looked at the police captain. No way was he going to look at Victoria. Despite the fact she'd glanced at him, he wasn't going to reassure her. That wasn't why he was present for her being questioned.

She of all people understood the fact that being a professional trumped whatever interpersonal thing they had going on. And even though he wanted to talk privately—and probably heatedly—with her right now, this took precedent.

The captain said, "Ms. Bramlyn, your fingerprints were found in your grandfather's apartment, along with signs of a struggle. Now he's missing."

Victoria said, "Is there a question in there somewhere?"

Mark pressed his lips together. Being belligerent wasn't going to get her very far.

The captain exhaled through his nose, a quick sniff of disapproval.

"Of course my fingerprints were there. I visit frequently."

"There's no record of you traveling to Florida. Anywhere."

Victoria said, "The dictates of my position, as well as my career history, necessitate that I do certain things…under the radar."

He glanced at his phone and thumbed the screen. "Is that so? And the struggle?"

"I left the culprit tied up in a shed. The detectives released him, despite the fact he clearly had information as to my grandfather's whereabouts."

"Clearly."

"He told me, himself, a few days later, that Oscar Langdon and my grandfather had gone drinking, after which Langdon likely killed him and then buried his body somewhere."

The Captain's eyebrows rose. "Oscar Langdon."

She lifted her chin. "Also known as FBI Special Agent Colin Pinton."

"You cannot be——"

The director cut him off. "She is, in fact, correct. Langdon is an FBI agent, or he *was*."

The captain frowned. "So a known terrorist likely kidnaps and kills your grandfather, and you're spending your time at a park in Seattle. Enjoying a relaxing Saturday night."

"It's complicated."

"Oscar Langdon is an FBI agent, so I'm going to concede that point." He blew out a breath.

The two detectives didn't look all that impressed, mostly with Mark and his boss. Victoria was an unknown component. Mark figured they had basically no clue who she was. Whether they would eventually get the whole story was something else entirely.

He prayed they never wound up in a position where she owed them anything. He'd saved her life, and in return? She had manipulated his, gained him a promotion just so she could position him within her committee in order for it to be as effective as it possibly could be. Was he glad that dirty FBI agents had been exposed? Of course. Did he wish she'd used someone else to do that work? Also, of course.

Mark knew he couldn't have the good without the bad in anything. It was a trade-off. Always. He just wished Victoria's actions in his life didn't feel so much like he'd been a pawn in some game he didn't have the clearance to know about.

"Langdon is manipulating all of you," she said. "He's orchestrating this because I won't leave him alone. This is a setup."

"Why does he care about you?"

"Because I'm a thorn in his side." She stood up, making every cop in the room flinch toward his gun. She lifted one side of her shirt. "And I won't die."

When they'd all gotten a half-decent look at her bandage, she sat back down. "Langdon has a nuke, and we believe he's going to use it."

"Where?" the Captain barked.

"If I knew that, I wouldn't be sitting in a park with the intention of drawing him out so we can arrest him when he tries to kill me."

The captain blinked.

Welcome to my world. Mark said, "Do you have any idea where your grandfather is right now?"

She turned to him. "No."

"What about Langdon, anything you can give us that will help us find him?"

He saw her flinch, though it was only a slight flex of the skin around her eyes. "No."

There was more to that answer, he knew. Mark didn't wait for her to elaborate. He told the room, "I have people looking into scientists with the know-how to put the components of the nuke together."

His director said, "Assuming Langdon didn't already get it put together."

Mark shrugged. "We can assume because he hasn't used it yet, that it's either not ready or he's waiting for something else."

The police captain said something. Mark was only half listening, arrested by the look on Victoria's face. As though she'd just realized something.

Mark didn't know what that was. He said, "Ms. Bramlyn needs to be out looking for Langdon, not answering questions about a man who doesn't deserve the kindness of her looking for him." He shrugged, realizing he'd revealed his personal knowledge of her grandfather and the kind of man he was. "Especially not when we're looking at a present threat."

The needs of the many outweighed the needs of one man— one who was probably already dead. Yes, Mark would stand beside her if the time came to bury him. But the fact was, he'd never liked the guy, and he never would. He wouldn't be the one grieving, and it was entirely up to her what she did with the knowledge that he was still missing and presumed dead.

Victoria wasn't a bad person. Otherwise their lives would have gone much differently. He never had to wonder if she might turn, or go bad. There was no way. He knew her too well, even before she had all that spy training. She might keep a lot from him, but she never lied.

What he *didn't* know was what she was capable of. No one did, until they were pushed to those circumstances. What extent would she go to in order to stop an attack and bring Langdon in?

They were learning what Langdon was capable of. The lengths he would go.

How far would Victoria have to go in the pursuit of stopping him?

"I appreciate your help on that." Her soft voice jolted him from his rambling thoughts.

Mark said, "I have a job to do, and I'm going to do it." That meant FBI business, and an FBI investigation to find and stop one of their own. Not going off with her old team on missions she deemed were necessary.

She jerked in her seat. It actually looked like she'd been hit.

Victoria was the one who lived her life confident in her ability to walk away free at any time. She probably thought the same, even about this situation. Mark, however, was going to be the one who did it—who walked away. They were done. He didn't want to be manipulated anymore, no matter that he entirely agreed with her aim. One hundred percent, no question. She absolutely should have formed that committee and gone after Langdon. He'd seen in her in that prison, so he wasn't going to argue.

And having an ally who worked over at the Seattle office of the FBI was probably invaluable to her cause.

He just didn't much like it that he'd been the one maneuvered.

"One more thing before we call this meeting to an end." The director of the FBI turned in his chair and pinned Victoria with a stare. "Just one thing, so we can all leave knowing you have nothing to do with Langdon except wanting to stop him."

Victoria braced. He saw her do it, like she knew what was coming and needed to prepare.

"Langdon's people have a tattoo on their arm. Inside, forearm."

She pulled up her sleeve to reveal...nothing. Mark had never seen a tattoo.

"It's ultraviolet. So we'll need a special light." He got up and moved to a table in the corner, coming back with a thing that looked like a cross between a flashlight and a handheld document scanner.

The director grabbed Victoria's hand. His knuckles went white with the force of his grip.

Mark stood. "Sir."

Victoria stared hard at his boss as he flipped on the light and moved it over the skin of her arm.

And stopped.

"I guess we have our answer."

"That's not—"

The director interrupted her protest. "I want this woman taken down to holding."

25

Seattle, WA. Saturday 10.47p.m.

Okay, this was just ridiculous. Victoria shot to her feet. "Mark!"

He was already halfway to the door while the rest of the men in the room stood as though she was the enemy combatant they needed to restrain. Detain. She wasn't the enemy here. Clearly all of this was nothing but a distraction. Langdon looking for ways to slow them down and get them running around, dealing with other things rather than the search for him.

"I'll leave you to this," the police captain said. "Seems like you have your hands full." He shot her a disapproving look.

Fact was, if she'd wanted her grandfather dead, she would probably have done it a long time ago.

No, that wasn't true. Even though Mark was right, that he had treated her horribly, she'd also never actually killed anyone on purpose. Neither did she intend to.

He walked out with his detectives, leaving her with the FBI director and Mark, who had stepped to the side for the cops to leave and now turned to the door again.

"Mark."

He turned back from the door, his face strategically blank and giving nothing away. Least of all any feeling. She *hated* that look on his face.

"You know I don't work with Langdon. He put this on me before South Africa." She flexed her arm. "That's what I don't remember." She had to take a breath. "I woke up in prison with it."

"You were in prison?" The director's question resonated in her.

There wasn't the time to explain it all to him, though she figured she'd be forced to. Probably through hours of questioning. Hours they didn't have.

Victoria clenched down on her back teeth. She didn't care what the director thought of her. All she cared about was Mark's opinion, and he was giving her nothing. "Langdon is still playing me, hedging his bets, and finding any and every way to take me out. To stop me from ruining his plans by finding that nuke."

"But he didn't kill you years ago, and he could have."

"Genevieve asked him not to." She had considered the woman a friend, and it had been reciprocated. Right up until Genevieve pulled that gun on her and the sergeant had been forced to take her out. Victoria always took the action that would get the result, regardless of her feelings. She couldn't do what felt good, because that didn't guarantee success. Nor did comfort.

She said, "Langdon is out there, and he's going to use that nuke as soon as he can."

Mark nodded. "We're pushing to find him, but we also need as much information as we can get."

What did he mean by that? Did he think she was hiding something?

The director said, "Obviously you've been working with Langdon this whole time. It's why you have so much sway, from paying off key people and doing whatever you want with no oversight."

Maybe he thought Mark was one of the people she'd "paid

off." She might not mind a little discomfort personally, if it got the result she needed, but she didn't want Mark's life to be harder because of her. She wouldn't do that to him.

Not after what he'd done for her.

Back when Victoria joined the CIA, she'd told them the whole story as Mark had told the FBI. The police report listed it as an accidental death. But the people who needed to know had the full story. She couldn't have risked being in a situation she shouldn't be in—all because she hadn't disclosed the whole story. Victoria had triggers. She also had hard limits on what she would and wouldn't do as a spy. It might make her a tough case, but she'd more than made up for that with closures.

The bad guys she'd brought in.

The assets she'd found.

The lives saved.

"I'm the one who brought Langdon to you." She turned to face the director. "I'm the one who brought all of this to light. The connection. The corruption in *your* agency. Langdon is a special agent, and you had no idea. Your people never saw it until I read you in."

The director didn't like that much. Too bad he needed to realize who held the power here. He sniffed. "You can defend yourself all you want, that tattoo says you're one of Langdon's people."

"It was put on me while I was unconscious. It's Langdon's insurance policy that he can do exactly this." She pointed her finger at the table. "And it comes to light now, when we're so close to finding him? You don't find that suspicious?"

"Are you close?" the director said. "Seems to me like we still have no idea where Langdon is, and no idea when or where he's going to use the nuke."

Like that was the point? Victoria wanted to cry out her frustration. A guy like this would only think her offensive actions were the result of being an emotional woman, who would then dismiss her as being—probably—in love with Oscar Langdon.

Because clearly a woman in a relationship couldn't think objectively.

"We are close." Mark waved his phone. "We've found a report of a missing scientist with the skills to build a nuke out of the parts Langdon has. Now we need to find out where he's been taken. A fresh case, with fresh leads. One that will lead us right to Langdon and the weapon he has."

The director mushed his lips together.

"Tell me," she said, "why you see any advancement of anything Mark Welvern is trying to do as an affront to you, instead of a win for the whole FBI?"

"We don't all have powerful people in high positions to put in a good word for us."

She glanced at Mark and saw the muscle in his jaw twitch at the director's statement. He knew. She saw it. He knew what she'd done.

He knew.

Mark folded his arms.

"I needed an ally. Someone I can trust." She wanted to move closer to him, to touch his elbows and implore him to believe her. To see the truth in her words. "There's only one of those in the world."

"Kind of handy that I'm an FBI agent. Talk about right place at the right time."

"You're the one who believes in God." She'd even thought about that. Considered it one of those "God things" her team talked about. They all believed now. With Mark having the same faith, she'd felt left out.

But knowing she was going to go it alone made it easier to focus on the task at hand, catching Langdon.

He said nothing.

"I'm going to have a couple of agents escort you down to holding. You'll be there until we're ready to question you."

A power play by the director. She was used to men like him flexing their muscles. Proving that the woman was clearly emotional enough to betray the oath. Never mind that nearly all of the corrupt FBI agents they'd uncovered thus far had been men.

And what about the director? Seemed to Victoria that if Langdon wanted the search delayed, then it stood to reason having a key player in a position pull those strings furthered his end.

She'd have to get Talia to take a deeper look into this man.

Victoria turned to Mark. "Call Jakeman." When he didn't move or change expression, or even say anything, she added, "Please."

Finally he nodded. "You'll need a lawyer."

"I don't want a lawyer. I want to know that he and General Hurst are safe."

The director butted in. "Because your actions have put them at risk?"

"I've done nothing but what I was asked to do in order to keep this country safe." Her hands curled into fists by her sides. Victoria didn't bother trying to calm down. "Why do you think Langdon has been trying to kill me?"

The idea she was working with one of their ten most wanted criminals was ridiculous. Mark should know her better than that.

The director referred back to his file. "In what capacity? All I can see here is that you've been employed by the State Department for—"

"Long enough I should have retired already."

"Years working in…*records*." As though using that tone was significant in downplaying her role, which the director apparently had no idea about. "Then all of a sudden, you're promoted to director level. Probably had someone put in a good word for you, right?"

"I don't have to explain my resume to someone who doesn't have the clearance to know. But I'll tell you this." She lifted her chin. "The majority of the work I did in *records* is redacted."

The director made a face, as though he'd tasted something sour. "The CIA? Seriously?"

"For the record, I never said that. I'm a state department director and as such will not be going to one of your holding cells. I'll be afforded the respect I've earned, director. You know nothing about me. But you still insist on being a dog with a bone, gnawing away while the house is on fire."

She glanced at Mark and saw a tiny glimmer of humor in his eyes. It didn't reach his face, though.

"I'll step out for a moment," he said. "I don't have director-level clearance, and I need to make a call."

A breath of fear moved through her, worry over Jakeman. The man wielded a considerable amount of power in his position. He commanded troops and had protection. She still worried whether he was safe.

Victoria had long ago come to terms with the fact that the fatherly affection he felt for her was similar to the feelings she had for him. She loved his wife, but Mary Anne was all about her role in society and the charities she fundraised for. Victoria was way too boots-on-the-ground. Their daughter, the one she'd rescued, had a fiancé and was doing well, had moved on with her life. Jakeman had become a friend. Then an ally and a colleague. At times he had filled the empty position of father in her life. Something that was about mutual respect.

She turned to the director. "Yes, the CIA. Seriously." He might as well know. "Which makes it highly suspicious to me that you, who should be looking into a missing corrupt FBI agent of *yours*, is instead pointing fingers at me in a witch hunt."

"You think I'm one of these dirty agents?"

"Maybe not. Then again, in your own way?" She shrugged. Accusation wasn't her thing, but he could read between the lines. Langdon wouldn't get found without her being on the streets. "Putting me in holding won't get you anything."

"Because you were trained to withstand torture?"

"Is that what the FBI does these days?"

He sneered. "You aren't going to trap me."

Victoria leaned closer to him and said, "Ditto."

He wasn't going to push her around. There was no way she would allow that to happen.

Mark shoved the door open and found them almost nose to nose glaring at each other. "Jakeman's people picked up. Then I got transferred to the NCIS director locally."

She turned to him.

"Jakeman is fine. He's on a plane back to Washington tonight." Mark hesitated a second. Long enough she knew something was seriously wrong. "General Hurst is dead."

Victoria's stomach clenched. "How?"

"Hit and run. He was getting out of his car outside his house, and an SUV ran into his motorcade. They opened fire when it became clear he wasn't dead. There were six casualties."

Victoria slumped into a chair and shut her eyes, but it wasn't enough. She covered her face with her hands. Still not enough to shut out the images her mind conjured up. General Hurst, his people. His family? Bodies jerked and fell to the ground as the sound of gunshots rang through her mind.

"We need to find Langdon."

26

Bellevue, WA. Sunday 12.16a.m.

Mark slammed the driver's door. Probably a little more forceful than was necessary, considering Victoria's glance as she rounded the hood. They crossed the road together, the purposeful stride of two cops with a possible lead.

Dakota stood in the open doorway. "Come on, I'll show you what we've got."

"How is Josh?"

"Not much change." Dakota shrugged. "They're going to call me if I'm needed."

They were all on duty because of this bomb threat—Langdon and his nuke. Dakota should be with her fiancé, but if she was here then there was a reason for it. One she didn't need to justify to him.

Mark moved to the side and allowed Victoria to go first. She gave him that glance again. "Thanks."

He didn't say, "You're welcome." He figured it was implied. Too much had gone on today. Or yesterday, considering it was now Sunday. He blew out a breath. This had been a long week. A long few months. And in the middle of all that, he'd been shot—a reminder of the toll this whole case had taken on him, making him overtired, especially on the days he had to work through the night. Not to mention the lingering ache in his stomach.

"You okay?"

Mark stepped over the threshold to stand by her in the hallway. "I feel old."

Her eyes smiled. "You are old, but then so am I."

"How's your stomach?"

She shrugged. "You?"

"I'm feeling a pity party coming on, but there's too much work to do." And yet, he'd stayed silent in the car. They should have been having this conversation on the drive over. Getting back on that footing of their friendship, the solid foundation they had of knowing each other for so long. Of having gone through some insane experiences together and always having each other's backs.

Now she'd been implicated in Langdon's crimes. Maybe she didn't care because she knew the truth, and she figured there was no way she'd end up in jail, but he just couldn't find the same confidence.

She was out here partly to prove the director wrong because he couldn't accuse her without proof, and, as yet, had none. The police in Florida had since rescinded the BOLO and pulled her name from their suspect list since Mark sent them that email. He just hoped he didn't regret sticking up for her.

Truth was, Victoria was only free because she was under observation. The FBI was going to be close enough to cuff her until this was over, no exceptions. He'd have preferred it was another agent standing that near to her. But if he reassigned it then she would know something was up. He'd have to explain to her that they didn't trust her.

She stared long enough at his face he wondered if she was going to speak. "Couldn't it be a compliment that I helped you get the assistant director job? I knew you could take on that job *and* help me at the same time."

Mark said, "But I didn't get it on my own merit. I got it because you pushed my name to the forefront."

"The director would never have signed off on it if you didn't have the merit to get the position." She shrugged. "I'm pretty sure the only person who was surprised you got the job was *you*."

Mark wasn't sure about that. They didn't have time to talk about it right now, though. Dakota was waiting for them. "Go ahead."

He turned to shut the front door and saw a car pull up down the street. Tines was here on assignment from the director. He resisted the urge to wave to her. He made sure she saw him, though.

The house was single level with a long hallway to the left, leading to the bedrooms and bathroom. An office had been set up in one, and Talia was at the computer. The dining table was round and covered with mail and papers. A lamp in the corner of the living room was on, the shade ripped.

"Struggle?" He glanced at Dakota.

She nodded. "Front door was picked and left open. A chair overturned. The lamp. That kind of thing."

Talia stepped into the hall. "You guys need to come see this."

They crossed to the doorway and crowded into the tiny office. She sat back at the computer and typed on the screen.

"Is that his email?"

"Yep." She tapped a few more keys. "Got some correspondence here from an internet handle we know is Langdon, or at the very least, a close associate."

"Really?" Mark took a step closer to try and read the screen.

Talia shot him a look over her shoulder. He moved back half a pace length. She said, "Langdon starts out by making friends, like he's a fan of the guy's work. Doctor Fredrick responds politely enough, and though he's tentative, Langdon doesn't let up. They eventually make a date to meet for coffee so Langdon can ask him about a research project he has going on. That was two days ago."

"You're sure it was Langdon?" It was all usernames and probably the dark web. How could she really know for certain?

"If she says it was him, then it was him," Victoria said.

Mark shifted to look at her. Why did she feel the need to use that tone with him when she was the one who'd lied? She claimed she always told him the truth. Actually, what she'd say was that she was always "truthful" with him. Maybe that wasn't the same thing.

Maybe she simply omitted what she figured he didn't want to know. Or what he wouldn't like, thereby avoiding the conflict that was inevitable.

She looked away. "Talia?"

Yep, there was guilt there. For the first time since the director dropped the bomb that his career had been manipulated by the person he trusted most in the world, he actually felt a tiny bit better.

If he didn't find the time soon to talk it through with her, she would probably just wait until he wasn't mad anymore and then simply go on as though nothing had happened.

Wouldn't be the first time she'd used that tactic.

"I'm looking for a way into Langdon's server, or his computer. His phone. Whatever he used to send these messages."

"Copy that." Niall strode into the room. "Finally got someone from his office on the phone. He usually works Saturdays but he has his son this weekend, so they weren't expecting him to come in."

"There's a child in his life?" Victoria's voice held the thread of a warning. A threat even.

Dakota came into view behind her colleague. "There's no evidence of a child living here."

"Maybe he doesn't stay overnight, just day visits," Mark suggested. Talia clicked keys in the background, typing faster than he could even think.

"My next call is to track down the mom." Niall motioned with his phone. "Make sure everything is copacetic."

"Do that."

On Victoria's order, he strode out to the hallway. She blew out a breath, and he saw her share a glance with Dakota. "There better not be a kid involved."

Mark said, "Any idea on the timeline of when the scientist was taken?"

"Near as we can figure," Dakota said, but not without another glance at Victoria, "He was taken either late last night or early this morning."

"Neighbors?"

"No one heard anything. Based on their comings and goings we were able to narrow it down as much as we could. Assuming it's accurate, all we really have is a serious guesstimation." She paused. "Are you guys okay?"

Like Mark was going to answer that? "Let's just find Langdon."

"We're fine."

He turned to Victoria, incredulous that she would brush off what was happening between them.

"Methinks Mark doesn't agree y'all are *fine.*"

"Okay then," Victoria said. "We are too busy to worry about it right now."

"Worry about what?" Talia sounded distracted, only turning to them when she reached the end of her question. She glanced at the three of them. "Oh. That."

"Except we have no idea what that is." Dakota waved a hand. "And if I demand to know, I'm the jerk who doesn't care about the missing man I've never met. I just care more about my friends."

"As we speak, he could be torturing him," Victoria pointed out.

"Lovely." Mark folded his arms.

"And his child could be with him." She faced off with him. "We could be looking for a missing child."

Yes, that would be as bad as she insinuated he should think it is. "As if a nuke wasn't bad enough?"

"Langdon will want every opportunity to get his nuke up and running. There are no lengths he won't go to."

"And how do you—"

Niall strode back in. "The kid is with his father. He's eight years old, has seizures that require medication and they were supposed to get that prescription filled today. Cops are on their way to the mom's house to meet up with her. She's understandably upset, so I spoke with her until they arrived."

Dakota turned to Talia. "Tell me where to point my gun. We're getting this kid back before *anything* happens to him."

Niall leaned over and kissed her forehead. "I'm with you."

Mark got on his phone while Talia typed, having a conversation with Dakota at the same time. Reading through the bulletins for the day, going back to this morning and then last night. Police cases and updates. Everything local he was privy to, which was a lot. He got to four in the afternoon—just a few hours ago—before he saw something.

"Take a look at this." He didn't show anyone the phone and didn't move or look up from it. "A pharmacy not too far from here was robbed this afternoon." He scanned the report. "Someone broke in the back and stole only one thing. A preprepared prescription ready for pickup." He read the patient's name.

"That's him, the child." Niall's face darkened.

Mark said, "The cops had no reason to believe it wasn't just random. Someone grabbing meds off the shelf and hoping they got something good. But they were going to call the mom first thing in the morning to make sure it wasn't related."

"It's related." Dakota moved to Talia. "What about surveillance?"

"I'll see what I can do. I might need my own system to run that kind of search, though."

"Head to the office if you need to," Victoria said.

"The Homeland Security office? It gets logged when we enter or leave. The boss will want to know why I'm there in the middle of the night on a Saturday when he already assumes I sleep with my fiancé, even though we're not married yet." Talia made a face that explained clearly how she felt about that.

"We need to find that child, Talia."

Mark decided to be helpful. "I can put a call in, explain you're working with me on an FBI case. Which is the truth."

She glanced at him. "No offense, but you're not his favorite person right now. The guy doesn't exactly trust the FBI."

Mark pressed his lips together. It would take time. He couldn't singlehandedly turn the tide of public opinion, least of all do it quickly. "I'll get it squared away."

Talia stood, gathering up her purse and her coat. "I'll find Langdon. A car. Something." She strode to the door.

"Talia?"

She glanced back at him. Mark said, "Thank you for your help."

After she left, Dakota and Niall headed out into the hall. Dakota muttered something about the forecast being frosty. Whatever that comment meant.

Victoria stared at the empty doorway. "You'll thank her for her help, but not me?"

"When have you ever helped me?"

She opened her mouth.

He shook his head, realizing the truth in what had been an off-the-cuff comment. "Don't bother. Seems to me like you've been helping yourself to whatever you need for a long time."

27

Seattle, WA. Sunday 3.42a.m.

Victoria gripped the phone as she shoved the bathroom door shut. "Your plane landed all right?"

"Yes." Jakeman sounded sleepy. Not surprisingly, as he'd already traveled back to Washington D.C. It was the middle of the night, and he'd finally responded to her texts. "We're in the car, headed to the safe house."

It grated on her that it was even necessary for him to be going to a safe house at all. Let alone in the middle of the night. "I can't believe Hurst is dead."

"It wasn't stupidity that killed him. He was careful, and he had protection."

"I'm still alive, aren't I? So are you."

"For the time being."

"You're planning on being dead soon?" She paced in front of the row of four sinks on the floor of the Homeland Security office where her former team—or most of it—now worked. Yet more stuff that grated on her. Never mind that she'd allowed them to be reassigned. She'd *thought* she'd gotten all the FBI agents involved, which should have included Langdon. Her job should have been over. Her friends reassigned to their new teams while she moved on.

All well and good, except...she kind of missed them. Seeing their faces every day. Being their boss. Bear was nice and all, but the conversation was a little one sided.

Not to mention the fact Mark was seriously ticked at her right now.

Jakeman sighed. His voice rumbled over the phone line. "Vicki." It almost sounded like he thought this was funny, when it definitely was not. "If I don't keel over from a heart attack at my desk, I'll get popped by some assassin. There's a slim chance I'll live to be an old...er man. But I'll enjoy it if I do, and I'll even allow you to say, 'I told you so'."

"There's nothing amusing about this."

"It's three in the morning. Everything is amusing."

"Respectfully, I'm going to disagree with you." She glanced at her own reflection in the mirror and had to wince. She looked seriously disheveled, in need of about three days of sleep...and probably a vacation wouldn't hurt.

"Don't start calling me 'sir' now. It doesn't suit you."

Victoria almost laughed. "I wouldn't dream of it."

"What else is wrong?" He paused. "We're almost at the house, so make it fast."

"I should let you go."

"Vicki, spill."

"I really don't like when you call me that. I'm a grown woman and not your child."

He made a pfft noise through the phone line. "Who's going to give you away when you get married? Anyway, you're changing the subject."

Like she could remember what they were talking about when he'd just said something like that? "It's not going to happen."

"What did you do?"

"So it could only be a nonstarter because of something I did?"

Jakeman said, "It's been a non-starter since the beginning. Just tell me what's changed now. Why have you written the whole thing off?"

"It's not me." She squeezed the bridge of her nose, forcing herself to quit arguing. Defending her actions wasn't going to change anything. Especially when Mark wouldn't even hear her. "He knows about the promotion."

"Ah."

She waited, but he didn't say anything else. "Did you fall asleep?"

"I was just wondering why you're surprised he found out. You knew it would happen, so what will you do now?"

"I don't know!" Great. Now she was wailing. It was official, she'd lost it.

"Does he know about the rest of it?"

"I don't think so." And thank his God for that. It was hard to keep track of so many things. That was how she figured spy work wasn't for her anymore. Maybe she should get a job as some kind of private security consultant. She could live permanently in her New York apartment, after she changed the name on the deed to her real one.

"That is all going to come out as well."

And things would be more complicated than they already were. She was coming apart at the seams trying to find Langdon before everything fell apart.

Then she could just…go. Mark would have a perfectly nice life without her. She needed to quit this thing where they were in a holding pattern together, and separately, and set them both free.

"I have to go, Vicki."

It was on the tip of her tongue to tell him again not to call her that. Instead, she said, "Please be careful. There are only two of us left now." The rest of the committee was dead, as was a US Attorney and one of the FBI agents. She had no interest in losing anyone else to Oscar Langdon.

"I know. I will." He paused. "Promise me you'll stay with your people. Have a care."

He didn't tell her not to go into danger. He also didn't tell her to let someone else look for Langdon.

Victoria was grateful for both things.

Jakeman hung up. The door to the last stall whipped in and hit the wall. Dakota strode out. She stomped to the sink and glared at Victoria in the mirror as she washed her hands. She tugged two paper towels from the dispenser so forcefully, Victoria wondered that the whole thing didn't fall off the wall.

"Just spit it out."

"I don't even know where to start." Dakota balled up the paper towels and tossed them in the trash. "You talk a good game. I'll give you that."

"But you figured me out?"

"I've put up with your…methods for long enough. Now I'm supposed to be all about forgiveness, and loving your neighbors and all that, but you're making it *really* difficult."

"Sorry." Her tone clearly stated she was not sorry.

Dakota sucked in a breath through clenched teeth. "Don't. It doesn't suit you. But you know what? I know exactly what you need, because I've lived it. Right now you're too busy making sure you don't fall apart to realize the answer is right in front of you."

"I'm trying to find Langdon."

"No, you're trying to have your cake and eat it."

Victoria couldn't figure that out in the middle of the night, running on next to no sleep in three days. "Just say it."

"You need Jesus."

"You're getting married soon," Victoria reminded her. Like Dakota had forgotten that her fiancé was in the hospital. "You don't need to worry about me."

Dakota made a face, waltzed to the door and hauled it open. Victoria's phone buzzed. She looked at the screen and read the text from Talia.

Whatever you two are yelling about, this is more important. I have something.

Victoria strode back to the office. "We weren't yelling."

Dakota slumped into a chair at her desk. Mark and Niall broke off their conversation and turned to look at her.

Talia said, "Yeah, cause we couldn't hear you."

"What do you have?" Victoria got herself another cup of coffee, trying to brush off the awkwardness

Mark met her by the pot with his empty mug. "Is Jakeman all right?"

She nodded and poured him a refill. "He's at a safe house."

They didn't need to have another drawn-out conversation with no resolution. She'd just had one of those with Dakota, and it hadn't made her feel better. Nothing would, until Langdon was dead or in cuffs.

She turned around and leaned her hips against the cupboards. "What've we got?"

Talia said, "I've got a car leaving the scene of that pharmacy robbery. Two blocks away there's a shot of the interior where we can actually see the driver's face. It's our scientist."

"And Langdon?"

"Come and see this." She clicked on her mouse.

Victoria wandered over and looked at the image on screen. A man, given the shoulders. His hood was up. "Could be Langdon, holding a gun on the driver. It's not the child."

She sounded about as convinced as everyone else was. But then Victoria had been chasing this guy a long time. She knew him better than anyone—an edge that she needed to pay off in her search for him.

Talia said, "There's a shot of the plate in one image, I ran it through the county database and it's registered to this guy." She pulled up a screen with a bunch of tiny boxes, name and address. Weight and date of birth. Then she clicked on a picture.

"I don't think he's the one with the gun." He was nothing like Langdon. An elderly man, listed as disabled. "Has he reported his car stolen recently?"

"No," Talia said. "Nothing. But the car passed an ATM

camera that's along the route on from the pharmacy to this guy's house."

"Do we think Langdon has the scientist and the kid at the old man's house?" Mark asked.

"If he does," Victoria said, "that means the old man is likely dead." And wasn't that a lovely thought. "So they rob the pharmacy. Medication means the scientist now agrees to build the nuke because his son isn't in imminent danger of needing a hospital. Where do they go?"

"We could drive by the house, see if the car is there?" Dakota lifted her feet and planted her shoes on her desk. "Can't hurt, right?"

"He probably stashed it out of sight." Would Langdon really bank on them being so far behind him that he didn't have to worry about the car being on the drive?

"What else do we have?"

She didn't like Mark's tone. "Fine, let's drive out there on the off chance that Langdon is holed up there." She had figured the nuke components were somewhere like a storage unit, or some kind of abandoned lab. "Anything about where the attack is likely to take place?"

"I'm running down scenarios." Talia looked grim. "I have a few options, depending on whether he just wants to kill a lot of people or if he's going to target someone. Business leaders. Government workers. Civil servants. That kind of thing."

"Keep us posted." She grabbed her coat and tugged it on. Right before it settled onto her shoulders, Mark clasped the collar and assisted her. She lifted her gaze.

"I'm just trying to help."

"You've been mad at me all day. Why change your tune now?"

He sighed. "We have to find Langdon, right? That's the priority. Besides, I'm too tired right now to be mad in any way that's not unfair. I know there's more you've neglected to tell me. I assume at some point I'll learn what all that is. Until then, there isn't much I can do about it, right?"

"Uh..." She shut her mouth before she said something she would regret. Or just spilled everything right then. No, that wouldn't help. It would only make things so much worse. "Let's go check out that house."

Dakota sat in the front seat of their car. Niall drove, with Victoria in front and Mark in the back, head leaned against the seat and his eyes closed. By the time they got to the house, he was snoring even.

Victoria's phone buzzed, and she read the text from Talia. "Nothing on the driveway. They're going to circle neighboring streets and see if they can get an angle on the backyard."

"Copy that." Niall made a right turn while she studied the map of the neighborhood on her phone.

Then she looked at every car on the street leading up to the house. "I see it."

Niall pulled over right when she picked up. Victoria said, "We have the car." She gave Talia the street name, so she'd know where.

"You think they're in there?"

Victoria thought it through. "Worth a look."

Mark sucked in a breath. "We found them."

"Let's go see."

28

Seattle, WA. Sunday 5:22 am

M ark flattened the Velcro tabs on his vest and followed Victoria toward the house under cover of darkness. The sun wouldn't be up for two or three more hours this time of year, so there were still plenty of shadows to hide in.

Niall paced beside him. "We're assuming this is a trap, right?"

"Probably." Mark kept his voice low but had to say what he was thinking. "Help me watch her back?"

"What do you think this team does?"

Mark didn't need unhelpful comments. He blew out a breath. "You know what I mean."

"I'm sure I do."

He would, since he'd lived that with Haley. They'd both been in danger. The only difference was that they'd come through it to find a relationship. Not something that would happen with him and Victoria.

A cat darted across the street. On the other side in an upstairs window someone had their curtains open, and in the window he saw they were watching a cartoon.

Someone's young child up early, on a morning no one wanted to leave their warm bed, so they snuggled in and watched TV.

Not that Mark would know. He was pretty sure his mom had never done that with him. Before she left. Now he barely remembered her, only that she'd had blond hair. His father certainly hadn't. The guy only ranked lower on the scum scale than Victoria's grandfather because he'd used his fists. But the abuse had been no less vicious than she suffered from her grandfather's biting comments, or the emotional manipulation.

"You need to get your head in this."

He stopped beside Niall, along with Victoria, at the front door. "Dakota is taking the back way?"

She glanced over, her gaze assessing him. "She's checking out the car first."

"I'll go around," Niall said, "in case we get a runner." He wandered off, not waiting for permission.

Mark had to wonder if he actually had it, at least loosely, considering this was connected to the research facility case. Looking into the fallout. Assisting them. He probably had permission from his boss to be here.

"You okay?"

"Is he going to get in trouble if it's on paper that he was here?"

Victoria frowned. "That's what you want to talk about?"

Mark didn't want to talk about anything. Now was hardly the time, anyway. "Let's go in."

With one last glance, she turned to the door and tried the handle. They stepped to the side to avoid any gunfire that might blast through the front door. Same reason they wore vests, vital things that might seem small at the time but might mean the difference between death and survival.

Victoria pushed the door open slowly, and soundlessly. The interior was dark, no sound and no movement. Yet. Despite the car being parked a few streets away, it didn't seem like anyone was still here. They could have ditched it and gone somewhere else in a new vehicle.

How would they find them?

Mark just knew they would. They had to, because the consequence of failure meant the loss of so many lives.

Enough people had died already. The US Attorney, Pacer. The corrupt FBI Agent, Vance Davies, who'd stepped in front of that car. General Hurst. Now three additional lives were in danger, between the car's registered owner who lived here, and the scientist and his son.

Victoria wandered down the hall. It was another single-story house, like the one the scientist lived in. This one smelled like the windows needed to be cracked and the house treated for mold. Entirely too much damp had settled into the air. In a climate like this it was common, but that also meant there were common ways to treat it.

Mark didn't want to contemplate the fact it was likely an applicable metaphor for his ongoing "relationship" with Victoria. Something bad had crept in, and they'd allowed it. Question was, would they both be willing to do the work to reverse it. Or was it a case of scrapping everything and starting over. Somewhere else.

He circled the bedroom, flashlight beam moving as he shifted his weapon. A closet? It was always worth checking everywhere.

Mark pulled the door open. "Victoria!"

Within seconds, she and Niall both entered the room.

"I found the homeowner."

Victoria looked over his shoulder and hissed out a breath between clenched teeth.

"Sorry."

She glanced aside at him. "Sorry? Are you responsible for this?"

He wasn't, but he also didn't like her feeling the impact of a loss related to her case. Instead of explaining all that he said, "Cause of death?"

"I'm not a medical examiner." She'd crouched and was now

almost nose to nose with the dead, old homeowner. "But it might have something to do with the bullet hole in his forehead."

Niall actually chuckled.

Mark shot him a look. As far as they knew, this was the first dead body they'd discovered where the person didn't know exactly what they'd been up against. The first person without a personal connection to the case, who hadn't signed up to fight Langdon knowingly.

He didn't want the scientist, or his son, to be next.

Niall's phone rang. "O'Caran."

Mark stayed with Victoria, who was now typing on her phone. An email. They needed to call the local police and report a dead body. "Don't touch anything." After all that talk with the police captain, and those two detectives, Victoria's fingerprints didn't need to be at the scene of a crime.

"Copy that." Niall hung up. "Dakota needs us at the car."

Victoria straightened, and they followed Niall to the hallway. "What is it?"

Mark left everything the way they'd found it, making sure the police would find as true of a crime scene as they could give them, even though they'd walked through the whole place and been the ones to discover the body.

Niall said, "She's already called an ambulance."

"Wait, what?" Mark caught up with them.

"The kid was tied up in the trunk of the car. Looks like he was given medicine and then dumped there for us—or someone—to find."

Victoria shook her head as they stepped out of the front door. "So Langdon dropped the kid off and then took his father to get the work done?"

There was something in her expression Mark couldn't decipher. They strode to the car, then drove to meet Dakota. She had the kid sitting on the hood and was talking to him when they all climbed out. She'd wrapped the scientist's son up in her coat to keep him warm.

Mark had to point out one thing to Victoria before they got into this. "He didn't 'drop him off' if he left him in the trunk. The kid could have been there long enough to have had another medical emergency." He didn't like the idea of finding a dead child any differently than finding an old man stuffed in his own closet.

The child and Dakota both looked at them as they approached.

Niall said, "Ambulance should be here in a minute. As will cops, which means we need a good explanation of why we broke into this car."

"It was unlocked," Dakota said. "I heard the sound of someone in distress."

She said it with so little emotion, Mark wondered if that wasn't exactly what had happened. "I'll call the police captain and let him know what we're doing. The responding officers can take all our statements, since we have nothing to hide."

He'd been at scenes where the Northwest Counter-Terrorism Taskforce left one person to tell the police a version of what had happened. But the team had been disbanded now, and they all worked at different agencies. He wasn't sure if the state department would actually claim Victoria Bramlyn as one of their own, a Director.

Dakota said, "Victoria, you wanna leave and we'll deal with this? Niall?"

Of course, Dakota would offer. Despite the argument they'd had at an audible level in the bathroom, she was still prepared to take the heat and be the one who explained it all.

Mark knew what there was in Victoria that had inspired so much loyalty in people she'd only worked with for a few years. He'd seen the same thing in her since they met. Life had thrown them more curve balls than he ever would've imagined.

Am I supposed to forgive even this, God?

Mark already knew the answer even before he finished asking

the question. He wouldn't be living out what he believed if he didn't extend Victoria the same grace he'd been given.

As he walked away and made phone calls to both the local police captain and his director, explaining what they'd found, he continued thinking on it.

Victoria didn't believe, but that didn't make her any less worthy of what he had the grace to give her. It was part of the reason he'd kept her at arm's length all these years and relegated them to that "friend" zone that had gotten such a bad reputation. But he'd had her in his life. They'd kept each other sane and safe, which was more than what a lot of people had.

Mark couldn't count the number of times he'd called her and talked through a case, just to have a sounding board. He had to admit, now that he knew she'd gotten him the assistant director job, it stung. He wasn't about to thank her for advancing his career, but it was done.

The only other choice he had, besides accepting it, was to resign, and he wasn't about to do that anytime soon.

The director was the one who asked the question, "Can the kid tell us anything about where Langdon took his father?"

"I'll find out." But he doubted the kid could give them actionable intelligence.

The ambulance showed up. Mark hung up from his calls and moved to where Victoria stood watching as they treated the kid and loaded him into the ambulance.

"What now?" Mark figured she had an idea, but he'd rather go home and get twelve hours of sleep before taking the next step. He didn't figure they had the time though, and the sun was up now.

He looked at his watch.

"Breakfast?"

"There's this place I usually go to before church." He met a couple of his friends there, normally. Guys he'd done bible study with who were similar in age and either single dads or had no kids and hadn't been married. Divorced people tended to fall through the cracks in a lot of churches, no one really knowing what to say to them or what to do with them in "family ministry." Mark tried to make sure it didn't happen to the guys he knew.

"That sounds good."

"Food?"

"All of it." She didn't lift her gaze, just kept it carefully nonchalant.

Mark wasn't going to let it go. "You want to go to church?"

Victoria shrugged like it was no big deal. "I need a flash of inspiration. Where else am I going to get it?"

"And you're not just doing that because I've been mad, and you think it's a way to soften my feelings toward you?"

"I get that you think I'm capable of running a game on you like that." She pressed her lips together.

Yes, she was entirely capable of that. No matter that he didn't want to believe she was. Life had proven him wrong too many times.

She shrugged. "Do you have a better idea of what we can do on a Sunday morning?"

"No, I do not."

She lifted her chin then, challenging him to turn down her offer of going to church with him. The last thing he wanted was for her to go for any other reason than genuine curiosity. Then again, did it matter the reason if she'd be there and listening?

Mark held out his hand. "Let's go."

Before she could take it, her phone rang. "Victoria Bramlyn." She listened for a second, and then her face washed pale. "Pops?"

29

Seattle, WA. Sunday 7.31a.m.

"Who else would it be?" His voice was shaky and laced with pain, but he still managed to sound irritated.

"Where are you?" Not to mention all the other questions she had. *How* was he? What had happened to him, and why was he calling her now?

This wasn't the time for him to guilt her into coming to Florida, but if she had to, then she would. If it was the right thing.

No one wanted family life getting in the middle of a case. She hadn't been given another choice when Langdon went after her grandfather and dragged him into the fray. She was going to have serious words with him when she caught up to him about making this personal when it never needed to be.

Over the line she could hear a muttering. "First thing you've said that was actually helpful."

"Just tell me." If he wanted to get to the point, then he should just do it. Calling him an "old coot" was much too affectionate.

"A park."

"Local to St. Petersburg?" Either he'd have to get a whole lot more specific, or she needed to have Talia get GPS on his phone.

And her friend was probably sleeping right now. Resting up so she would be ready for when they got another lead.

She turned to Mark and saw him on the phone, quietly asking for a trace on her phone. If that wasn't Talia, whoever he was talking to was going to have a hard enough time even finding her phone, let alone getting the number of the phone her grandfather was using to then trace it.

"Stupid girl. I'm in Seattle."

It was on the tip of her tongue to ask him how she was supposed to know that. "Do you know which park?"

"No. There's a fountain. I'm cuffed to a gazebo."

"Does the fountain have one of those cupid babies in the center, shooting an arrow?"

It was the same park she'd been at earlier…or was that yesterday? Maybe it was more than a day ago. She could hardly keep track of time right now and was desperately in need of sleep. Or at least an IV of coffee.

Langdon had to have known she was there, or he wouldn't have placed her grandfather there now. He had to be reaffirming the fact he knew her every move. She'd tried to draw him out but had been arrested instead.

How was he with the scientist guy making the nuke and also out directing her grandfather's location and movements? That could mean he still had allies. Or people he handed cash to which, although not as reliable, still got the job done.

"Yes, I see the little angel."

"Okay, I know where that is." She set off in the direction of the car they'd ridden there in with Niall. Did Mark even have the keys? She turned, glanced at him, and then turned back.

Mark waved Niall's keys at her. She followed him, mouthing the name of the park. Mark nodded and got on his phone again as they walked. Good, they needed as much backup as possible right now. Especially if Langdon was going to be there.

Trying to draw *them* out.

Was it a trap?

"…even listening."

"I'm here, Pops."

"When a man's telling you his last words, you pay attention girl."

She fisted her other hand. "Sorry. What do you mean, 'last words'?" Her question made Mark hesitate. He glanced at her over the roof of the car, both their doors open. They needed to get in and go but, in that split second, just stared at each other.

"Because I'm about to die." Her grandfather let out a sound of frustration. "Are you stupid, or just too lazy to pay attention?"

She climbed in the passenger seat. "I'm neither stupid nor lazy, Pops."

He huffed audibly.

"I told Mark you've mellowed with age." Mostly true, but not completely. "Don't make a liar out of me."

He glanced at her, turned the key, and put the car in drive. Victoria didn't meet his gaze. Instead, she listened to her grandfather launch into a scathing diatribe on his opinion of Mark Welvern.

She cut him off midstream. "We're on our way. Now tell me why you said you're about to die." Could be he was bleeding out, or about to die horribly some other way.

"I'm strapped to a bomb. The phone has enough battery for one phone call, and it's about to run out."

Victoria reached over and grasped Mark's free hand as her grandfather continued, "As soon as the phone call ends, the bomb will start counting down."

"How much time?"

"Until it starts, I have no idea. He seemed to think that was hilarious."

"I'm sorry." She'd been gearing herself up for the closure of burying her grandfather as soon as the case was done, and she'd located where Langdon had dumped his body. Now he was here. Literally, on the phone and in town.

He had no reply for her empathy, or her sorrow. She didn't

want to get bitter, not when she'd managed to keep that from happening all these years.

"We'll be there as soon as we can." She tried to estimate travel time. "Ten minutes, tops. Okay?"

"Not like I can go anywhere. I just hope I don't blow up before you get here, I'd like to see your face when it happens."

His tone made her press her lips together.

The phone went dead.

She lowered it to her lap, trying to process. Mark squeezed her hand, the one she realized still gripped his. "What did he say?"

"That he doesn't want to die without seeing my face."

"That's…nice."

"Yeah, except it was more like he wanted to rub my face in it." She explained about the bomb and the timer.

"So it could go off at any time."

She nodded, thankful he'd changed the subject away from the particulars of her grandfather's way of dealing with her.

"The nuke?"

"He didn't say." She blew out a breath. "I have no idea."

Mark made another call, this time to a captain. Bomb squad —why didn't she think to ask for them? She hadn't had much in the way of backup with the CIA, but she could hardly blame that. Her team was solid. They could aid her.

She just wasn't sure she wanted them mixed up in her mess. Not when Langdon had made this personal. Too many chances for it to bleed out of her containment and hurt someone else.

Enough blood had been spilled already.

She flipped the phone over on her leg, wondering if she should wake Jakeman. After accounting for the time difference, she then wondered if he'd gone to church or stayed in the safe house this morning.

He was devout enough to risk death for the sake of communing with the Lord, or whatever actually happened in a church service. She hadn't gone for a very long time. She was surprised at her feelings of disappointment over missing the chance to go with Mark.

As soon as he pulled up, she jumped out and ran to the gazebo. A cop car pulled up across the park, and she waved them over.

When they neared her grandfather, sitting on the steps of the gazebo and handcuffed to the wood slat, the cop held his arm out in front of her. "Whoa."

How could she get her point across quickly? "I'm a state department director." It didn't exactly scream that she knew what she was doing.

The other cop yelled out, "Hold up, sir."

"I'm with her." She glanced back to see Mark hold up his badge. "Assistant Director Welvern, FBI. And you could say it's been a long night."

She took a couple of steps toward her grandfather. "It's been a long *week*."

"I've wanted this to be over ever since you came to live with me." His grizzled face had aged far past his years a long time ago. Now he looked like little more than a shell.

"Sorry I ruined your life."

"Off saving the world, too good for the town you were raised in. The people who looked after you."

One of the cops tried to steer this around to the relevant topic. "Sir—"

Her grandfather jerked his chin. "You want them to die, too? Just for fun?" He flashed his dentures at her, as though this was at all funny.

"You guys need to back up." She waved them off. All three of them. Not just the cops, but Welvern too. "How much time is left?"

He tugged back his jacket with the hand not cuffed to the stair rail. The display looked like an old MP3 player, barely bigger than the gray screen with the scrolling digital numbers.

2:39.

2.38.

2.37.

"There isn't much time." The relief that this wasn't the nuke nearly brought her to her knees.

He said nothing.

"Do you want to die?" She moved closer, assessing the wires. Probably if she broke the circuit and attempted to disconnect the trigger mechanism it would explode. She caught sight of a wire going up his arm. Into the thick black handcuffs she'd seen European cops use—no chain between the hands, this had a solid piece holding them steady. This one was wrapped in a wire. "If we get you free of the cuffs, it'll blow?"

Her grandfather lifted his chin, almost amused at the predicament he was in.

Behind her, Mark said, "How long on the bomb squad?"

She didn't think he was talking to her. Victoria held her grandfather's stony gaze. "Where is he going to set off the nuke?"

One of the cops gasped. "Did she say nuke?"

"That has to be the threat they were talking about at roll call."

Mark said, "Bomb squad is five minutes out."

Her grandfather said, "I guess this is it."

Victoria said, "You knew there was no way out. And you're okay with this?"

"Gotta go sometime. Why not take out a bandstand in the process? Get in the papers, make everyone wonder about the mystery instead of *wasting away in a retirement home waiting to die.*"

"You told me you liked Florida."

"Is this what you're going to talk about?"

She ignored Mark's question. "Where is he going to use the nuke, Pops?"

"You think I'll tell you?" His eyes flashed, and he motioned with the fingers of his free hand. "Come closer and I will."

"Just over a minute isn't enough time for games."

"Hurry up then."

She took two steps, heard Mark's warning, "Victoria," and

kept going. Her grandfather snagged her elbow in a crushing grip that a man his age shouldn't be able to pull off. She hissed.

He growled. "Your boyfriend might have his own ideas, but I do as well."

"Let go of me." She didn't let her eyes drift down to the timer. That wouldn't slow it or help her get the information she needed. "Tell me where he's going to hit?"

"Victoria, forty-five seconds."

"Pops, please," she pleaded. "He's going to kill thousands."

He actually laughed. "And I'll go down in history."

"Be a hero. Not one of the villains." So far he'd been kidnapped but hadn't done anything to actually get himself labeled as an accomplice. "For once in your life, do the right thing." His grip on her arm brought tears to her eyes.

"Look at you, getting all emotional."

If there was ever a time to do so, she figured that time was now. "Just tell me."

"Twenty-six seconds," Mark said.

She tugged on her arm, fully aware she needed time to run out of the blast zone. Other options included the bomb being a dud, or it being powerful enough it didn't matter how fast she ran.

"Let go of me if you're not going to tell me where he'll hit."

"Tell them I'm this great hero."

She waited, and he whispered three words in her ear. Victoria ripped her arm from his grip and turned, running for Mark before they raced away from the gazebo together. She looked over and saw that the two cops were faster.

The bomb squad van pulled into the parking lot half a second before the bomb strapped to her grandfather exploded.

30

Seattle, WA. Sunday 7.46a.m.

M ark moved his head, his cheek mashed against grass. The world had descended into a dull rushing sound with only the hard ground beneath his body.

He groaned but couldn't hear the sound from his own throat.

Victoria.

Mark forced his body to move. He blinked and saw gray cloud cover. The bare limbs of trees. His arm moved, and he felt damp leaves beneath his fingers.

It took a minute to push himself up. Even longer to realize one of the cops was talking to him. He was crouched over his partner, head turned in Mark's direction. Mouth moving.

The world surged, and it was as though his ears came into focus the way his vision might. Sirens.

"...get to her."

Mark blinked.

"Now." The officer gave him no choice.

Mark looked for Victoria. His gaze skittered over what was left of the gazebo, the debris. The carnage.

Her grandfather had exploded into oblivion, almost taking

Victoria with him. And he would have, if she was any semblance of the woman she once was. These days she understood the value of living to fight another day. Of not allowing personal feelings to cloud her judgment.

The result was that he got another chance to talk over with her everything they needed to say.

The cop said something else and pointed over to Mark's left.

Victoria.

Mark tried to get up, stumbled, and wound up crawling over there on his hands and knees. It wasn't far, but he realized several things hurt. Probably he'd have to deal with those things soon. At the hospital.

But given the state Victoria was in, he'd be there anyway.

Mark turned his head. Two police cars. Flashing lights. Ambulance. He sucked in a full breath and yelled, "We need help."

Coughing spasms overtook him, but he paid it no mind. Just gathered her to his chest and held her while he waited for the EMTs to run across the grass.

He felt her move, her hands coming up between them. She grasped his arm and shoulder. He shifted to look down at her face as she looked up at him. Wound on her temple. Blood on the corner of her mouth. Still, she stared up at him like she was glad to see him.

Mark leaned down, his cheek against hers. She turned to tuck her face in his neck, her grip on him tightening. Sweetest hug of his life.

Why had he thought there would ever be another woman in his life that would ever evoke such all-encompassing feelings in him? His ex-wife, even in their "honeymoon phase," hadn't caused such depth of passion in him. He could consider it a cruel joke, God giving him the one thing he could never have.

Mark should've let her go so many times before. By all rights, they should have drifted out of each other's lives. But they hadn't. For one simple reason.

"I love you, you know." Her hearing was as obliterated as his, so she probably didn't hear him. But he felt the reflexive grip of her fingers.

She moved then. Hands to his face, she tugged his head down until they were almost nose to nose, gazes locked. "I know. I love you."

"I'm sure you'll hate me for interrupting."

Mark already did. He turned to the EMT and saw him crouch beside them.

"But the both of you look like you need some help."

"Her first." He made sure Victoria was going to get seen to. They both had so many scrapes, cuts, and injuries—old and new —that the EMT would likely have to figure out what was from the bomb and what wasn't.

"You guys cops?"

Mark said, "I'm FBI. She's state department." He'd never been sure how to explain what she did. "Is the cop okay?"

The EMT glanced aside where a colleague of his worked on the officer laying on the ground while his partner ran his hands through his hair. It didn't look good. "I can find out, but we do this first."

Mark nodded.

He looked over Victoria, asking questions as he went, and took her blood pressure. He shone a penlight in her eyes. "Was it really a bomb?"

"My grandfather."

The EMT started. "Your...what?"

Mark explained everything, though he had to be brief on how it related to Langdon, the corrupt FBI agents they'd exposed and arrested, and what was happening now. Victoria's role in all of it was unclear, and this guy didn't need to know how she fit in.

"Huh."

Mark shrugged. He wasn't going to explain more. That would be a breach of security. What they needed right now was someone on the other side who could breach Langdon's operational security.

210 | LISA PHILLIPS

A thought occurred to his sluggish brain. "Right before…" He blew up. "Your grandfather said something to you."

Victoria frowned. "You're right." A light illuminated in her eyes. "I need a phone."

The EMT cut him off before he could respond. "You *need* a hospital."

"And a phone."

Mark nearly laughed. "And that's why they pay her the big bucks. She gets the job done."

"Yeah, being one of the good guys is lucrative."

The EMT laugh. "If it was, I probably wouldn't have a second job hanging drywall on my days off."

"I renovate houses in the evenings and weekends."

"For real?"

Mark nodded.

The EMT slapped his thighs. "Okay, let's load up."

Mark helped him get Victoria to the ambulance. He gave a statement to the cops who'd shown up. The injured officer had been taken away in the same ambulance as Victoria, having suffered a serious head injury.

There was nothing Mark could do but pray for the guy. And yet, how powerful a weapon the believer wielded. Moving things in the heavenly places simply by talking to his Savior. He was never powerless when he had the means to pray over a situation.

The cop shut his notebook and eyed Mark. "You need a ride to the hospital?"

Mark shook his head and winced at the slice of pain. Mental note: head shaking not a good idea.

"I'm not sure it's a good idea for you to drive."

"I'll be okay," he said. "My car is here, but I won't drive if I'm not able. I'll call someone."

Niall. Josh. Normally he'd have called Victoria first but that didn't work under the circumstances.

Mark got a few side glances from first responders. He knew

they all wanted the full details on why a bomber had blown himself up in the park on a Sunday morning.

He hardly understood what had happened himself, given Victoria's grandfather had been missing. Presumed dead. Now he'd shown up here. And Mark hadn't heard all of what he said, but the guy hadn't seemed upset about it. Not that he'd been eager to blow himself up. It just seemed like he was perfectly fine with this turn of events, prepared to do what Langdon wanted as though he didn't have a better idea for the rest of his life, so he'd figured, "why not?"

Mark climbed in the driver's seat of the car and just sat there for a moment.

They were all alive, so far. Her grandfather's fate wasn't something Mark would lose sleep over. Not when he hadn't stood up to Langdon at all. And didn't seem to care that he hadn't. A man like that didn't deserve his grief.

Mark tossed the keys in the cup holder and dug out his phone. He just needed a minute, and then he would head to the hospital. He figured it was nothing more than shock but didn't want to risk losing it on the road.

He called the one person who might actually have the skills to hunt Langdon. Someone they should have called days ago, and would have if he hadn't still been mad at Victoria. Now things had gone too far. It was time for the whole team to step up.

"Alvarez."

He squeezed the bridge of his nose. "It's Mark."

"I know, I have caller ID."

"You don't… It's…" He didn't even know where to start.

"Is she still alive?"

"Barely." They'd escaped that explosion with only a fine line between them living to tell about it and being blown to smithereens.

"Where is she?"

Mark told him the name of the hospital.

"Go there. Stay with her."

Mark started the car engine. "You think Langdon will target her? Isn't he busy with the scientist?" He realized Sal didn't know any of this. "I mean to say, he's kidnapped this—"

"I know, bro. I'm up to speed."

Maybe his brain wasn't working right. "What?"

"I'm in town. I've been here for days, trying to find Langdon. And I'll tell you now, this guy is slippery. It's *beyond* frustrating."

"Thank you."

"Not what I thought you'd say. But don't thank me until I find him. So far I've managed to come up with zilch."

"Us, too." At least, that was how he felt. "Her grandfather said something to her right before he blew up." Mark cleared his throat. "She hasn't told me what it is."

But she'd told Mark that she loved him, just like he loved her. Knowing that helped—the same way their friendship and the fact they'd always been there for each other had helped over the years.

But it didn't solve all their problems.

"Find out. We need that information." Alvarez paused. "And she needs you, just like she needs the rest of us but refuses to admit it." There was no trace of bitterness in his tone.

"She needs us, and you just forgive her?" Maybe at another time he'd have been able to say it more eloquently, but he'd nearly been blown up, had hardly slept in two days, and it was barely nine in the morning.

"Yes, I have. She has her reasons for doing what she did, though I haven't excused her actions," Sal said. "What I've done is figured out there's no way I can stand before God when I can't forgive her. I had to, so I did."

"How?"

"Part of forgiveness is that conversation with God where you admit you don't want to forgive. That you don't know how. That's the start." Alvarez hung up.

Mark sighed to the quiet in the car as he pulled out and drove to the hospital. When was the last time he'd been the only one in a car? He felt strange being alone. Overwhelmed. In shock.

He gripped the wheel and concentrated, but it didn't help the itch between his shoulder blades. As though he was being targeted. The way he had been when that sniper took a shot at him.

He'd saved a life that day, but it had cost him weeks in recovery. Mark wasn't sure if he could go through that again.

Only for Victoria. He knew that much.

She was the only one who rooted for him to succeed. Even if his promotion had only been because she wanted an ally sitting behind his desk. He was who she'd come to when she needed someone in her corner.

Mark parked and strode through the hospital doors, straight to the desk. "Victoria Bramlyn. She was brought in by ambulance."

The elderly man typed with two fingers on the keyboard, and frowned at the screen. "She hasn't arrived yet."

"It's been at least an hour." He'd given a statement *and* talked to several first responders. Not to mention the call with Alvarez.

…there's no way I can stand before God when I can't forgive her. I had to, so I did.

She was the one who needed someone in her corner now. And Mark knew that the foundation of what they had was strong enough to weather *anything*.

"Can't help you." The man shrugged one shoulder. "She isn't here."

31

Seattle, WA. Sunday 9.03a.m.

Victoria's body swayed with the motion of the ambulance. Every time she closed her eyes, all she saw was the EMT's face. The surprise. The flash of the gun, and the way his body jerked as he fell backward.

The rear door had a hole in it now. She didn't even want to look at it, or she'd see the blood that wouldn't leave her mind's eye.

"Did you have to do that?" She lifted her gaze at him.

He gripped the wheel with those thick fingers. EMT jacket, ball cap. Like he was one of them. He wasn't. He was the corrupt FBI agent, Colin Pinton. And the wanted criminal Oscar Langdon.

A man who led a double life, playing both sides of the fence, until those two lives turned on each other. He'd made his break in the chaos.

"You should have just disappeared."

He spoke then. "Look over my shoulder for the rest of my life? Expecting to turn any corner and see you standing there, holding a gun on me."

"I wouldn't bring a gun."

"No, you wouldn't."

She shifted, her bruised body stiff against the hard dividing wall between the rear of the ambulance and the cab. "You didn't need to dump that guy's body."

Only he probably figured he'd had no choice. Like he'd had no choice to kill Pacer, and General Hurst—all the others who had died, while she'd managed to fight off her attackers and live to tell about it.

"And you didn't need to involve my grandfather."

Langdon barked a laugh. "That guy was a hoot. Told me stories about you as a kid for hours and managed to drink me under the table." He chuckled. "Haven't had a night like that in years."

"So you strapped a bomb on him and cuffed him to that gazebo?"

"His idea." Langdon sniffed as he turned a corner, making the whole ambulance sway.

How long before someone noticed she'd never made it to the hospital? Until the EMT's body was discovered where it had been thrown out of the back of the ambulance onto the side of a deserted road?

Now he wanted her to believe her grandfather had chosen to die like that? Part of her wanted to scream in frustration, determined to refuse to believe it. But a bigger part of her knew very well that it could be the truth. Her whole life with the old man had been complicated, never knowing what he was going to do or say. What he would find unacceptable. What he would allow. What he would berate her for.

Now he was gone. All the family she'd ever had who had paid her any attention at all. Given her any "care" at all. Done. Dead.

All she had left was…

No. She couldn't think about him. Right now she needed to focus. Get out of these bonds, get Langdon subdued, and get him to tell her where the nuke was. That was her only job right now.

Victoria looked around again for what seemed the millionth time. No weapon had appeared since the last time she surveyed the interior. Medical instruments had all been put away. She had her shoes on, but would Langdon see if she pulled one off to strike him with it? Probably. Victoria knew his skills almost as well as she knew her own.

What she needed was to keep him distracted. "Where is the scientist you took?"

"Found the kid, I assume?"

"Did you think my team wouldn't find him?"

Langdon shot her a grin. "Always put too much stock in your friends. It's easier to go it alone."

"You don't think I should have trusted Genevieve, is that it?"

He shook his head. "Different."

"So I should ditch everyone I've ever brought into the fold and go it alone?" Maximum damage. Maximum carnage. Langdon would want a splash—because why else would he need a nuke? Talk about overkill, his plan to murder so many with this bomb he had. He would also want everyone to know it was him.

She said, "If I did that, then it would be just me. Swinging in the breeze."

"Think I'll get hung? Not likely."

"I found you, didn't I?"

"Under the circumstances," he said. "I'd like to think it was obvious that I found you."

"Unless that was my plan all along."

He barked a laugh again, the harshness of it echoing in the cab. Victoria slid the lowest drawer out with the toe of her shoe and looked inside. IV bags. That was a bust, unless she could find a tube…

Victoria knew of more ways to kill a person than anyone ever should, that was for sure.

"Did you kill the scientist?" Had he finished the bomb?

"What do you care? You're here, I'm here." He paused, probably thinking through the sale and whether she would buy whatever line he came up with. "Things could be good."

"Kill me now." There was no way she would go with any other option.

"You don't mean that."

"Try me." She waited, but he didn't take her bait. "Or better yet, I'll kill you. Yes, that would work."

"Don't be like that. I've got more reason than you to be mad. You're the reason Genevieve is dead."

"I'm not responsible for what happened to her."

"You were there," he said. "You could've stopped it. Saved her."

"From the men *you* sent." Now Oscar Langdon's woman was dead. And the man just kept driving the ambulance, dry eyed and irritated that she was dead. "She probably knew where money was stashed, am I right?"

She figured it was worth a guess for the sake of having a few more seconds to keep searching these drawers one by one.

"You were supposed to stand down." His voice rang through the cab. "Instead, you fought back, and now she's dead."

"We both loved her."

"Funny way of showing it. But don't worry." He glanced back and sneered at her. "I have plenty of ways you can make it up to me."

Yeah, no thanks.

He chuckled, then looked back at the road. Sure, she'd broadcast how she felt about his "invitation" all over her face. He knew she didn't want anything to do with that kind of thing between the two of them.

Langdon was like a child whose toy had been taken away, or broken. Now he was acting out, but he had access to much more dangerous means of retaliating.

The man she'd fallen for was nothing like this guy, sitting in the driver's seat of an ambulance that might as well be carrying the nuke he planned to use. Colin Pinton had been a good man. A good federal agent, or so she'd thought. Long enough to be fooled into allowing her feelings to be part of the picture.

Victoria tried not to have too many regrets in her life. Things she wished she'd done differently, or not done at all. Colin Pinton was the one time she couldn't deny she'd willfully ignored all those tiny, niggling signs and jumped in anyway.

"I'm not going anywhere with you."

When she was in love with Mark and always had been?

"Then you die when the bomb goes off."

"Fine." Much better than the alternative.

"And everyone will learn that you were in league with me the whole time. All about our sordid past, and how you died for the cause just like you intended to."

Victoria's stomach tensed. "Jakeman will never believe that."

"Welvern will," he fired back. "I'll make sure he regrets every day he did anything for you, and every feeling he ever had for you."

She didn't even want to think what would happen when—or if—Mark found out she was with Langdon. As though she'd ever give up her life to go with this guy and live on the run.

"Why tarnish my reputation? Because of Genevieve?"

"Partly." He pulled the ambulance to a stop. She couldn't see where they were or what kind of buildings surrounded them. Just a gray stucco wall. He said, "But also because while everyone's unpacking your life, they're spending less energy trying to find me." He shifted in the seat and turned to her. "Maybe I'll make it look like I died too."

A nuke would obliterate everything. The fallout would be chaos, and yet he wanted the rhetoric to be about a spy gone bad?

Victoria would have taken up that fight had it been about anyone else. Just like she was certain her counter-terrorism task force would never accept it. They knew her. Not everything about her life, and what she'd done, but she had been real with them. Genuine. They knew *her*.

"Either way, I'm gone and your fate has been decided."

Victoria had never been a fan of that assessment. About as much as she was a fan of allowing some all-powerful creator to have control over her life.

A few times she'd wondered if giving up that control might have helped her get out of a jam, but she'd always managed it alone. By the skin of her teeth. She was capable of a whole lot, and not helpless if she could ever prevent it. Who wanted to be?

Mark was all about humility and kindness. And catching bad guys. He was the epitome of what all good cops strove to be, and it went right to his core. She knew him enough to know he was the opposite of her. Victoria could handle a lot more gray area than Mark would stand for. Thus the source of the conflict between them, the reason they'd been unable to figure out how to have a real relationship that went deeper than friends.

Langdon climbed between the two front seats, into the back where he'd tossed her onto the floor.

He bent his head towards the cord he'd used to secure her to the leg rail of the bed.

Victoria whipped up her hands, let the tube drop so it was slack, and wound it around his neck. She pulled it tight.

Langdon jerked in surprise. He grabbed her neck and squeezed his fingers around her airway while she tried to constrict his with the tube. Both of them gasped. Evidently this was what the end would be. Locked together like this. If she was going to die anyway, maybe she could at least take him with her.

She squeezed tighter.

So did he.

Langdon's lips pulled back to reveal gritted teeth, a gleam in his eye. She didn't like that look. "You'll never—" He gasped. "Find it."

She squeezed harder.

"Boom."

Black spots flashed in the edges of her vision. If she lost consciousness, Victoria would never know. She'd condemn hundreds, possibly thousands, to their deaths. And for what? The satisfaction of knowing she'd killed him?

She loosened her hold on the tube.

He gasped. "Kill me and you'll never be able to stop the bomb." He didn't let up on her neck. He just kept squeezing.

Victoria reached up and grabbed his hands, trying to pull them away from her neck so she could breathe.

He didn't let go.

He wouldn't allow her to pry his fingers from her. No matter how hard she scratched at his hands. His arms.

Langdon's grip finally loosened, and she managed to suck in air. It hurt. But he hadn't let go because she'd made him do it.

His breath wafted over her face, and he spoke close to her ear. "I'll let you know when I've decided that your time on this earth is done. That's when you'll know it's the end."

32

Seattle, WA. Sunday 10.24a.m.

M ark heard his dog bark as soon as he got out of the car. Just that sound reassured him, for whatever unnamed reason, that things would be okay.

He twisted the key in the lock and stepped in, dumping his backpack on the bare floor of the hall. Bear raced over.

Mark gave his dog a rub down. "Is she here?"

No, that would be too easy. Still, he couldn't help but hope. The kind of hope that had nothing to do with what was possible, and everything to do with what was not possible. The kind of business God seriously loved to do.

Mark straightened to listen and look around for evidence of her.

Carpet would be down in a couple of weeks.

He shook his head, dismissing that unhelpful thought. It figured that his brain didn't want him to embrace reality. Hadn't helped when he had launched his father off Victoria and onto the corner of the coffee table. When the sheriff declared his father's death accidental, Mark had swallowed all that he had to say and pushed every feeling down.

Since that day, he'd been avoiding what was real, pretending that he only wanted a friendship with Victoria.

Bear trotted to the back door and nudged the bell with his nose.

Mark let him out and stood in the open doorway, long enough for his dog to take care of business and then meander back inside between Mark's leg and the door. Mark just looked at the gray cover of clouds and the trees. Felt the movement of the breeze on his face.

"Incoming!"

He spun around, hand halfway to his gun before he realized whose voice that had been.

Victoria's former team had let themselves into his house, moving down the hall to where he stood off at the side of the kitchen. Actually, only part of the team.

Talia dumped her giant, gold purse on the counter. "Shut the door, Welvern. It's cold."

Mason moved to the coffee pot, lifted the lid and dumped the old grounds in the trash he found under the sink.

Niall and Haley strode down the hall. A dog barked. Neema. Then his dog barked. Niall moved toward the noise, trailing after them. "Dakota is at the hospital with Josh. She asked us to watch their dog."

Mark held out his hand. "Let them figure it out."

He turned the corner to the living room. The two dogs had faced off with each other, but their heads were angled to sniff each other's necks. Tails wagging. They danced around each other, and Mark observed enough butt licking—which wasn't something he needed to watch—to know they would be fine.

He turned back to the hall. "That's nasty, Bear. She's a lady."

Haley was grinning, holding an empty mug ready for a refill. Niall clapped him on the shoulder. "You look like crap."

Mark ignored that. "How is Josh?"

"Not much in the way of change, but they say his body knows what to do. It's all a waiting game now."

Mark followed Niall to the kitchen. He stood in the doorway because there wasn't anywhere else to stand that wasn't already occupied by another person. "Why does this feel like a party when it very much is not one?"

Talia lifted the lid of her laptop and settled onto one of his barstools. "Because we have information you need to know."

"I should go upstairs," Mark said. "Do a sweep." He'd only just arrived home and hadn't secured the whole house.

Niall headed toward him. "I got it."

Soon as he'd passed Mark, Haley said, "He needs to move. He doesn't like standing still, or sitting down, when one of our own is in danger."

Mark was pretty sure the last time he'd spoken to Haley she'd been mad at Victoria for all the secrets she'd kept from them. Now they were rallying to do what? Find her? He turned to Talia. "So tell me this information."

Haley was the one who said, "We're just waiting on two more. Then the whole team will be here."

Mark rubbed the spot on his stomach where he'd been shot. Allyson and Sal were on their way?

Haley said, "Do you need something? Ibuprofen?"

He shook his head. What he needed was something much stronger, which he'd never take anyway because it was too risky, even just once. Just a personal choice based on his father's tendency to become reliant on any and every substance he could get his hands on.

Mark also figured he needed about forty-eight hours of sleep. But before that, he needed to know where Victoria was.

The door opened. "Hola." First in was Allyson Sanchez, formerly of the ATF. Though, judging by the glints on her finger, she may well already be Mrs. Salvador Alvarez.

"They're here!" Haley rushed to hug Allyson. "Was it amazing?"

Allyson nodded. "*So* amazing."

Sal stepped in, shut the door behind him, and then petted

both the dogs who insisted on sniffing his boots. Both he and Allyson did look more tanned than usual, and happier than he'd ever seen them.

Sal clapped him on the shoulder. "In case you need honeymoon ideas, bro. Belize." He squeezed Mark's shoulder. "Trust me."

They congregated in the kitchen, Niall back from his sweep of upstairs. Mark called for the dogs, and let them outside.

"Will somebody *please* now tell me where Victoria is?" Mark folded his arms on his chest. Then he had to unfold them because Mason handed him a steaming cup of black coffee.

"You're welcome."

"Like, right now."

Mason turned to his fiancé. "Honey?"

Talia paused typing on her computer. She clicked the mousepad and pulled up an image. "This, we believe, is Langdon."

Mark strode to her side and peered from close up at the screen. "Can't tell if it is or not."

"Right." She clicked again, and the image zoomed in. It focused and…

"That's Victoria."

"He has her tied up in the back of the ambulance." She squeezed his forearm. "We weren't sure what happened, so I was tasked with tracking it from when it left the scene of the explosion. Langdon disabled the GPS, but I followed them from surveillance. Traffic cameras. ATM cameras. That kind of thing. Found the side street where he shoved the EMT out of the back and then took off. Cops who showed up said he was already cold."

Cold. As in dead.

Not something he *ever* wanted to be said about Victoria. Not if he could help it. *God, help me.*

Mason squeezed his shoulder.

"We need to get her back."

Talia nodded. "There's more. Unfortunately. And you're not going to like it."

"You dug something up."

He figured the information she'd dug up was likely the strings pulled to get him the FBI assistant director's job. But it could easily be something else. He knew a lot about Victoria's history, but nowhere near everything. They probably knew things he didn't but maybe no one on earth knew everything.

If she died today, all those secrets would die with her.

"Genevieve Moran wasn't just Victoria's friend." She pulled a picture of her up on her screen from whatever French authority had conducted a medical examination of her body.

"Right," Mark said. "She was Oscar Langdon's woman."

"That's what we all thought, and it's true, but it's still not the whole story."

"I was digging through everything I could get on Colin Pinton from the FBI's files. That got me to a phone he had, not his work number but—"

"You hacked his personal phone?"

"NSA," she said, as though that explained what the FBI hadn't been able to get access to. Because they had no records of a personal cell phone that they'd found. "So I went through his phone records to see if anything popped. And let me say, something popped all right." She took a breath, then continued with a wary expression on her face. "From what I can surmise, Colin Pinton began a relationship a few months before he transferred to California. With an employee of the state department."

"Victoria."

Talia nodded. "She dated Pinton before she…you know, dropped off the map or whatever."

"Before Langdon dumped her in that prison." He scratched at his jaw, putting the puzzle pieces together and working the implications of a relationship. "So Colin and Victoria start to date around, or during, the time Victoria was actively trying to get close to Genevieve. Then when the operation to grab Langdon goes down, she's dumped in South Africa. Because of Genevieve, or because of Langdon?"

"Who cares?" Haley was probably as itching to get on the hunt for Victoria as he was.

Mark shot her a look. "She never knew Pinton was Langdon, right? That means they dumped her in prison so she wouldn't find out. Probably to safeguard whatever deal they had going down that night." Save her life, but get rid of her. Maintain their secrets. "They should've killed her."

Haley pushed off the kitchen counter toward him. "Excuse me?"

"They left her alive when they should have killed her. She came home and set up a committee specifically to nail this guy, and to have it done in an official and permanent way. To make sure he goes down for all of it."

"But he's got her."

"And the tattoo on her arm," Mark said, "that's the final nail in the coffin of her career. He's going to paint the picture that she turned and is now responsible as well. Or that the nuke was her idea all along, and he was the one coerced."

"They can't do that!" Talia's face reddened. "People will think she's guilty!"

As opposed to simply being a woman who had fallen for who she'd thought was a good man, had been betrayed, and now stood to lose everything she'd built? "I'm going to help her get free of this." It was true. None of them had to hear him say it to know he would do whatever it took. "We all are. Isn't that why you guys are here, so we can pool our skills and resources and do this together?"

He couldn't find her without their help. Mark knew there was a reason God had brought them into his life, probably for this. Right now. So they could help him get her back. *Thank You.* Seeing His hand in this, Mark felt like there was actually hope they'd be able to bring her home.

Niall closed in, wound his arm around his fiancé's shoulders and hugged her to him. He looked at Talia. "Mark is right."

"I know we're going to find her." She didn't sound happy about it. "I just can't believe he'll make it so she's blamed. So people doubt all the work she's done and who she is. The good. For this country."

Niall nodded. "Me either."

"Seems like Langdon hedged his bets all around, hiding his identity as an FBI agent. Working both sides. Seems like he had contingencies ready and waiting so he could flick one thing and set something in motion wherever and whenever he needed."

Talia pointed her finger at him. "That's good. I'm going to look into that."

"She knew where he was going to set off the nuke." Mark squeezed the bridge of his nose again, and then ran his hands down his face. "Victoria is the only one alive who knew that."

They looked shell shocked. He felt the same, having been essentially blown up earlier that morning. His whole body felt like he'd been hit by a train, and he suddenly felt the urge to send a sympathy card to anyone who'd actually experienced that. Or family members who had lost someone that way.

"Anderson."

They collectively turned to him as Mason turned away slightly to take his call. Probably all wondering, as Mark was, who it was on the phone. If it was related to Victoria's abduction. Whether they would learn something from it, or get a lead.

"Thank you." He hung up. "Jakeman's safe house was hit. There are unconfirmed reports coming in that everyone there is dead."

33

Seattle, WA. Sunday 10.57a.m.

Victoria blinked. The rush of her inhale filled her ears and she looked around. Breezeblock walls, no window. Single bulb illuminating the room.

That's when you'll know it's the end.

But she wasn't dead. Yet.

She tried to relieve the tension in her screaming shoulders but couldn't move her hands. Rope bit into her wrists. Her feet were also bound to this metal folding chair. She gritted her teeth. Not a chair she could snap or bust out of. Nothing around her to cut the bonds.

She didn't have many options if she wanted to get out of here.

The short clip of a person's shoes on concrete tapped down whatever hallway lay on the far side of the closed door. It might as well be in Madagascar out there, for all that she could access it.

The walker—a man, by the sound of it—passed the door without stopping. Without speaking. He continued down the hall, retreating from her ability to hear. About his business without paying her any mind.

She blew out a breath. A bead of sweat rolled down her fore-head, and she slumped down in the chair.

She wasn't going to get out of this. Not without him coming in here and her getting him to participate in the escape process. Easier said than done, but it wasn't impossible.

There weren't a whole lot of options for her.

He'd intended to kill her, but only as much as she had been intending on killing *him*. A stalemate, kind of like her in this chair. Then when he'd talked her into standing down, he'd whipped out a stun gun and zapped her.

She was supposed to be finding out where that nuke was. What he planned on…

She knew. Her grandfather had told her where Langdon intended on using it.

Where Colin intended on setting it off.

She shut her eyes then, forcing her mind—for the first time—to process the fact it was the same man. For as long as she'd been chasing him, Victoria had striven to separate them in her mind. She didn't want to feel the jabbing knife of that betrayal. Not right now, not then, and hopefully not ever. But it wasn't going to help her to do that anymore. It was time to fully embrace reality, not just the world the way she wanted to see it or believe it was.

He'd lied to her.

Victoria made a face, alone in the room. No one could see it. The truth was that he'd fooled her, and that hurt more. The reality that she hadn't realized he was lying to her. Meaning, she cared about someone who didn't even exist, which meant she hadn't cared about him at all. To any degree. Mostly she'd been coming off a time when Mark had been lamenting the impending end of his marriage. Then, next phone call, he'd sounded excited because they'd been working on things. Patching it up.

She'd responded like any warm-blooded woman in a long-term relationship with her job. Rebounding with the first guy she met that she thought was a good guy. A nice guy. The fact he'd been an FBI agent had been a gray area she'd not wanted to think about too much. Fact was, she was around government and federal types all the time because of her job. She'd been in Europe. It was an insular community.

Mark had gotten a divorce. Victoria had run the mission and had woken up in South Africa. All around it had been a bad idea, hindsight being 20/20, and all that.

The door handle rotated and was pushed open. She lifted her chin and watched as a familiar face came in. Not one she'd been intending to see.

"Jakeman." She cleared her throat and swallowed.

He didn't look happy to see her and stumbled into the room. Hands behind his back.

Langdon followed him. Gun pointed at her friend. Folding chair in the other hand. He jerked it open and set the legs down, then shoved Jakeman to a sit. "Good. We can get started."

He set his foot on top of Jakeman's shoe, holding it in place, and brought the butt of the gun down on his knee.

Jakeman brought his head down right as Langdon straightened. Their skulls glanced off each other. Langdon roared. "I should put a bullet in you for that."

"So do it." Jakeman spat blood onto the floor.

"I'm *trying* to work. So just shut up."

"Am I invited to this party?" Victoria figured if she got his attention long enough, he'd give Jakeman a breather. With the added bonus that Langdon might forget to secure her friend to his chair. "Or is it just for the two of you?"

"I don't need your help." Langdon swung the gun around. Now that she knew he wasn't imminently going to use it, she could cross a few scenarios off her mental list of what might happen.

"Why are we here?"

She wanted to ask why Jakeman was here, too, but this would be a good start.

Langdon sucked in a series of long breaths. Trying to calm, or compose, himself. "All who knew about me, and who caused all this, are done. Both of you being the ones left—you got voted to go down with the ship as it were."

"You're going to blow us up with that nuke?" She had to know what Jakeman knew.

He gasped. Evidently he'd been missing that part of the puzzle.

"Right now?" She also had to know the timeline.

"I'll let you know when it's going to happen." Langdon sneered at her. "You'll know when that is because all of a sudden things will get really hot."

"And us?" She motioned to Jakeman with her head. "We just get obliterated while you run away?"

Langdon shrugged one shoulder. "Seems like a decent plan to me. I'm just finalizing the particulars."

"And the scientist?"

"I didn't need him anymore."

"So he's dead as well?"

Langdon pushed out a breath. "Does it matter, Victoria? You're going to be *dead*."

And he got to choose the time and place. This man thought he controlled the end of her life, with her powerless and tied to a chair.

"And everyone in the world will think you and Jakeman couldn't handle the secrets anymore. You were so tormented by your sordid relationship that you weren't able to hold it in any longer. So you decided to end it all with a nuke. Blow up your whole world and let it all go down in flames so that your passion could live forever."

Cold prickled the skin on her arms.

"Mark would never believe that."

She glanced at Jakeman.

He shook his head. "Not just Mark. All of Victoria's friends. And all my family."

Langdon took a step toward him. "You think I can't fake a relationship? Like I've never done that before?" He laughed.

Jakeman flinched and shifted away on the chair.

Victoria bit her lip to keep from telling him not to make it too obvious that he wasn't secured to it. "Don't do this!"

Langdon twisted back to her.

"Don't make it worse than it has to be. Just…go. Do you really need to set off this bomb and make up a bunch of lies, just to get away?"

"Yes."

He walked to the door, stepped out, and threw it shut.

Victoria started. Then she shut her eyes.

"He's really going to do this."

She looked at her friend. A man she had been very careful in her association with, as she was when connected to anyone of his caliber. There was zero point in a person like her, who strove to live under the radar, getting the spotlight shone on her entire life, just so the news could have a headline story.

Now all that would have been for nothing. Everyone would think she and Jakeman had been embroiled in some kind of love affair.

Her only hope was that Mark and her team, the people whose opinions she actually valued, would know it wasn't true. They would never believe it.

Unfortunately, given the fallout of a nuclear bomb, they would also be dead. Which kind of negated their faith in her. Especially considering their deaths were on her.

Langdon might be the one pushing the button, but it was her responsibility to stop it.

Victoria wasn't going to submit and allow him to have that kind of control over her life. Just as she'd hesitated giving that kind of control to "the Lord," as her team referred to him. In a situation where she had no power, because Langdon had it all? Absolutely she would give that to God. She'd rather He was in authority than a homicidal ex. When there was no Langdon, and Victoria was the one who had say over her own destiny? That was another question.

But right now...she had to worry about right now. Not wait for a peaceful day, where she had time to mull over all the repercussions of what amounted to a Hail Mary play.

God. Okay, so this was weird. *I have no other ideas. They all say you're all powerful and all that other stuff...so help. Don't let a nuke blow up Washington state. Help me stop it.*

She didn't feel any different. But the amount of times Victoria's team had told her about their new or renewed faith could probably fill a book—a rewrite of all those basic things, the "foundations" as Haley had called them.

Still, she had no idea if that even worked. Maybe she needed a backup plan.

Victoria looked over Jakeman, assessing him for injuries while also refusing to meet his gaze. After what Langdon had told them his plan was, she didn't want to make things any weirder between them.

"Can you get up?"

"Do you think he's going to come back?"

She shrugged. "I know you're the one who's mobile, and I'm tied to this chair." She didn't want to have to break her thumbs, especially considering she wasn't certain that would actually enable her to pull her hands from the ropes that bound them. Not given how tight they were around her wrists.

He rolled over on the floor, groaning. "I'm far too old for this."

"What are you now, eighty-something?"

"I'm fifty-seven, and you know that. You were at my birthday party." He hesitated before saying anything else and narrowed his eyes. "That was a good distraction." He straightened where he was sitting.

"You're welcome."

"Mary Anne has been making me do yoga, you know?"

Victoria shook her head.

"If we were lovers, you'd know that."

He was making jokes? "This isn't funny."

"No, but this might be." He contorted his legs, locked

together, and pulled his feet through his hands until his hands were in front of his body rather than being locked behind his back.

"Smooth."

"Things you'd know."

"Jake—"

"Yeah, yeah." He stood up. "I've never stood a chance...not since Mark entered the picture."

"Does your wife know you feel that way?" Was he really trying to distract her with this ridiculousness?

He laughed, straightening one leg with the other bent and his foot off the ground. "You know she loves you."

"This conversation is getting really weird. Anyway, Mark entered the picture in third grade, so..."

He touched his bound hands to his chest. "So I really never did stand a chance? You break my heart."

Jakeman had to hop to her, sweat rolling down his face. He never once made even a sound of pain even though his knee had to be shattered. He leaned against her chair and looked at her back. "Plastic ties." He straightened. "You know, I had this knee replaced a couple of years ago. It's metal, so I know it's not broken."

"That doesn't make it better." Besides, they needed to get out of here. Not take their sweet time having a conversation. "You'll have to—"

The door swung open.

Jakeman rushed Langdon with an awkward gait. Langdon swung his arm and punched him in the stomach.

Jakeman gasped and fell to the floor.

Langdon stepped back into the hall for a second, then came out with a tripod and video camera. "Time for your last words."

34

Seattle, WA. Sunday 12.04p.m.

M ark pushed open the door to his office and pulled up short. "I didn't expect to see you here, sir."

"It's a Sunday, Welvern. And you can call me director."

He blinked. Was he supposed to laugh? "Are you working the Langdon case?"

The older man leaned back in Mark's chair, the thick mustache like a caterpillar crawling over his top lip. "I have another matter. The real reason I'm on this side of the country."

This was a long way from Washington D.C. and honestly sometimes felt like a completely different world. Policing wasn't much different here, but it still seemed as though each state—each city and town—had its own individual culture.

"A case?"

"An event we need to safeguard. I'm afraid the clearance level doesn't extend down to you."

It had to be seriously high level then, considering Mark was the assistant director over the whole office. But that wasn't what he wanted or needed to talk about. The reason why he'd come here.

"I got a report that the residence where the secretary of

defense was spending the weekend has been hit, that there may not be any survivors."

The director's mustache crawled again. "I'm sure he's fine."

"Langdon has to be involved. He must've attacked or kidnapped him as he's done with Victoria Bramlyn. Or he just killed the man." Killed them both.

"You think he's targeted them like that?"

Mark said, "Victoria was taken before she could even reach the hospital."

"I'm sure she just left and is back on the case already. She is a spy."

"She'd have told me. Then there's the surveillance footage we have of her tied up in the ambulance, also an indicator she didn't just leave."

Mark immediately bit back regret for saying that out loud. He wanted to reach out and squeeze the guy's neck. Why, he wasn't all that sure, considering the director was on his side. The side of right, and the law. It was just that every ounce of frustration he had pent up inside him wanted to be channeled at the person sitting across from him in his chair. The person making his job that much harder than it needed to be.

He'd already had Talia look into the director's personal life. She hadn't come up with anything incriminating. He wasn't linked to Langdon, despite the fact he'd been Colin Pinton's boss for years. Mark figured it was unlikely they'd even met, considering how huge the FBI was.

Without evidence, there was no reason to suspect the director of anything that would betray the office he held.

Mark said, "The job you're here to oversee...could it be what Langdon intends to hit with that nuke?"

The director huffed out a breath. "That seems to be more than assumption at this point. We only have circumstantial evidence that Langdon may have a weapon of mass destruction, and definitely nothing that tells us when or where he plans to use it."

"Victoria knew." Mark slid his hands into his pockets. "Now she's gone."

She'd been about to tell him. So close to knowing where Langdon planned to enact his destructive plan, and now he was so far from knowing, he might as well be in a different solar system.

"Seems convenient." Caterpillar mustache.

That thing just loved to crawl along as he worked his mouth. The director's version of a disapproving frown. "Whether that's true or not, Langdon is still the priority."

"Mmm." The director lifted both brows this time. "Yes."

"And the thing you're here to oversee? Could that be a target?"

He shook his head, not even pausing to think it over. "I'm sure it's not. The whole thing has been kept under serious wraps."

"And yet you don't agree that finding Victoria should be our priority?" It could just be Mark's priority—and it very much was —but his boss had apparently dismissed that idea. As though she'd simply ditched them and gone back to her job. Even considering that Mark hadn't officially worked with her much, he could still say with confidence that she hadn't.

Mark continued, "She's the only one who has all the information we need. Her personal connection with Langdon makes her the perfect person to assist in finding a man we should have caught days ago. We're the laughing stock of federal agencies right now, with all this corruption right under our noses and we knew nothing. We did nothing."

The director stood, shoving the chair back as he did so. "Tread very carefully right now, Assistant Director Welvern. Ensure you do not step into insubordination territory with that tone, and your attitude."

"Sir—"

The director lifted one hand, palm out. "Very carefully."

Mark pressed his lips together.

"Your association with Director Bramlyn has colored your career in a way you clearly weren't prepared for and still don't seem to fully comprehend. I understand you were childhood friends. Such longevity can often cloud our ability to see the truth when it's so plainly in front of us."

Mark wasn't ever going to believe that somehow Victoria was dirty, or that she was secretly working with Langdon. No way. Never.

All it served to do was make Mark more and more suspicious of his boss and *his* loyalties. And though Talia found nothing, he still wasn't sure enough to suspend all his doubts and give this man full trust.

The way he did with Victoria.

That was a knowing kind of trust. She wasn't infallible, but he knew her well enough to know what he needed to worry about and what he didn't. Those known unknowns that kept him up at night—not the things he didn't know were coming, but the things he was sure would. With Victoria, it was all known. She would be there. And she would work for the right outcome, whether that cost her her life or her friends.

Of course.

She hadn't gone off on her own. Langdon had her tied up— not that he considered that something insurmountable for her. But there was no way Victoria would reach out to one of them. Not if it would put their lives in danger. Especially not if she thought she could take care of Langdon and the nuke herself. Did she have that kind of explosives detonation training? He had no idea. But unless they could help in a way she needed them to in order to put an end to this threat...

There was no way she would call, even if she could.

Mark's phone buzzed in his pocket. He lifted his wrist and looked at the face of his smartwatch. It scrolled with a new text message.

DONE.

Mark said, "The threat is clear. I strongly suggest you ensure the security for the case that has you here, or whatever it is that you're overseeing."

The director said nothing. Mark strode out, straight to the elevator, and headed to his car. When he'd pulled out onto the street, he used the screen on his dash to call Mason.

The secret service assistant director picked up before the second ring. "She's working on it."

"Dumping his phone?" Mark felt a quick pang of conscience at the fact they were essentially hacking the director's life. But the man had insisted on keeping his secrets. He could have read Mark in on the reason he was coordinating something here. Whatever it was could very well be the event Langdon intended to use his bomb, for maximum effect.

The fallout was almost too huge to comprehend. Initial explosion, plus the ramifications that would continue for months. Years. A whole generation. This would be so much bigger than 9/11, something no one wanted to see repeated anywhere on American soil. And this time, it wasn't a *foreign* threat to the US way of life. It was a homegrown enemy determined to hit them with firepower for no reason but spite, just for insisting that they bring him in. Whatever it took.

Mark gripped the wheel with one hand and the back of his neck with the other as he weaved through afternoon traffic.

"If there's something there to find, she'll get it."

He turned a corner, headed for the secret service office. "Anything on the GPS for the ambulance?"

Mason was quiet for a second. "Talia wants to know if you'd rather she looked into what the director is doing, or if you want her to spend time trying to reboot the GPS on the ambulance."

He worked his mouth side to side. It was likely Langdon had dumped the ambulance somewhere, considering it was way too noticeable. Not a low-key getaway vehicle. So he'd gotten rid of it, and was holed up somewhere.

Mark didn't want to think about what was happening with Victoria.

He wanted to rage. Scream. Slam his hand against the steering wheel. Push the gas pedal to the floor. But what would all that solve? Victoria was the one who'd taught him by her own example that allowing emotion to overtake him wouldn't benefit the situation. He'd get distracted in his own head and someone could get hurt. What he needed was focus.

She was the one who knew Langdon. She had the skills to bring him down and the knowledge of what his plan entailed. Mark had to trust her and provide whatever support he could.

The way they'd leaned on each other for years.

Since the night his father died and Mark had been forced to pack away that rage over what the old man had been intending to do with Victoria. Did he feel the weight of guilt over being responsible for his death? Sure. He'd gone to counseling on and off over the years, some of it at the request of the FBI. Did it matter that the old man had been emotionally and physically abusive? No, that didn't give Mark the power to judge him and sentence him to death.

It had been a horrible accident under terrible circumstances.

But it still stained his soul. A soul that had been washed by the blood of Jesus. Bought by redemption. Redeemed.

The worst of who he was had been made new in Christ.

And now he prayed Victoria would know the same peace he felt, even in the midst of what was happening to her.

"Okay, she got something."

Mark waited.

"The director is in town because he's overseeing security for the Western Governors' Association. They're having a last minute, private meeting tomorrow night at an undisclosed location that Talia's working on finding."

"About what?" Langdon, maybe. The truth was, Mark didn't think they'd know what the reason was. Not until they got there.

He could try calling the governor of Washington, but the guy always had his lieutenant field the calls he didn't want to bother with.

"Your guess is as good as ours."

Mark tapped the steering wheel with his index finger. "Can you get us in?"

"This is an FBI operation from the look of it," Mason said. "My office didn't even know it was happening—and won't—considering this was a completely illegal breach of another federal agent's official phone."

He heard Talia say something in the background but couldn't make it out. He could guess, though. Probably the same wording Victoria would use if she ever cared to explain herself. Which didn't happen often. Something about the ends justifying the means.

"You need to get us into that meeting." Mark didn't have the clout. Not with the director overseeing all this and keeping it to himself.

"You think this is where Langdon will go?"

"Do we have any better ideas?" Mark headed for his house so he could shower and make a plan. It had nothing to do with seeing Bear, or that being the first place Victoria always went when she needed him. "Get me into that meeting, Mason."

"I'm going to regret this."

The line went dead.

35

Seattle, WA. Sunday 1.52p.m.

"And that's why I'm doing this."

Off camera, Langdon stood with his gun pointed at Jakeman. He stepped to the tripod and touched a button. The red light blinked out. "I guess that will have to do. There isn't time enough to make another one."

Victoria squeezed her eyes shut. He'd adjusted her sleeves so it didn't look like she was tied to the chair. He'd also brushed out her hair. As though that would make her look put together when her makeup was probably smeared across her face by now.

She looked down at the skin of her arms. Tiny fingers danced across every inch of that organ, over her whole body. She was about to scream. To claw herself free of whatever he'd injected into her that was now crawling under her skin.

She felt crazy.

She probably looked crazy.

"Mark will never believe it."

Langdon moved the camera out into the hall. "If I do this right, he won't be alive to see it."

Victoria screamed out her frustration.

Langdon just laughed. "You know that's how I like it, darling."

She hadn't, and probably could have died in peace never ever knowing the darker side of this man. But he'd insisted on dragging it all out into the light, destroying her whole life—ending it, even —only to then make a break for a new life where he did...what? Sat on a beach somewhere? Or terrorized unsuspecting people who then had to live under the thumb of some third world warlord?

This man was going to continue this destruction until he was put in the ground. And the price would be high.

A tear rolled down her face.

The price would be so high.

"I'll have to edit the video. That's going to take time." It was like he was talking to himself. "But it'll get me maximum dramatic effect and help sell the whole story. The bomb will obliterate everything, so they'll never find your DNA. You'll be a myth, a legend. *The body was never discovered.*" He used a sensational tone.

"Because your bomb is going to incinerate us."

Langdon shrugged. "Everyone will see it. You'll be famous, and dead. Does that make you infamous?"

She said nothing.

"You'll go viral. Victoria Bramlyn, trending."

She couldn't think of anything worse.

"Viral." He paused. "Huh, maybe I should have thought of that and got a bioweapon instead of hanging onto that uranium." He shrugged. "I couldn't sell it. What else was I supposed to do?"

"There isn't some kind of...nuclear device amnesty program?"

He laughed, and it sounded like his amusement over her comment surprised him. He shut the door, the sound of his laugh echoing down the empty hallway.

She still hadn't figured out where she was. Did it matter?

He didn't come back for a while. Victoria fought the urge to try and snap the ties. "Jakeman."

She could feel blood trickling down her feet. Pooling on the floor. Enough her foot sat in something wet and sticky, but she wasn't about to bleed out.

The secretary of defense only moaned.

She looked down again, trying to ease the itch all over her legs. She caught sight of the inside of her elbow, the spot where Langdon had injected whatever this was that made her feel crazy. Sound crazy. Look crazy.

She tried to breathe through the sensation. The alternative was losing her mind.

Jakeman moaned. Langdon had hit him pretty hard, then kicked him. Enough he stayed down as Victoria read from Langdon's prepared notes, everything he'd wanted her to say for the video that would be the nail in the coffin of her life, her work. Her reputation and the respect she'd built. Even Jakeman's wife and daughter, assuming they were still alive, would lose faith in them. If they for one second thought it was true, then Victoria had lost this entire battle.

There had to be something she could do to stop him.

Langdon strode in and walked right to her. He bent to a crouch and she heard a light *snick*. The ties on her right foot loosened, falling to the floor. She jerked and tried to kick him.

Almost nothing happened. She barely managed to do more than twitch her leg and grunt.

He laughed, loosed her other leg, and stood. Her hands were secured together and tethered to the chair legs at the back, under the sweater he'd covered her hands with.

He cut them free from the chair, but left her hands bound.

Then Langdon backed up. He pointed the gun at her then flicked the barrel toward Jakeman. "Get him up."

Victoria considered the situation. "You're assuming I can walk."

Debatable, at least she figured as much. Not even in control of her own body right now. *God, is this the kind of stuff You help with?* She imagined it probably was, but she had no idea how that worked. She wasn't a Christian in the sense Dakota had explained. Hadn't really ever had that desire, or seen that she necessarily had a need. Maybe life had simply never been this intense. She'd never found herself this close to the wire with no way out.

Did God accept people on those terms? She had no idea.

"You'd better walk, or I'll drag you out myself." Langdon sniffed. "Get him up. It's time to go."

"Where?" She gritted her teeth and tried to get up, knowing she had to find her balance and move, even if that meant dragging her feet in order to avoid retaliation on her or Jakeman. "Where is the bomb, Colin?"

The skin around his eyes contracted.

"We had a good thing, right? For a while." Yeah...until he threw her in a South African prison to keep the lid on his own secrets.

She'd jumped in with both feet, mostly just for the sake of distracting herself. Mark had been happy. Married. To say Colin Pinton had been a rebound didn't exactly qualify the bad decision she'd made but it covered enough of what it was.

Victoria couldn't say precisely that she'd known something was off with him, but she must have had some slight feeling or premonition. Maybe that was why she'd resisted his attempts to take things "to the next level." In the end, it had been a good thing she had resisted, considering what happened instead. But the truth was, she'd had blinders on. Too absorbed by her own hurt feelings and also trying to find it in her to be happy for Mark, to see what had been right in front of her face.

"Get him up." Gone was any trace of the Colin Pinton that she'd known. This man was Oscar Langdon, international criminal.

She took a step and winced. Her whole body was sore and hypersensitive. The tingling sensation wouldn't let up. How long would it take to leave her system? She wondered if she'd be dead before she felt normal again.

No.

She wasn't going to allow that to happen.

"Where's the bomb?" That was part of what she had to do, disarm it so no one would get hurt. He needed to tell her. Then she could take him out and go shut down the bomb before it went off. "When are you going to use it?"

He sighed. "Let's go meet destiny."

"Lang—"

"The bomb is already at the ranch."

A thought niggled at her, but the incessant itching overwhelmed her ability to recall whatever it was. "A ranch?"

"*The* ranch. Timer is already set, everything is in place and ready to go. You're just icing on the cake, darling." He sneered. "The video's been sent, and the bomb will detonate at midnight, regardless of where we are. Doesn't matter. There are enough variations of this plan, because I've figured them all out. There's no way I'm going to fail. Doesn't matter what you try and do."

"Tonight?" The Western Governors' Association. "Their meeting isn't scheduled until tomorrow." She remembered that much from her last email update. It was an extremely secure event, a house full of the most powerful people on the West Coast, all gathered together to pat each other's backs and brainstorm what they were planning next.

She remembered thinking it was a waste of taxpayer dollars.

Langdon said, "They'll all be there tonight, why wait?"

A shiver went through her, and it felt like her skin hummed. She wanted to itch herself all over. And she would have, had she been able to. Too bad it wouldn't help. She knew nothing would make this go away. Unless she was able to claw her skin off. If she had no skin, she'd no longer have to worry about the itching from the stupid injection any longer.

She would recover, eventually—if she didn't destroy herself in the process.

Or...she'd be dead from his bomb.

Victoria didn't want to think about the fact he'd basically incapacitated her from being able to defuse it. She might have been able to do it, given some of her training, but it might just be impossible with the way her faculties were functioning at this moment. If she got near enough to disable it, she would probably twitch and set it off instead.

Langdon prodded her with the gun. "Move."

She hissed out a breath as the feeling of the barrel moved through her. Like a wave of ants.

"Get him up. Time to go, the clock is ticking."

She moved to Jakeman and saw his eyes open, staring at her. His gaze then shifted to glare at Langdon. Victoria wanted to reassure him, to tell him that she had this. Langdon wasn't going to take them anywhere. She knew now where the bomb was. In a second, the tables would turn and she would have the upper hand.

He thought he'd incapacitated her, but Langdon didn't realize what she could withstand. There was a whole lot more to Victoria Bramlyn then he ever gave her credit for.

So what if he had a gun? He would quickly find out that didn't matter.

Victoria would stop him.

She helped Jakeman to his feet. Hands bound like hers. Legs unsteady. They clung to each other for a second, years of friendship leaving them able to communicate without words. In this together. She was going to take care of it. No need to worry.

Victoria turned, holding onto Jakeman's arm with her bound hands. It would be awkward, but she was determined.

Probably Langdon would see it coming.

She said a silent prayer that this would work. That she would get Jakeman free of him, so that she could get to the bomb.

They took a lumbering step toward Langdon.

Another.

Victoria shifted. She saw his gaze track her intention. No turning back now. She swung up in an arc with her hands, intending on clipping the gun before she hit him in the face. Would she get shot? Too late to guess. She slammed the gun.

He twisted.

Something heavy hit her from the side—behind her shoulder —and she got bumped.

Jakeman launched himself at Langdon. She cried out. They toppled to the floor, Jakeman on top of Langdon. The secretary of defense roared in frustration and pain.

Victoria sank to her knees and tried to grab the gun from where they both fought over it. She leaned on Langdon's shoulder but ducked her head so Jakeman didn't hit hers with his own as he swayed. Why did he go and do this? She'd been taking care of it. Taking care of both of them. It was her job.

Langdon gritted his teeth.

She couldn't get Jakeman off without pushing him. She wanted to scream at him, ask what he'd been hoping to accomplish.

The gun went off.

Jakeman's body jerked. Langdon shoved him off. Victoria fell back to a sitting position on the floor.

Langdon hauled her up by her arm, fingers wrapped tight around her bicep. She cried out as he dragged her up toward the door and into the hall.

She craned her neck to look back over her shoulder. "Jakeman!"

He lay on his back, blood on his chest. Gasping. Eyes wide.

"Jakeman!"

Langdon just laughed.

36

Olympia, WA. Sunday 7.32p.m.

"Yes, Mr. President. I understand completely." Mason hung up and stowed his cell phone, shaking his head.

Mark shut off the SUVs engine and waited for him to explain.

"I guess we're in. They have no choice but to unbar the door." The secret service assistant director opened his car door. "He said, and I quote, 'You get my Vickie back.' Has to be the weirdest conversation I've ever had."

"With the president?" Mark couldn't say he'd ever had the honor.

"No, pretty much the weirdest conversation of my life."

They strode together to the front door of the ranch house where the Western Governors' Association meeting was being held tomorrow. No point in waiting until then, considering they had the time to set things up so they'd be ready when Langdon got there. With Victoria.

Both pulled out their badges, letting the Washington State Police officers at the front door know exactly what they were dealing with—two assistant directors of federal offices who had spoken with the president and weren't going to take no for an answer.

The first to speak was a sergeant. Lined face, handlebar mustache. He'd have been a heartthrob forty years ago. Now he just looked like he needed slippers and a recliner. "You two from the gate?"

Mark nodded. They'd given their names, flashed their badges at the camera, and waited for their information to be checked by whoever was on the other end.

"I kinda thought you guys were joking about that." But he stepped aside and allowed them between the two oak doors.

Calling it a ranch was like calling a buffet a snack. The place was really an estate with multiple buildings. Barns. Cottages. It would probably be more accurately called a village, and if they had their own post office and residential sheriff, then he wouldn't have exactly been surprised.

"Down the hall, to the left."

The other officer watched them depart with narrowed eyes.

Mark muttered, "Whatever." They were here and that guy's opinion didn't matter much when lives were on the line.

"What's that?"

He didn't explain. He already regretted his attitude with Victoria still missing. He couldn't waste time being petty. Instead, Mark said, "Are the governors here already?"

"Washington is in residence all this week and next. The rest trickle in this evening, one straggler with a delayed flight tomorrow."

Mark nodded.

"State police chief. Seattle PD commissioner. They're here as well, along with thirty-five staff. Housekeeping, catering. All that."

A man stepped out at the end of the hall. "FBI and Secret Service?"

Mark said, "That's us. Seems pretty quiet around here."

The man waved them into a room. Mark went first, followed by Mason. He pulled up short at the noise and the number of people crammed into this small room, then felt Mason jab his finger into his side. He stepped out of the way and Mason entered. They stood side by side while men and women in suits and badges turned in their direction.

"You mentioned there was a threat?"

Okay, then.

"You're FBI right?" The first man strode over, holding out one hand.

Mark shook it.

The guy had dark brown hair, silver at the temples. Tan pants, white shirt. Badge hanging from a chain around his neck. Sport watch. "I'm Governor Templeton's head of security."

"Mark Welvern."

"I've heard of you from the lieutenant governor."

Mark nodded, hoping it was good enough.

"How's it feel to be one of the last ones standing?"

"Like I should've brought some backup of my own."

Mason slapped Mark's shoulder with the back of his hand. "What am I? Oh, wait. I'm the Secret Service assistant director." He even folded his arms.

"Let's find that nuke. Okay?"

Someone across the room spat out a mouthful of coffee.

"Then we can work out which of us has more seniority."

Mason huffed in disbelief. "You think you outrank me? Your army of ants was corrupted with the red kind that bites, thinking they're gonna get away with it. But you're right. There's a *nuke* to disarm, and we need to find your woman."

The governor's head of security glanced back at the room. "Anyone else feeling as out of the loop as I am?"

Mark explained the situation as quickly as he could, impressing on them the timing factor. "We have no idea when he's gonna show up or where that bomb is right now."

Everyone there gathered in.

"A nuke, seriously?"

Mark nodded while one guy slipped out the back of the room.

He got it, this was heavy. "I'd like to walk through every room in every building. Get a sense of the place."

The head of security nodded. "Sounds good. We should start evacuations, right?"

Mark wasn't so sure about that. "If he's here, or watching, we could tip him off that we know something and he'll change targets. We might never find him." Or Victoria.

There was some discussion. That many cops in one room, all from different departments, it got sticky on the issue of who was the senior giving orders. A few of them clearly distrusted the FBI, and given the current climate, he didn't blame them.

"This isn't about me, or the FBI. This is about all of us stopping an attack."

Mason said, "Besides. I'm the one the president put in charge. So we go through me until further notice. Let's move out. I want a sweep, and I want all security double-checked. We make sure Langdon isn't here already. I'll get you all Victoria Bramlyn's picture, and you call me immediately if you find her."

Mark nearly sagged with relief but refused to give any of them the impression he was seriously exhausted. This was almost over, right? Until then, he had to continue pushing through to the end.

Give me strength, God. Help me find her.

God was in the business of supplying needs. Mark trusted Him to do this now, just as He'd done so many times before.

This might be the most important one.

Five minutes later, Mark entered a barn with the governor's head of security. "What did you say your name was?" Maybe the guy had told him, and he'd been so preoccupied with everything going on.

"In the grand scheme of things, is it really relevant?"

Mark glanced over his shoulder. It was a rare man who could admit his own place was a humble one. Most just kept quiet about it. He spotted an expression in the guy's eyes he didn't understand.

Mark turned his attention back to the interior of the barn and a hall of stalls that were way too clean to actually house horses. Sure enough, over the first stall he spotted a vintage Corvette.

Under his jacket, Mark reached across his body like he was scratching an itch on his ribs and unsnapped his gun.

"See any nukes?"

"Nothing yet." He kept moving like he was more interested in getting a look-see at all the cars. One was so brand new he was pretty sure it was a prototype. It looked like a sports car from the future. He couldn't help whistling. It helped to sell the idea he was distracted, not trying too hard to look for a bomb despite his earlier tone. Mark reached the end of the line of stalls and then spun around.

Gun up.

The man whose name he still didn't know had a gun of his own. "Now why did you have to go and tell them all about the nuke?"

"Colin."

Wig. Prosthetic disguise like they used in theaters. Or spycraft. Probably his own mother wouldn't have recognized him.

Langdon would have killed her if she had.

"That's not who I am." He held out his free hand, palm to the roof. "The time has come to be reborn."

"So you blow up this whole place, and all the people here, and you take off and go live your life as someone else?" Where was Victoria, and Jakeman?

If Langdon was here already, that meant the two of them likely were as well. "Tell me where she is. Where the bomb is. *Now.*"

"Because you think I'm going to just give everything away?"

"Where's Jakeman?"

That got him a reaction. "Not doing so well, last I saw of him." There was a gleam in his eye and a slight smile on his lips.

Jakeman wasn't okay. Mark listened to Langdon—his words, as much as what he didn't say, watching his body for the telltale sign he would attack.

They stared for a while at each other, each holding their guns, carefully aimed. Langdon knew what Mark could and couldn't do, in accordance with his sworn oath. What he didn't know was what Mark might be prepared to do. In the name of justice.

"Where is she?"

Mark saw it in his shoulder. A tiny flex of muscle that heralded his intention to strike.

Both of them launched forward, guns forgotten except for the express purpose of hitting each other. Far more satisfying, and Mark didn't need to be investigated for discharging his weapon.

He grunted, the air punched out of his diaphragm. Doubled over, he coughed and then slammed into Langdon, both arms wrapped around his waist as they toppled to the floor with the force of Mark's tackle.

Langdon responded by slamming his gun down on Mark's back.

He grunted again and rolled, shoving Langdon's head on the floor, hard enough it bounced off. The man's eyes went glassy. Mark reached for his opponent's gun. He shoved it away, where it slid under the door of one of the stalls.

He holstered his own gun and then moved to flip Langdon to his stomach.

"All this fuss for you?" Mark readied to roll the guy.

Langdon twisted, sweeping Mark to his back, fist already primed.

Mark found himself staring up at the ceiling, blinking away the spots in his vision. Langdon moved closer. Mark kicked out at him, punched, then tried a couple of palm strikes.

Langdon grabbed Mark's head, hands on either side, and slammed it down on the floor.

Mark roared. He managed to roll Langdon in an old wrestling move he used to practice in high school. It was more of a gut reaction to being in this position than a planned attack.

He shoved Langdon away, both of them breathing hard. Mark

swiped at the wet on his mouth and saw blood on the back of his hand.

He drew his gun and pointed it at the now-unarmed man. "You're under arrest."

"Take me in, the bomb will go off. You'll never find her."

"So tell me where she is."

"Only after I walk out of here."

Mark shook his head. "Not happening." Mark figured at least that meant they had time before the bomb went off. Time was good; it meant they also had a chance to fix this.

To stop him.

Langdon chuckled. He lay back on the floor of the barn, breathing hard.

"Face down. Hands on your head." Mark climbed to his feet. It hurt, and he didn't bother hiding that fact.

Langdon glanced at him. "You'll never find her."

A fission of cold fear cut through him, dividing hope from despair until hope had nothing to keep it alight. *Lord.*

"Hands on your head." He practically screamed it at Langdon.

"Welvern, what do you think you're doing?" It was the FBI director.

He didn't turn around. "This is Oscar Langdon, and if you tell me he's the head of security for the governor's office, then I'll know you're in on it." Then to Langdon he said, "Hands. On. Your. Head."

"Mark." Mason touched his arm.

"He needs to tell us where the bomb is."

"He will."

Langdon only grinned up at them, blood lining his lips.

"You got him." Mason moved beside him. "Now let us take care of this."

Mark realized he was breathing hard. The back of his head didn't feel good, and he could feel wet warmth on his neck there.

"Cover me?" Mason moved toward Langdon.

"Yep."

Langdon moved. Metal glinted.

A knife.

Mark fired his weapon. Two. Three times.

Mason's body jerked. Langdon's.

They both fell to the ground.

Mason rolled to his back, blood coating his stomach.

Mark landed on his knees between them. "Hold on," he told his friend. Then he turned to Langdon. Three shots, center mass. He wasn't going to last much longer.

Mark got in his face. "Tell me everything."

37

Olympia, WA. Sunday 10.14p.m.

Gunshots. Victoria heard them. She whipped her head around but couldn't make out anything else. The shots had been muffled. Barely audible. Maybe she was just kidding herself.

She tipped her head to her shoulder and continued her attempt to push the bandage up off her eyes.

It was tight.

What else was there to do?

The last thing she'd heard was the slam of the car door. He'd shut her in here, tied to the headrest, sitting on the backseat. His words...

She couldn't think about that right now. She needed to see.

Finally, she managed to get the blindfold to move up into her hair, leaving her one-eyed. She used her other shoulder and her elbow, making sure she didn't shift too much on the seat. An action like that could be deadly. She eventually got the rest of it up onto her head.

If it wasn't for the fact it would take out everyone else in this place along with her, she might not mind so much. The bomb would go off, and it would all be over. Jakeman had probably bled out by now. Those shots could have been Mark or one of her other friends.

Everything, lost.

One lone tear rolled down her face, and then the dam broke.

Victoria sobbed into the quiet car. Not knowing if they were alive, or dead, was even worse than the certainty that she'd have to wake up tomorrow and face life without the people she loved and cared for.

She cried until the emotion had been spent. Minutes. An hour. Who knew? She was all alone, as she had been many times in her life. Except now she had people in her life she wanted to spend more time with. A man she wanted to finally admit her love for. What was the point in denying or burying it any longer? She didn't care about the fallout or the consequences. She didn't care if their lives didn't mesh or if it would take work to figure out.

She just wanted Mark.

God. Mark belonged to Him. She could live that life. He didn't make it look easy, he just made it look peaceful. *I need that now. Maybe it's not possible.* She sucked in a choppy breath. *But I want what he has, and I want him.*

She'd heard the "gospel" enough times she got the gist of it. Her need for a Savior. His sacrifice, out of love, so she could be His child.

Victoria looked around, waiting for some divine assistance in figuring this whole thing out. Her fingers were numb. Outside the car, all she could see through the seriously tinted windows was wood paneling.

At any other time, she'd have marveled at the interior of this car. It was basically a work of art, though the back seat had hardly any legroom and...

Victoria shook her head. The dash looked like the cockpit of an airplane. So many high-tech buttons and screens, dials and knobs.

And a cell phone.

She could see it in the cup holder.

Victoria let out a cry of frustration. That was what he'd been talking about. Whispering in her ear, all excited like. Rubbing his body against hers. Gross. She'd wanted to be sick and couldn't believe she'd ever thought Colin Pinton attractive. Maybe she'd just thought he was a good guy.

Maybe that was worse.

So blind.

Not anymore. She lifted her feet and bent her legs, reaching with her toes. *Pressure plate, you see. One little pound change in the load on that seat and...boom.* She shuddered, praying small movements weren't enough to set off the bomb. Maybe he'd been lying about that. But there was far too much risk to try it just to see if he was or not. It would put thousands at risk. She'd have to grab the phone without shifting her weight too much, or without lifting her backside up off the seat. She pressed her feet together, the phone sandwiched between, bringing her knees slowly towards her chest.

Victoria gritted her teeth. "I really hate you, Oscar-Langdon-Colin-Pinton-whoever-you-are." Gone now. He'd left. Gotten away with it, tying her up at ground zero so he could set her up and then kill her.

Not if she could help it.

The phone slipped out from between her feet. She cried out and watched it tumble between the center console and the passenger seat. *Please be where I can reach it.*

She was already sitting upright, hands bound to the headrest. She'd tried to get the headrest off first but hadn't been able to get purchase on the little button on the far side to release it up. Shove it off. Get her hands free.

The frustration was about to make her scream. Instead, she channeled it into the adrenaline she needed. No shakes—oh, please no shakes—just pure mental focus. Victoria stuck one foot between the center console and the chair and felt around for the phone.

One call. And when they hang up, or the phone battery dies, boom.

Talia. She needed to get a message...something...to her

friend. The woman could wring miracles out of technology. Langdon hadn't done nearly enough homework on Victoria if he didn't know what her team could do.

Or she'd managed to keep them a secret enough, he just hadn't been able to find anything out on them. The Northwest Counter-Terrorism Task Force had been, in many ways, a black ops mission. Good on paper, all above board. But in the light of day, they were nothing but the blurred shadow in the corner. For their safety. For the mission.

For this.

Victoria found the phone. She stabbed at the corner with her toes and shoved it back toward her, where it slid out onto the floor near her other foot.

She exhaled the breath she'd been holding. *Thank You.*

Grabbing it with her feet again, she lifted it and held it to her bound hands so she could grab it. Only twenty-six percent battery. She swiped the screen awkwardly and then typed out a text to Talia's phone number.

A series of numbers, a variation of police ten-codes that she would know. Emergency. Don't call. Team member in danger. Bomb. Terrorist. No time to waste. Technology compromised.

In all it was three messages.

Seconds later the phone screen flashed.

"Can you hear me?"

Victoria's exhale sounded like a sob. "How did you—"

"It's not a phone call, I just hacked the mic. You're right. There's a line of code to run a program at the conclusion of the next call."

"It'll detonate the bomb." Her voice seemed too loud, echoing in the car.

"Not anymore."

Victoria nearly started crying again. "Talia. He left Jakeman for dead."

"Mason has been stabbed."

Victoria gasped.

"You said Jakeman? Where were you?"

"I… have no idea." Was her friend dead now?

"Everyone else is okay so far as the last update. They got to Langdon and he's dead, that's how Mason got hurt." Her voice trailed off to a mutter, which included the words "good riddance." The only thing Victoria heard until Talia said, "Huh."

"What? Is Mason going to be okay? Did they take him to the hospital?"

"Full medical center on site. He's been carried over there."

"Talia."

"Talia...hello?"

"What? Oh, he was texting me. He's mad Langdon got the jump on him, that's all. But says Mark took him out. I've also told Mark you're here. He's now barraging me with messages, asking for a location."

"There's wood paneling on the walls, and I'm in a car."

"I know that. I think he's in the same building. We're figuring it out."

"And the bomb?"

Talia made a noncommittal noise. "That might prove a little hard…er… There it is."

The car's headlights illuminated, and then began to flash. The alarm sounded.

Victoria tilted her head to the side so her ear was against the soft part of her shoulder. "That's really loud."

It shut off. A figure appeared by the window, and Victoria let out a little squeal.

"I guess you're not impervious to fear as everyone thought."

"I'm not…" She saw the figure reach for the door handle. "No! He can't. Tell him not to open it."

He stepped back. It was Mark.

Victoria whimpered. "Tell him he can't open it. The bomb will go off."

Mark reached into his pocket and pulled out a phone. He held it to his ear. She saw his lips moving but couldn't make out anything.

He hung up. The window was so darkened she couldn't make out his face on the other side of the glass. She couldn't even put her hand against the glass. Or her forehead. One was bound, the other meant too much movement.

Another tear rolled down her cheek, and here she'd thought they were all spent.

"Did you hear that?"

Victoria said, "No. What?"

"Mark." As Talia said his name, the man himself leaned down and peered through the glass from close up. She saw his eyes widen the second he spotted her.

"He's here." She needed her hands free so she could...do *something*. She wanted to mouth the words she'd like to say to him. He might not be able to hear her, but he could understand well enough.

"Where's the bomb?"

"In the trunk."

Mark pulled out his phone, looked at the screen, and then moved to the back of the vehicle.

"Tell him not to open it." She twisted as far as she could without moving her backside. It hurt a lot. "It's...There's..."

"Okay, hang on." Talia went quiet for a second. Then she said, "Can you hear me?"

"Yes. What?"

"Victoria."

"Mark." Her whole body sagged.

"We need to get you out of there."

Talia said, "Agreed."

Victoria shook her head. "You can't. The bomb is in the trunk. He said it would detonate at midnight—"

"It's almost eleven."

"If you open the trunk, or any of the doors—even the hood— a separate device will activate. It will flood the car with gas, and you won't want to hang around to watch what happens to me after that."

Mark said, "Why do that? Why not just set off the main bomb, unless it's a dud? Maybe the scientist couldn't get it going so this is his attempt to distract us so he could get away."

"Or it *was* his plan," Talia said. "If he wasn't dead, we could ask him."

"You'd have had to torture it out of him. And that might have taken days." Victoria knew enough about Langdon to know that. Because the same could have been said about her, except that she believed she never would break.

Not unless it was Mark's life in jeopardy.

"Get everyone out of here. Evacuate the whole county if you have to. No one within a hundred miles." They had to do their best to get everyone to a place they'd be safe. Minimize the loss of life. At least, as much as was possible.

Mark's voice rolled through the phone line. "I'm staying."

She saw him then, standing by the car. Tall. Strong. "Nobility will only get you killed."

"If you die, I die."

Talia made a frustrated sound. "Let's plan on both of you living full lives and all that's going to entail. Okay?"

"We need help."

Mark was right. Victoria said, "I need to make a call. There's only one person I know who can figure out how to get to that bomb. I just pray it'll be in time."

"We're all praying."

"Talia." Victoria blew out a steady breath, pleading with God. "Get me an open line and dial this number."

38

Olympia, WA. Sunday 10.52p.m.

"I 'll make the call."

Mark squeezed his hands into fists as Victoria replied to Talia's comment. "He won't talk to you."

He stood there, powerless to do anything as she prepared to call another one of her friends who could help her. And he couldn't do a thing. Now wasn't the time to get worked up about it. "Just give Talia the number."

She did. The line quieted, and he knew Talia was gone. Or she'd muted herself at least. Victoria said, "You shouldn't be here."

He knew she was talking to him. It was there, in the tone of her voice. The intimacy of a lifetime sharing the best and worst of each other.

"I'm not leaving." He got on his phone, keeping the line open but checking in with Mason and the FBI director—neither of whom would appreciate being left out.

They both needed to evacuate to a safe distance, they needed to take everyone at the ranch with them, and they needed to do it as fast as possible. No waiting. No delays. Just get out before it was too late.

She sighed as the confirmations came in. They were announcing the evacuation.

He heard the knowing, even in that audible exhale. Along with the resignation that there was nothing she could say that might change his mind.

Whatever happened to her, happened to him. That was simply how it was going to be.

He looked at his watch. "Do we know how much time there is?"

"Langdon didn't tell you that?"

"I was too busy shooting him so he couldn't stab Mason—*again*."

"He said midnight."

"I asked him where you were. Where the bomb was." Mark stared at the dark window, knowing she was there. Not knowing how much she could see of him. "He just sneered, and then he died. Like it was all a big joke."

He looked at his watch again. "If midnight is right, then we have an hour."

"Not enough time for them to get here."

"Who?"

"People who know what they're doing with a nuke. Now will you just go?"

"No."

"I don't know why you're just standing there."

Mark crouched and looked in the window from up close again, phone to his ear. He probably looked like a creeper from her point of view, but he needed at least a half-decent glimpse of her face. She was tied to the seat in front, hands bound up by the headrest of the passenger side.

"I'm not going anywhere."

"So you've said."

"You think I'd leave you like this?"

He saw her shake her head, his nose touching the glass. Saw the long exhale. "You have enough time to get to a safe distance."

Talia got back on the line before he could say anything. "The sergeant is on the line. He wants to know why you're interrupting his bacon sandwich."

The laugh that burst from Victoria was like a single bark. Surprise. Amusement.

"I'll put him through."

"Working on owing me triple?" The voice that burst onto the line was gravelly, sounded like a grunt, and was clearly amused.

"If I'm still alive in an hour, I'll owe you big time. But I'm not watching your dog again. She's mean."

He chuckled. "Biting means she likes you."

"I'd love to banter." She paused. "I seriously would love nothing more than to shoot the breeze with you right now, but I'm in a situation."

She outlined everything. From some kind of altercation, a car chase in France with details Mark hadn't been privy to, something about him having tied her up to get her back into the US, to the man behind it.

"Oscar Langdon?"

"He was the one last dirty FBI agent they were looking for."

The Sergeant let out a low whistle. "Got yourself in a mess. One Jakeman didn't fully brief me on."

"Jakeman was left for dead. Langdon is dead."

More whistling.

Mark said, "What we need your help with is a nuke."

Talia explained it was wired to sensors in the car that could tell if the doors or trunk were open.

"Got someone that can look under the car?"

"That would be me," Mark said.

"Can't believe you let me go to Last Chance, Vic. I'd have helped."

"I know." Her voice was quiet.

Mark's was not when he said, "Last Chance?"

"Who're you?"

"FBI assistant director Mark Welvern."

"Huh." The sergeant said, "We had a training op in Last Chance County."

"I grew up there, with Victoria."

"Guys." She broke in. "The nuke?"

Talia came back on the line. "Josh and Dakota found the scientist. He's dead, and it was a mess. They think Langdon lost his cool."

Mark paced away from the car toward the stall door. It wasn't a big space, but the barn wall rolled up like a garage door so the vehicles could be displayed or driven away. He said, "Tell me what I'm looking for on the underside."

While the sergeant told him what to look for, he thought it through. If Langdon was mad, and the scientist had been murdered...didn't that indicate he might've failed to do what Langdon wanted?

Maybe there was a bomb. Whether it was a functioning nuclear weapon, he wasn't sure. At least, he couldn't be convinced with any level of certainty.

"That's not what I'm seeing." Mark traced the wires with his fingers, being careful not to loosen anything.

"So it's hidden."

Mark spotted something, high up by the wheel. "Hang on." Yep. That was it. "I found the sensor mechanism for the rear side door."

The sergeant had him describe it. Then he said, "Do you have any wire clippers?"

Mark pulled out the multi-tool he carried in his pocket. One Victoria had given him for Christmas after his old one was confiscated after he'd tried to go through airport security having forgotten it was in his backpack.

Talia made him shine his flashlight camera to the mechanism. He didn't need them all conferring over what to do, taking forever. Dragging it out. He said, "Be quick."

The sergeant made some comment about the wires. Talia replied. That techno speak he didn't understand and had no desire to learn. It was like a whole different language.

Mark gritted his teeth while they figured out what he should do. He was just about to remind them that the clock was ticking when the sergeant said, "Cut the red one. As far away from the mechanism as you can."

Mark didn't wait around. He tucked the phone on his chest so they could see what he was doing, traced the wire away from the metal box, and cut.

Two seconds later he exhaled. "We didn't blow up."

"You should be able to open that door now."

"And the trunk?"

"Slide the phone on the ground. I'll look."

Once Mark had it in the right place, he got up and pulled the passenger door open. Victoria looked like she wanted to cry—and like she already had been. He crouched in the open door, wary of the pressure plate she'd told them about. "Hey, beautiful."

A flash of disagreement flared in her eyes. "It's good to see you."

He wanted to kiss her. Would even that alter the weight pressing down on the seat by just one pound? He didn't know.

"Why did you—" A high-pitched beep interrupted her. "Guys!"

Mark leaned in, holding onto the roof. The front windshield was now a display filled with four digits and a colon between.

09:56

09:55

09:54

"We're counting down," Mark said. "Nine minutes, fifty-three seconds to go."

"Yes." Victoria whipped her head around to glare at him. Like that was going to work. "Good idea. Go."

"I need to get into the trunk, sergeant." He moved away, headed for the phone.

"Mark, will you just go!"

He slid back so he could see her through the open door. "No way, honey. We do this like we do everything important. Together."

All in all, he was pretty pleased with that. It came out quite eloquently.

"I've done plenty of important things without you."

Mark figured that was probably true. "Not one thing in my life that I've ever done without you has been anything even close to important."

"I don't even know what that means."

"I'll explain later," the sergeant said. "After we get the two of you out of there."

"Victoria?"

"Yeah?" She'd stopped yelling now.

"I love you."

No one said anything. "I'd love you more if you *left.*"

"Is that true?"

"No." She gave him that, but grudgingly.

Mark smiled to himself under the car, ready to be done with this so they could figure a few things out. Like a serious change of relationship status.

Talia said, "Everyone except the two of you are out of the blast radius."

"Copy that." Mark laid back down on the ground. "sergeant?"

"Mark, will you just *go!*" It sounded like she was crying now.

Maybe it was because she was so happy that they'd finally admitted aloud that they loved each other, but he figured that was unlikely given the way it sounded. A guy could dream, though.

He slid under the car and set the phone back on his chest, facing the underside. Similar mechanism. More wires this time. "Red?"

"Only if you wanna die."

"Given I've finally just said I love you to the woman I've loved since I first figured out what that means…I'm going to say no. I don't especially want to die now."

"The inside black one."

Mark shone the light on his fingers and counted along. "This one?"

"Next one."

He took it. "Okay."

Victoria yelled, "Six minutes!"

He cut the wire. "Done."

"Pop the trunk. Slowly. Look for wires."

Mark set the phone in his shirt pocket, facing out. Not perfect, but it would have to do. He pressed the button for the trunk, crouched, saw no wires, and lifted it up. The whistle couldn't be helped.

"Four minutes, fifty nine."

Mark said, "I see that."

"Describe it."

"Huge bomb. On top is a laptop."

"Laptop?" Talia sounded excited now. "Get your phone hooked into it. Or will he have thought of that…" Her voice trailed off.

"Talia, we're under four minutes now."

Inside the car, Victoria whimpered.

"Type this." She rattled off a series of letters and numbers, keystrokes he had to type in that were given almost too quickly for his fatigued brain to figure out. Were it not for the adrenaline, he'd probably have been to slow. But also because of the adrenaline, he had to make sure he didn't fumble a key and get something wrong.

"Done."

"Press Enter. Then you get Victoria and run."

"One second." Mark left the command on the screen and went to the car interior and snapped her free of the ties securing her to the headrest by her wrists.

Then he moved back to the keyboard. He pressed Enter on the laptop. "Go!"

Victoria dove out of the car, stumbling on her feet. He caught her around the waist, and they raced through the barn to the heavy door at the end.

Mark slammed into the bar at a run.

Outside hit them like a blast of air-conditioned air. The crisp night temperatures of winter, nature so still and calm, readying itself for the first prickles of ice to settle overnight.

The explosion rocketed into the sky, breaking apart the barn as it enveloped it in a ball of deep orange.

Mark grabbed Victoria and pulled her close.

The force hit them.

His world went black.

39

Victoria came awake to the sound of beeping machines, dimmed overhead fluorescents, and the sound of heavy breathing. Her mouth tasted like old orange juice.

She tried to move but was tucked in tight by a heavy layer of sheets and blankets.

"Hey." The voice was throaty, and she felt weight settle on her left side. Warm fingers threaded through hers and gave a quick squeeze.

"Dakota."

"Yeah. The others are here, too. Talia and Haley. We just told them we're all sisters...by adoption."

Victoria squeezed her eyes shut for a second.

"I'll explain it when you're more awake. It was pretty funny."

A light in the corner blinked on, and Victoria saw Talia's outline heading into the bathroom. She needed to pee but had the feeling there were medical procedures at work and right now she didn't need to worry so much about that.

"Are you in pain?"

Victoria turned her head and saw Haley's face. All the women were here, except...Allyson's face came into view at the end of the bed.

"Victoria?"

"I'm...I don't even know." Her brain hadn't exactly woken up yet.

Allyson shot her a sympathetic smile. "You'll get there."

Victoria lifted her right hand. A cast covered her arm from elbow to knuckles. She'd broken it. She raised her other hand. IV tube feeding medicine into her elbow. Abrasions on her wrist.

She'd been tied to the headrest of—"The car."

Dakota shook her head. "You guys blew that sweet ride into tiny pieces, along with the building. All that's left is the crater you both rolled back into. The one they had to dig you out of."

Victoria frowned, figuring that was enough for Dakota to know she needed more of an explanation.

It was. Dakota said, "Took a whole day. By the time they found you...well, it wasn't pretty."

"How's Josh?"

"He's awake. There's a little movement, so they're hopeful."

Victoria turned to Allyson and lifted her brows. The former ATF agent said, "Sal and I found Jakeman. He's alive. He's at the naval base in Bremerton in intensive care. His wife has been calling every couple of hours, asking for updates on your condition."

"So he's okay?"

"He will be."

That was enough, at least. "Thank God."

Dakota's brows twitched into a frown, but she didn't say anything further. "Niall and Haley located the scientist. Don't know if you heard that."

Victoria couldn't remember if she had or not. Where was Mark? Surely if he had been hurt too badly, they'd tell her, right? She would be the first to know.

"Anyway it looks like Langdon was so mad he cut the guy all up and didn't care about the mess."

"Unhinged."

"What did you see in him, anyway?"

More than one of the women there shot Dakota a look. Talia gasped, as she headed out of the bathroom to the tune of the toilet tank refilling. "Dakota."

Victoria shook her head. "He wasn't Langdon. He was Colin Pinton." She couldn't refrain from asking any longer. "Now someone tell me where Mark is."

"Next door. And that's all I'm prepared to tell you until you hear the rest of it."

Victoria let out a long sigh and shut her eyes.

Dakota chuckled. "I see you're just going to pretend to fall asleep."

"Langdon is dead?" She didn't bother opening her eyes.

"Yes. Mark killed him."

Victoria's eyes flew open as she started recalling details and she turned too fast to Talia. "Langdon stabbed Mason." Her voice sounded strained, and she couldn't hold back the moan at the end.

Talia nodded. "Should I get a nurse?"

"Just tell me how he is. First."

"Recovering. Just like Mark." There was something in her gaze Victoria couldn't make out because of the dim light. "I'll get the nurse."

Victoria pushed out a breath through pursed lips. "I'm not sure I've ever felt like this. And I think I was blown up twice in one day recently."

Dakota shrugged.

"I should actually check that record book." Haley pulled out her phone.

Allyson glanced between the two of them like she thought they were insane.

Maybe they all were. Victoria kind of felt that way. "How is Mark?"

Allyson said, "They'll know more when he wakes up, but they think he'll be okay." She pressed her lips together for a second.

"He was found on top of you, like he shielded you from the blast."

That was supposed to make her feel better?

"He took the brunt of the explosion."

Victoria wanted to see him, but she wasn't exactly sure she could move at all right now. She'd lifted each of her arms a moment ago and now felt like she really was going to fall back to sleep any minute now. No joke this time.

"I'm pregnant." Allyson blurted it out.

Dakota nearly fell off the bed.

Haley dropped her phone on the floor.

"Sal didn't want to wait." She lifted both hands palms up. "It happened on the first go around."

Victoria smiled, feeling it overtake her whole face.

Allyson smiled back.

"Does he hate me?"

Allyson shook her head. "If he did, would he have come here to find Jakeman?"

"No."

"Would he have gone straight from dropping Jakeman off at the closest hospital to tracking down Langdon's hotel room in order to secure the nuclear material with the help of some guy who goes by "sergeant" and says obnoxious things like, 'tell Vickie she owes me big for this'?"

Victoria said nothing.

"He doesn't hate you. He just doesn't always agree with you." Allyson shrugged. "But families work through that stuff. They work it out and, in the end, it makes the bond stronger than if they'd never weathered through."

"Congratulations."

"Thank you."

Victoria turned to Dakota. "How about you? I lied about what the task force was doing. I used all of you."

"Did you watch our backs?"

"Of course."

"Were we doing something valuable that saved lives?"

"Yes, but—"

Haley said, "Did you need each of us, and the skills we brought to the team?"

Victoria looked at each woman in turn. "All of them."

The door opened, and Talia came in. A nurse with heavy makeup and pink scrubs followed her in and took Victoria's vitals, shone a light in her eyes until that was all she could see and asked her a whole bunch of questions, including, "Who is the president?"

"I should call him. Tell him I'm okay."

"Uh…"

Talia waved a hand. "It's fine. I hear he calls her "Vickie." Her body shook with a giggle. "Vickie."

Victoria frowned at her, trying to look authoritative.

Talia patted her. "I'll make sure that's included in *all* the reports."

"The doctor will be in shortly." Nurse lady wandered out.

Dakota shook her head. "She was a ray of sunshine."

Haley said, "Probably needs more coffee."

Allyson groaned. "Decaf for me if someone is going downstairs. I have to visit the throne room for a second, splash some water on my face."

"Do you need a mint?" Haley moved to her purse.

"In a sec, please."

Talia squeezed Victoria's hand. When she looked at her friend, Talia said, "I'm glad you're all right."

Victoria turned her head to the side, showing Talia her cheek. She even lifted her chin a little bit. Talia leaned down and planted her lips there. "I guess you'll just have to see the doctor with purple lipstick on your face."

"Wouldn't be the first time."

———

Two days later

DAKOTA PUSHED Victoria's wheelchair to the side of his bed. Victoria had to swallow the rush of emotion that stuck a lump in her throat.

Now that she'd decided to forego being the kind of woman who never showed emotion and certainly didn't need anyone else to be perfectly dialed in on what she was feeling, it felt like all the walls had come down. The emotion was flowing freely.

Victoria swiped at the moisture that trailed down her cheek.

"We're all praying." Dakota squeezed her shoulder.

Victoria nodded, not speaking in case she just dissolved right here. Mark lay still, his chest moving in a low rise and fall she could barely make out. She reached out and laid a hand on his sternum just to feel it.

He was alive.

I love you.

The tube down his throat. Machines tracking each beat of his heart so they'd know if it stopped. Long term problems that could come even if he woke up. Possible brain damage from the head injury.

"He saved your life."

"Just like Josh did." Victoria bit down on her molars to hold back what she wanted to say.

Dakota sighed.

"Am I really worth the two of them doing that?"

"That's up to you."

Victoria moved her hand from his breastbone to his forearm, then entwined her fingers with his. She bowed her head and laid it on their hands. Her lips moved as she silently entreated the God that Mark served with his whole life—even when it had been infuriatingly frustrating to her—that He needed to fix this.

They'd come so close to getting everything they'd ever wanted with each other. Life. Love. Now all that was in jeopardy. Even having gone this far with each other, they still weren't at the finish line. Life kept moving it. Shifting it farther away with each step they took.

When she could no longer sit hunched over at that angle, Victoria sat up. She had to blink to bring the room back into focus.

For a while, she just stared at his face.

Shouldn't he have woken up? She'd been hoping he would if she came in here, and if she prayed.

"He'll wake up soon."

She didn't need Dakota to try and convince her. "I'm praying as well." That had to be enough. Maybe she shouldn't be making it so God had to prove Himself to her. But it wasn't like she had any power over Mark living, or…

She swallowed against that lump again.

"Well…good." Dakota squeezed her shoulder again. As though physical touch was going to reassure her.

Victoria didn't want to know what it was like to live in a world where he didn't exist. Where she desperately strove to keep his memory alive. Where she had to grieve him *and* the dreams she'd carried since childhood. Dreams of marriage. A life shared together, with him.

Things she might have to watch die, right along with the man she loved.

So good.

So noble.

He'd fought that fight for years, knowing he wasn't the kind of man who could live any other life. She'd crossed so many lines, she didn't even know what her limits were now. Case in point, she'd lied to everyone she cared about trying to bring in her ex-boyfriend. The man she didn't want to admit to anyone that she'd gotten close to—a rebound after she'd thought she lost Mark for good.

Victoria pushed out a long breath.

"We should get you back to your room."

Victoria nodded, not wanting to argue. They were checking

her out soon. Sending her home with her bruises and a bottle of pain killers—as though she were all better.

As though she had anywhere to go.

Jakeman's wife had come by the previous day. They'd talked. Mostly Mary Anne had cried and Victoria had sat there awkwardly patting her hand over the fact her husband had almost been killed. He would pull through and was already sitting up in his own hospital bed.

Mary Anne didn't know who Mark was to Victoria. She didn't know what Victoria might have to face.

Mason was recovering as well, though given the knife damage, it would take longer than Jakeman's bullet hole. And Josh was on the long road to recovery.

Victoria had spoken to the sergeant on the phone earlier that morning to thank him for helping.

Dakota pushed her back into her room. Victoria didn't want to sit in bed staring blankly at the TV screen, not really watching it, pretending she was all right.

She turned to Dakota, ignoring the pulling sensation in all the shattered places with every movement.

Her friend frowned. "What?"

"Call Haley. Go sit with Josh. I need to get out of here." She knew then exactly what she wanted. "I need to see Bear."

EPILOGUE

Last Chance County.

Seven months later.

Bear emerged from the water, dripping. The sun beat down overhead. His long hair lay flat, and he padded through the pool of his own deluge.

Four feet away from their picnic blanket, he paused.

Mark flinched. "Don't do——"

Bear shook, wringing his whole body like the spin cycle on high.

Victoria held up both hands, curling her legs into her body so she was hidden behind her knees and hands. She still squealed as she got soaked, then started laughing.

"This isn't funny."

She turned to him as Bear trotted to his side and lay down with an old dog groan. "I was thinking I needed a way to cool off. It's pretty hot out."

Mark's gaze met hers. The smile encompassed his whole face,

relaxing him in a way that was more frequent now and made him look like the young man she'd once known.

Still, the past few months had been more about wrapping up their careers and figuring out what was next than talking about anything resembling a future that was about *them*. Victoria fought back the frustration daily, talking to God about it in her journal. Reading her Bible and finding solace in the pages.

She was growing.

Things were good. She should be happy.

Still, there was something between them. She wondered if he felt it, too. "Okay?"

He pointed to the lake, a distant expression on his face. "They're at three minutes already."

"Shame." She'd thought the sergeant's team would set a town record this time.

As if on cue, an explosion rocked the underwater. The spray spewed up into the sky. Folks gathered on the shore, clapping and cheering for the sergeant and his team.

"This was a good distraction. A good idea, coming to watch them compete." They'd done it. They breached the bunker.

She glanced back at Mark. "Thanks—" She saw what he held, loose in his hand.

A small velvet box.

Closed, like he was still mulling it over.

"This wasn't about finding something to do while we wait to hear that Allyson has had her baby."

Mark shook his head. She spotted the scar above his ear.

Haley was also pregnant, as was Talia. Both weren't due for a few months, though. So they had time. All the wedding presents and shower presents had made it an expensive year, but also one where she'd enjoyed being in Seattle. Close to her friends. Minimal travel had been strange at first. Being close to her friends, fully a part of their lives, made the unfamiliar feeling worth it.

Josh was making strides every day. He was already taking

Neema on short walks, and in a few more months should be fully recovered from the spinal injury he'd sustained saving her life.

"I knew it was big," she said. "Coming back home this week."

"Coming *here*."

"To the watch party?"

"You don't remember." He shook his head. "This was the place where I first saw you. Hacked up jeans you made into cut-off shorts. A raggedy white tank top. Long hair down your back. Bare feet."

"I sound like…" She laughed. "I don't know what I sound like. I probably wouldn't remember that girl if I saw her now." She shook her head. "This is what you want to talk about?"

"It's perfect." He scooted closer, shoving the cooler out from between them while Bear watched. "Who we are. All we've been through." The skin around his eyes contracted. "I've always loved you."

Victoria leaned in and pressed a kiss to his lips. "Same."

Mark chuckled, his breath warm against her lips. "Marry me."

He shifted the box between them, and she realized it was wider than it needed to be. When he opened it, she saw why.

Set inside was a thin white gold band next to a ring set with a huge blue emerald. Beside them was a wide band, the same white gold color.

"Say yes."

"Of course I'm going to say yes, I've been waiting for you to ask me for *years*."

"You don't have to wait much longer." He glanced to the side.

Most of the crowd had cleared out, leaving three people standing to the side. Two men and a woman holding a bouquet. She also had a tote bag over her shoulder.

"Reverend Hills." Victoria blinked.

"The president wanted to come." Jakeman grinned. "I took great pleasure telling him 'no'."

Mark chuckled. The reverend looked sideways at Jakeman like he was crazy.

Mary Anne stuck one hand on her hip. "Well?"

Mark turned to Victoria. "What do you say?"

He held out his hand. She took it, and they stood. "Right now?"

"Right where it all started."

Victoria touched his cheeks, pressing a kiss to his lips. When she leaned back, she said, "I'm *not* wearing cutoffs."

Mark laughed.

"Good thing I've brought you a dress," Mary Anne said. "And I rented that house back there." She pointed back, over her shoulder. "So you can get ready."

Victoria turned back to Mark one last time before she took the first step toward the rest of her life. "Are you sure?"

"Do you love me?"

"Since I met you, and every day since."

He kissed her that time.

HALF AN HOUR LATER, with their friends as witnesses, Victoria Bramlyn married Mark Welvern on the sand at the lake where they first met.

At the same moment, in a Seattle hospital, Tori Ellen Alvarez was born.

————

Hope you enjoyed this series, please be leave a review at your favorite retailer!

Start the next series by Lisa Phillips, *Last Chance County*, starting with *Expired Refuge*. Turn the page NOW for a sneak peek!
Also Available in Audiobook

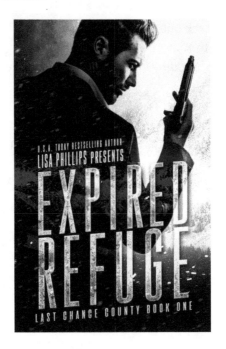

She'll never accept his help.
He'll never stop trying to protect his town.

Mia Tathers is an ATF Special Agent. It's not like she needs Conroy to protect her. However, when it becomes clear someone is recreating her biggest mistake, Mia has to face her own inability to forgive Conroy for what he took from her. It's the only way she'll stay alive.

In this town, Police Lieutenant Conroy Barnes is the one who fixes problems. When a blast from the past shows up, bringing danger with her, he vows to keep her safe. But the clock has expired on her refuge. Death is knocking, and Conroy is determined not to let it in.

Welcome to Last Chance County!
Find *Expired Refuge* now:
books2read.com/u/bzZpq2 or lastchancecounty.com

ALSO BY LISA PHILLIPS

Sign up for my newsletter and stay informed on new releases, participate in events, and get free stuff!

https://authorlisaphillips.com/subscribe

Find out more about LAST CHANCE COUNTY at

https://lastchancecounty.com

Find out more:

https://authorlisaphillips.com/northwest-taskforce

Or, buy the complete series at a discounted rate!

Northwest Counter Terrorism Box Set

ABOUT THE AUTHOR

Follow Lisa on social media to find out about new releases and other exciting events!

Visit Lisa's Website to sign up for her mailing list to and stay up-to-date, get free books, and be included in special promotions!

https://www.authorlisaphillips.com

CPSIA information can be obtained
at www.ICGtesting.com
Printed in the USA
LVHW040730110522
718473LV00002B/296